Praise for

KATE RHODES

'Beautifully written and expertly plotted;
this is a masterclass'
GUARDIAN

'Gripping, clever and impossible to put down'
ERIN KELLY

'Clever, atmospheric and compelling, it's
another masterclass in plotting'
WOMAN'S WEEKLY

'Rhodes is a published poet
and every one of her sentences sings'
FINANCIAL TIMES

'A vividly realised protagonist whose complex and
harrowing history rivals the central crime storyline'
SOPHIE HANNAH

'An absolute master of pace, plotting and character'
ELLY GRIFFITHS

'Kate Rhodes has cleverly blended a tense plot with a
vivid sense of the raw, beautiful landscape of the Scilly
Isles, and every character is a colourful creation'
RACHEL ABBOTT

'Kate Rhodes directs her cast of suspects with consummate
skill, keeping us guessing right to the heart-breaking end'
LOUISE CANDLISH

'One of the most absorbing books I've read
in a long time – perfectly thrilling'
MEL SHERRATT

'Fast paced and harrowing, this gripping novel
will leave you guessing until the end'
BELLA

Also by Kate Rhodes

The Locked-Island Mysteries

Hell Bay
Ruin Beach
Burnt Island
Pulpit Rock
Devil's Table
The Brutal Tide

Alice Quentin series

Crossbone's Yard
A Killing of Angels
The Winter Foundlings
River of Souls
Blood Symmetry
Fatal Harmony

KATE RHODES

HANGMAN ISLAND

SIMON &
SCHUSTER

London · New York · Sydney · Toronto · New Delhi

First published in Great Britain by Simon & Schuster UK Ltd, 2023

1 3 5 7 9 10 8 6 4 2

Simon & Schuster UK Ltd
1st Floor
222 Gray's Inn Road
London WC1X 8HB

Simon & Schuster Australia, Sydney
Simon & Schuster India, New Delhi

www.simonandschuster.co.uk
www.simonandschuster.com.au
www.simonandschuster.co.in

A CIP catalogue record for this book
is available from the British Library

Hardback ISBN: 978-1-3985-1034-0
Ebook ISBN: 978-1-3985-1035-7
Audio ISBN: 978-1-3985-2286-2

Typeset in Sabon by M Rules
Printed and Bound in the UK using 100% Renewable Electricity
at CPI Group (UK) Ltd

MIX
Paper | Supporting
responsible forestry
FSC
www.fsc.org
FSC® C171272

For my brilliant daughters-in-law,
Jess Fulcher and Harriet Churchward

Round
Island

St Helens

St Martin's

Bryher

Tean

Northern Rocks

Tresco

Samson

Eastern
Isles

St Mary's

Bishop Rock

Annet

Gugh

ISLES OF
SCILLY

Western Rocks

St Agnes

Bryher

Tresco

Shipman Head

Badplace Hill

Louis Hayle's
house

Site of activities
centre

Hell Bay Hotel

Hell Bay

New Grimsby Sound

*Shipman
Head
Down*

Hangman Island

Ben's
house

The Rock Pub

Porthcawls' Cottage

Lucy Boston's shop

The Town

Arthur Penwithick's
house

Boatyard

Gweal Hill

Church Quay

Trenwiths'
cottage

Green Bay

Nathan Kernow's
house

Penny Cadgwith's
house

Samson Hill

Rushy Bay

Hell is empty, and all the devils are here.

WILLIAM SHAKESPEARE,
The Tempest

PART ONE

1

Friday 25 August

Jez Cardew knows he's in danger the moment his eyes open. He's lying on his back, soaked to the skin, with pain throbbing inside his skull. The stars look blurred and out of place. A midnight-blue canopy hangs overhead, glinting with light, like a child's drawing covered in too much glitter. When he drags in a breath, the sharp tang of brine hits the back of his throat. All he can remember is leaving St Agnes, alone on his father's boat, then blacking out. Now there's smooth fibreglass under his fingertips instead of the cabin cruiser's scratched varnish.

He succumbs to the darkness, and when his eyes open again, there's a figure up ahead in the wheelhouse. Relief floods through him; a local fisherman must be ferrying him home, but he still can't understand how he's ended up on someone else's boat. There's a burning pain at the back of his skull, and trying to sit up makes him dizzy. When he touches the wound, he can feel blood coursing down his neck.

'Who's there?' he calls out.

Silence hangs on the summer air as the wind holds its breath. The shadow man doesn't reply. Jez peers over the gunwale, but there's no sign of land, which doesn't make sense. The Scillies are grouped so close together, you can always see lights from neighbouring islands, but now there's only the ocean's dark expanse.

'Answer me, please,' he yells out, suddenly afraid. 'Where are we going?'

'Offshore.' The voice is a soft murmur.

'I need a doctor.'

There's a loud burst of laughter. 'You won't get one on the Atlantic Strait.'

Jez tries to stand, but tumbles back to the deck. He feels himself drift in and out of consciousness. His strength is finally returning when his eyes open again. The boat has anchored. There's a sharp pain in his left wrist; he didn't notice before, but someone has bound it with twine that cuts into his skin, too tight to loosen. His confusion is mixed with wild panic. The sea's motion rocks the boat from starboard to port. It rises with one swell, dropping with the next, the waves' murmur filling his ears like whispered threats.

'What the hell is this?'

He can just reach the pager he always carries in case there's a shout from the lifeboat house, but it's no use to him now. Its only purpose is to signal that a boat is in trouble, but he's the one in need of rescue. Fear surges in his stomach again when the figure in the wheelhouse turns round. It's too dark to see details; he can only listen as the man winds the anchor back up from the seabed, setting the boat adrift. He is dragged to his feet by his free wrist, and hears another peal of laughter as he hits the gunwale.

'Come on, you hero. Show me how brave you are now.'

Jez battles hard to stay upright, but he's shoved backwards, plunging into the sea. The brutal cold cancels his pain, and waves roar in his ears; the sound is ugly, like a football crowd jeering. He spits out brine, thrashing his legs to stay afloat. His left wrist is tied to the gunwale, and now the boat's engine is churning. He's dragged along in its wake, fighting to keep his head above water. He can't die like this. Not before he reaches thirty, on a calm August night when he's just found his path.

The boat comes to a halt again ten metres ahead; its lights shine like a beacon, promising safety, yet the man on board seems determined to watch him drown.

Jez tears at his wrist, but the knot won't shift. His training as a lifeboatman has taught him to conserve energy in a crisis. Lie on your back and float like a starfish, the trainer said, but instinct makes him tread water, to keep the cold at bay. Maybe this is a mate's sick idea of a joke. He manages to drag himself along the rope back to the boat, but when he tries to climb on board, the man kicks him away. Panic saps his strength. There's no land in sight; he keeps hoping for a glimpse of the islands, but he's surrounded by miles of unbroken sea.

He cries out for help as the boat speeds away, even though his only witnesses are the waves and sky. A current pulls him under, and pain sears through his wrist. The hymn sung at his grandfather's funeral echoes in his mind. *Eternal Father, strong to save, whose arm hath bound the restless wave . . .*

The melody plays on, but the words are lost as the boat's engine reaches full power. Black water surges over his head; he struggles to breathe, but the sea's embrace is too powerful to resist.

2

Saturday 26 August

I can think of better ways to spend an off-duty morning in late summer. I'm standing in Janet Fearnley's living room in Hugh Town, with arms outstretched like a scarecrow, while she jabs at me with pins. I should be grateful that Scilly's best seamstress is prepared to adjust my wedding suit only a week before the event, but I'd rather be on the beach. My junior colleague from the police, Eddie Nickell, smirks at me from his seat in the corner. He's become a friend since he joined the local force, even though his sunny disposition grates on me occasionally. We share a passion for sea swimming, and have seen even more of each other since we both joined the lifeboat crew. Eddie has agreed to be my best man, because my brother Ian will be cutting it fine, flying in from America hours before our wedding. Eddie's suit fits his slim build so well, no changes were required, while I'm the poor sod being stuck with pins.

This is the first time he's seen me attempt to look smart, which seems to amuse him no end. The heat only adds to my discomfort. It's just 10 a.m., but the temperature is rocketing, even though the window's wide open.

'My husband, Trevor, was an outdoor type, like you,' Janet says. 'He always hated being cooped up indoors. Are you planning to do the swimathon again?'

'I've signed up, but there's been no time for exercise since Noah came along.'

'How old is he now?'

'Three months, and full of beans.'

'You'll have to teach him to swim.'

'He loves the water already.' I watch her hands flying across the fabric. 'Has the lifeboat festival been keeping you busy, Janet?'

'It's taken a while, with events all over Scilly, but it's got off to a great start.'

I catch sight of a boxful of RNLI badges on her table. 'Did you send me some of those a few days back?'

'I got a packet too,' Eddie chips in. 'Someone had drawn a figure dangling from a yardarm on the note, like a kid playing hangman. I thought it was some kind of joke.'

Janet looks surprised. 'That's odd. I got a thousand made, to give away for donations; no one on the committee mentioned doing a mailshot.'

'Maybe they're meant for kids on the off-islands. I didn't see a note with mine,' I reply. 'It looks like most families are helping the festival one way or another.'

'We're determined to beat last year's total.'

'You always do.'

'It feels important, since losing Trevor.'

'Everyone appreciates the work you do.'

Janet lost her husband only last year while he was on a sea-fishing trip, alone on his boat, yet she's finished grieving, in public at least. The woman's over seventy but still making immaculate wedding dresses and suits. She's worn the same steadfast smile for the past half hour, while she adjusts my jacket. Janet is a typical Scillonian; she's lived on the islands all her life and remains positive through good times and bad. Maybe the classic books on her shelves help her to relax; I can see *Paradise Lost*, *Romeo and Juliet*, and several poetry anthologies.

When I look out of the window, three islanders manning a stall by the side of the road selling cakes and home-made lemonade as part of the week-long festival. There will be a play by local kids at the town hall, stand-up comedy and gigs in the pubs, as well as several fetes. I see evidence of Janet's involvement all over her living room: rolled-up posters, raffle prizes, and stacks of flyers.

'Are you looking forward to the wedding, Ben?'

'Not the dressing-up bit; the picnic on the beach is more my style. I hope you're coming?'

'I wouldn't miss it for the world. Nina's dress is a beauty, if I say so myself. She'll make a perfect bride.' Janet points at the mirror. 'Take a look at yourself now, Ben.'

I don't spend much time gazing at my reflection, for obvious reasons. My face proves that sleep deprivation is the new normal, thanks to my son being an early riser. Janet's full-length mirror shows a man pushing forty, with a giant frame, a mess of black hair, dark smudges under his mud-green eyes, and an ugly five o'clock shadow. Eddie appears to have sprung from a higher species. He looks tanned and relaxed, while I frown at the mirror.

'The jacket's great,' I say. 'Shame about the rest.'

Janet rolls her eyes. 'No false modesty, please; you and Nina should model for *Bride and Groom*.'

'I could pass as a caveman right now.'

'More like Poldark, on a grand scale. Two more minutes, then you're done.'

The woman's fingers move at the speed of light, pinning and tucking, while I keep my arms raised.

I can see my fiancée from the window. Nina stands further along Hugh Town beach, with our son in his buggy, her chocolate-brown hair glinting in the morning sun. I watch her stoop down to show Noah some stone or shell she's picked from the sand. It's a relief to see her looking well. She almost died giving birth to him three months ago, but no one would guess it now. Motherhood suits her, and Noah was born content. He wakes at four every morning, ready for life's adventures. I can't explain why our family life still feels like a house of cards. Maybe it's because the cardiologist in Penzance insists on seeing Nina every three months, to check her heart function, even though she appears fit and healthy. I can tell that my wolfdog, Shadow, is unsettled too; the creature suffers from wanderlust most days, but now he's glued to Nina's side, his pale fur drenched with brine.

'It's too quiet out there,' I mutter under my breath.

'How do you mean?' Janet peers up at me.

'Nothing's stirring, not even the wind.'

'It's a lovely summer day. Enjoy it while it lasts.'

I take in the view while she works her magic on the mid-blue fabric that I chose for myself and my uncle Ray. The off-islands shimmer in the distance, shrouded in heat haze, the Atlantic a pool of molten silver with barely a ripple. A crowd of island kids are building sandcastles, clearly overjoyed that school won't reopen for another two weeks.

'We're almost done, you'll be glad to know,' Janet says.

There's a sudden bleeping sound, which triggers a rush of adrenaline. Instinct makes me pull off the jacket immediately, scattering pins. Eddie's RNLI buzzer echoes mine, and he's already on his feet. We often miss rescue missions when we're patrolling the off-islands, but today there's no avoiding it. Janet remains calm as I apologise for rushing away. Every islander recognises the alarm call for lifeboat crew, and she's run the RNLI support team for years. She wishes us luck before we sprint downstairs from her flat on Fore Street, and I shout back, asking her to let Nina know I'm on a rescue.

We're only a few minutes from the two-hundred-year-old lifeboat house, poised above Hugh Town Harbour. Nina won't be thrilled if I'm late home. I'm on holiday from police duties for the whole week, and promised to ferry wedding paraphernalia home to Bryher on our boat, but it can't be helped. I joined the crew last year, even though my attitude to risk has changed since Noah came along. I push my doubts aside as we burst through the doors of the lifeboat house. We're among the first to arrive, so we're bound to be on today's mission, whether or not the call-out's serious.

The coxswain, Liam Quick, is too busy pulling on his oilskins to greet us. He's around fifty, athletic, with a mariner's weather-beaten face, mid-blond hair and a short-lived smile. He's the only full-time professional member of the island crew. We all know how passionate he is about his job; he takes every shout seriously, even when the risk to life is minimal. The coastguard loudspeaker is blaring at full volume, giving nautical coordinates for a missing boat. My temperature rises even higher as I pull on my kit. It's punishing on a hot day; the yellow and black suit has wrist and neck seals to prevent water getting inside, plus boots with steel toecaps. The final touch is a pre-inflated life jacket and a safety helmet, known as a Gecko.

I'm sweating by the time another crew member appears. Constable Isla Tremayne is out of breath from sprinting here. Our boss will be outraged that most of his five-strong police team are going on a rescue, but Madron's temper is easy to ignite. My old school friend Paul Keast arrives next. I'm relieved to see him. He's been a lifeboatman for twenty years and is always solid in a crisis. I'm busy listening to the cox's briefing when the next two crew members roll up, so I don't catch their faces, but the rescue is already underway. A vessel is missing off the coast of St Agnes, with two local men believed to be on board.

The lifeboat is anchored in the bay, forcing us to pile into our D-class speedboat to reach it. The festival organisers will be pleased about passers-by seeing us in action, leading to bigger donations. I feel a rush of excitement as the launch slides down the runway and hits the water. It rattles my bones as it scuds along at top speed, soon reaching the islands' main lifeboat. Its seventeen-metre-long hull is dark blue, but the fo'c'sle, deck and wheelhouse carry the RNLI's distinctive day-glow orange, making it visible for miles. All mariners associate that luminous colour with safety, even when the lifeboat is just a pinprick on the horizon in a force nine gale.

Every crew member follows the drill as we jump on board. Liam is skipper and Stuart Cardew acts as navigator; he's already staring down at the GPS system when the engine fires into life. I remain in the wheel-house as spare man, to run messages to the rest of the crew, grabbing the handrail when the twin engines activate. They're so powerful, the floor shudders. The bow thruster ignites, giving us an extra burst of power as we set off to locate the stricken vessel. We hit top speed in moments, twenty-five knots per hour, and I can't hear much through my Gecko except the engines' roar. St Mary's Sound passes in a blur, with the spikes of Bartholomew Ledges spearing from the sea like blackened teeth. It's a reminder that the waters around Scilly are full of hazards. The islands are the peaks of a submerged mountain range, with hundreds of sharp crags just beneath the surface. No mariner can rely on their GPS system alone to avoid shipwreck; they have to understand the tides.

I hear a tinny voice on the radio announcing that the rescue helicopter has been scrambled. It will take fifteen minutes to cross from the mainland. More details are already blaring from the radio. Two men set off on a cabin cruiser from St Agnes late last night, but no one reported it missing until now, which strikes me as odd. Why would any boat get into trouble on a flat, calm sea? Surely they had a phone or radio to summon help if the engine failed?

When I peer out of the window again, the islands have vanished; we're sailing west into open water. The sea is feigning innocence. Its appearance is more like the Mediterranean than the cold Atlantic. It's powder blue, glassy with sunshine, no other boats in sight.

3

Sam Austell arrives late for the shout. The lifeboat is just an orange speck on the horizon. He'd love to be on board. Two other men are in the boathouse, listening for news of the mission, but their closed body language announces that he's not welcome, even though he's been in the crew for six months. He catches sight of his face reflected on the computer screen when he peers at the coordinates sent by the coastguard. He's pale and scrawny, even though he's in his mid-twenties, and takes good care of himself. He still resembles the drug dealers he hung around with in Penzance before his stretch in prison. It's no surprise that some of the lifeboat crew objected to him joining.

When he glances around, he witnesses reminders that local volunteers have risked their lives at sea for a hundred and fifty years. The waters here are among the most dangerous in the UK, especially when the Atlantic delivers harsh winter storms to the islands' shores. A picture on the wall shows Bishop Rock lighthouse, three miles west of Scilly, with a giant wave crashing over its roof, even though it's fifty metres high. The board beside it records every rescue mission, resulting in lives lost or saved, for the past century. Names of volunteers who won bravery medals are recorded there too. It's a roll call of the great and the good in Scilly. Sam would love to join that band of heroes one day, if he can persuade the crew to acknowledge his existence. When he asks for details of the shout, only one man replies. The other scowls at him like he's filth stuck to the sole of his shoe.

'Your mate Jez Cardew's missing, on his dad's boat.'

Sam is too shocked to reply. He was with Jez until around 9 p.m. last night, but he never heard him return to the house they share with their landlord. He takes a slow walk back to the room he's rented since leaving his mother's cabin on Bryher after she nursed him back to health.

Hugh Town beach is dotted with fishing boats stranded by the tide, their mooring ropes lying slack on the sand. Families are strolling in the sunshine eating ice cream, like all's right with the world. Sam stands on the pathway, gazing at the shallow waves, hoping his friend is safe. He inhales one more lungful of peace, then heads home. A woman rattles her collection box at him, bearing the RNLI's logo. Instinct makes him drop spare change into the slot. Even he might need their support one day.

His accommodation looks best from the outside. It's a two-storey terraced building on Quay Street, made from local grey stone, which would have been a fisherman's cottage years ago. The property belongs to Callum Moyle now, and Sam is grateful to him for providing him and Jez with building jobs and a place to stay. Many islanders would never allow an ex-offender inside their home. The place is no palace, but it's his only option for now. The living-room wallpaper carries a floral pattern that's decades out of date; the air smells of tobacco and stale beer, with old pizza boxes littering the coffee table. The carpet is stained and dusty, full of sand trodden in from the beach.

He peers inside Jez's bedroom upstairs. It's a mess, as usual. The door hangs open, with his entire life on display; clothes are heaped on the floor beside the steel-capped boots he wears on building sites. Sam prefers to keep his own space neat. It's a habit he learned in prison.

When he enters his room, he notices straight away that something's missing. His phone should be on his bedside table. He's still searching for it when someone raps on the door. Callum Moyle barges in before he can reply, making him uneasy; his landlord rarely stands on ceremony, and Sam has noticed tension between him and Jez for months. Moyle is ten years older than his two lodgers, in his late thirties, with a strong build. He's thick-necked and muscular from years of physical labour, his brown hair razored close to his skull. He has few friends, due to his abrasive manner. Sam can't understand why a man who owns a property and a small but successful building business always seems fed up. This morning, Moyle's eyes look bloodshot, proving that he spent too long in the pub last night, his smile verging on a sneer.

'Where's lover boy?' he asks.

'On his dad's boat somewhere. The lifeboat's searching for him now.'

'That's shit timing,' Moyle says, his grin fading. 'It's screwed my plans for the day. I want that kitchen finished, fast.'

'He's been missing all night, Callum. He could be in trouble.'

'I've still got a contract to deliver.'

'You gave us the weekend off.'

'Change of plan, we need to keep going. You can have the morning, but be there by two, all right? Bring his lordship, when he gets back from his adventure.' Moyle grabs a padded envelope from the table and thrusts it into his hands. 'This came for you yesterday. Don't leave your crap lying around, all right?'

Moyle struts away, and Sam's sense of helplessness increases. He needs the work, even if that means never getting time off. He still can't believe that Jez is missing, and now his phone's gone too, with his whole life locked inside. He must have dropped it somewhere last night.

Sam opens the envelope in his room. The contents don't make sense: a handful of RNLI badges and a handwritten note, with a child's version of a hangman scene in the corner. A stick-man dangles at the end of a rope, head bowed forward on his broken neck. The words below are scrawled in uneven capitals:

'ONE FOOT IN SEA, AND ONE ON SHORE,
TO ONE THING CONSTANT NEVER.'

Why would anyone send him an anonymous message that makes no sense?

He stares out of the window. Hugh Town Harbour looks tranquil. Its quaint fishermen's cottages are protected from high tides by the quay's long arm, yet Sam has never felt more vulnerable.

4

The sky is still cloudless as we bump over flat water. Isla and Paul are on deck as lookouts because the portholes below deck give a restricted view, due to the boat's safety design. Every feature on board has been tested to destruction. I know for a fact that the vessel is almost unsinkable; it's self-righting, even when partly flooded, in the worst sea conditions imaginable. I've been on board in a gale-force storm. The boat did a 360-degree roll, with no injuries to crew or kit. It felt like being locked in a giant washing machine on spin cycle, yet we only sustained a few bruises.

When I scan the deck, everything appears in good order. There's a hydraulic haulage system to lower the small Y-class boat into the water, for cave rescues and going ashore, and dozens of life jackets and buoys are neatly stowed away, yet that's not where my concern lies. The coastguard has told us that two young men are missing on a vessel that should have returned to St Mary's last night, and they may already have come to grief. We're close to the Atlantic shipping lane, where any drifting vessel is in danger. Several small craft have been sliced in two by freighters over the past ten years. Cargo ships are so powerful, they take a mile to slow down, and fishing vessels may not be sighted in bad weather. I keep my eyes glued to the ocean's surface. Any broken timbers floating past will signal bad news, but so far, the water's clear.

The rescue helicopter is buzzing overhead already. Its downdraught blows hot air in my face and scatters ripples across the water's surface. The chopper can assist for up to three hours, over a two-hundred-mile range, before having to refuel. The air crew have a better chance of spotting the boat or a casualty than us, using a thermal imaging system that picks up swimmers as red dots on the sea's cold surface. I stare out at the horizon, but it's not long before my eyes start to play tricks. The sun's dazzle makes judging distances a challenge. The smallest wave can look like a body rolling in the water.

I go back into the wheelhouse once the speed drops; we're following the course a stricken vessel would have taken last night, at the mercy of tidal currents. The skipper keeps both hands on the wheel, gazing straight ahead. Liam Quick's 20/20 eyesight has earned him the nickname 'Hawkeye', because he's spotted so many victims in the water. I can tell how at ease he feels, after hundreds of missions. Stuart Cardew looks much less relaxed. The man's a likeable character, around fifty-five, well known across the islands. He teaches music at Five Islands school and plays folk tunes in a local pub every month. I've listened to him strumming his guitar since I was in my teens. His grey hair is always tied in a ponytail, and his full beard makes him look like Captain Birdseye. There's none of his usual laid-back manner today; his skin is grey as he watches the GPS tracker for blips on the radar. He flinches when I touch his shoulder.

'Are you okay, Stuart?'

'I've had better days. The wife doesn't know I'm here.'

'Want me to navigate so you can call her?'

'I'd rather keep busy.'

The penny drops when I study his pinched features again. 'Is it your boat that's missing?'

'My son borrowed it for a trip to St Agnes with Sam Austell.' His frown deepens. 'He promised to get it back to Hugh Town Harbour this morning, but never did. They're not answering their phones.'

'You're sure they didn't stay on St Agnes overnight?'

'I've called people already. The boat's not been seen.'

'Remember that shout last year when a yacht slipped its mooring? We spent hours searching, but the skipper was having lunch ashore with mates, safe and sound. This'll be the same.'

'Let's hope you're right.'

'Jez can handle himself at sea, Stuart. He won a medal for it, remember?'

KATE RHODES

His frown remains in place. 'I wouldn't trust Sam in a crisis, that's the trouble.'

'Don't worry, he passed his RNLI training with flying colours.'

Cardew seems immune to comfort, and reassurance won't help until the boat's found. He remains a hundred per cent focused on the satellite's green dots pulsing on the screen, like he's forgotten how to blink.

I know how badly the crew would react if two of our youngest volunteers were lost. Some members weren't thrilled about Sam Austell joining, but Jez was awarded the RNLI's highest medal for bravery, for jumping onto a sinking trawler in terrible conditions. Heroism doesn't matter today, though. There's an unspoken bond that unites us; it comes from regular training sessions, shared goals, and dangerous rescue missions all year round. I see the team as an extended family.

Jez Cardew is Eddie's cousin, with the same blond good looks. He's in his late twenties, a builder by trade, and is dedicated to his role as a lifeboatman, like all the other men in his family, even though he seems relaxed about everything else in his life. Sam Austell is a different case entirely. He's always been a troubled soul; his life spun out of control a few years back and he ended up in prison on the mainland for drug dealing. I had to argue hard for him to be accepted into the crew after he was released because I knew it would help him reintegrate. They agreed eventually, but some still question the decision.

Michael Kerrigan is the first crew member I see down in the hold. He's the islands' only Catholic priest, known as Father Mike by the islanders and trusted by everyone. It helps that he's always approachable. He's in his fifties, but he still referees at local football matches, and visits the Ship pub most weekends, to play darts and enjoy a quiet pint. He told me once that people share their woes over a drink more easily than in a confessional booth. He offers me a gentle smile, then checks his phone, like he's still worried about needy parishioners, even though we're miles out at sea.

Eddie is standing close to the window, his nose millimetres from the glass. My deputy no longer looks like a bright sixth-former hoping for A grades. His shoulders are slumped when he turns to face me. He must have heard the news about his cousin from the radio blaring in the wheelhouse.

'I saw Jez with Sam Austell last night, at the Turk's Head,' he says.

'What time was that?'

'Eightish. Me and Michelle took our boat over to St Agnes; Jez was there when we arrived. I haven't seen much of him lately, except on shouts.'

'The pair of you always seem close.'

'The kids keep me busy most nights, but Jez is more like a brother than a cousin.' His gaze returns to the open sea. 'We were in the same year at school. I checked GPS for his phone, just now. There's no signal coming back.'

'Maybe it's switched off. Did you speak to Sam last night, too?'

He shakes his head. 'He was in his own world; I think he left after one drink.'

'Track him down, can you, if your phone's still live.'

'I got hold of Callum Moyle just now. He says Sam got back early, but they haven't seen Jez.'

'Have you told the cox Sam's on shore?'

'Not yet.'

'I'll let him and Stuart know. Did you see Jez sail away from the pub last night?'

He shakes his head. 'We were inside, paying the bill. I'll keep calling people for more info.'

Eddie grabs his phone – he's always at his best with a task to complete – but there's a shout from above. We both rush up the metal steps from the hold and see Stuart Cardew still looking tense, the anxiety on his face increases when he and the cox hear that Sam Austell made it home safe, but no one has spotted Jez yet. The helicopter pilot is announcing new coordinates, which blare from the radio. They've sighted a small boat drifting one mile to our west.

'Not in the shipping lane, is it?' Eddie asks.

Cardew shakes his head. 'It's too close for my liking, Christ knows why he hasn't sent a mayday. Maybe the radio's buggered.'

'Does Jez often borrow your boat?'

'Two or three nights a week. The Turk's Head on St Agnes is his favourite pub these days. Why the hell did Sam go home back separately, if they set off together?'

'We'll find out. They both live with Callum Moyle, don't they?'

'Those two are a bad influence; Callum only cares about money, and Sam's a troublemaker. I keep telling Jez to move.'

'Try not to worry, we'll soon track him down.'

When I go on deck, the lifeboat is gathering speed, with half a mile of wash reeling behind us like a comet's tail. It will only take two minutes to reach the cabin cruiser, and tension is lifting from my shoulders already. Chances are Jez will be on deck wearing an embarrassed smile, but help is on hand if he's injured. The helicopter overhead is keeping pace with us. The downdraught spits brine into my eyes, and a paramedic is sitting in the open doorway, dressed in the air ambulance's scarlet uniform. There's no way I'd swap places with him; it takes far more bravery to drop twenty metres onto a shifting boat deck than to sail over a flat sea.

I catch sight of the cabin cruiser at last, and my system floods with relief. It looks perfectly intact as it expands on the horizon. The wind's picked up in the last few minutes, but not enough to cause problems. The cruiser is riding each swell with ease. I'm feeling optimistic when Stuart Cardew appears at my side.

'Can you see him yet, Ben?'

'Maybe he's below deck.'

Cardew peers through his RNLI binoculars.

'What the hell's he playing at? He must have spotted us by now.'

I'm holding my breath as we sail closer. The lifeboat keels gently from side to side when we slow to a halt, making conditions tricky for the skipper as he brings us alongside. One minute the boats are almost touching, then the current widens the gap to three metres. This is the moment when most accidents happen, during a transfer onto a stricken vessel, so the RNLI has strict safety protocols. If you fall between two boats, it's easy to lose a limb or get crushed to death.

I'm about to volunteer to jump when Cardew suddenly heaves himself over the barrier, vaulting the gap without even a safety line. It's not a clean landing either. He almost falls as he drags himself over the handrail, but I can't blame him for his impatience; I'd do the same if Noah was stranded on a boat drifting towards the shipping lane.

I can see the cruiser's name on its prow, written in faded black paint: *Happy Daze*. My uncle Ray owned one just like it when I was young. My brother and I would somersault backwards off the bow to impress girls on summer days like this, but there's no sign of joy when Stuart Cardew reappears from the hold. He raises his palms to the sky, like he's checking for rain. The boat is empty, for no good reason, and the detective in me needs to know why.

I follow the safety protocol this time, throwing a line to Cardew, bringing the two boats parallel. There's shock on his face when I jump on board; his skin is so white I make him sit on the bench by the wheelhouse before checking the vessel fully. The mooring rope is still coiled in a neat circle on deck, the anchor clipped to the prow. My fears for Jez Cardew increase when I ask Stuart to check if any life jackets are missing. Four are still strapped to the wall on deck, which means he's unprotected, if he fell into the sea. Whatever happened last night must have caught him unawares. When I twist the key in the ignition, the outboard motor fires into life immediately; there's no shortage of fuel or any problem with the radio. The boat is in good working order, but when I enter the cabin below deck, there's no trace of Jez, only the hot reek of boat diesel lingering on the air.

The chopper is already spinning in a new direction, churning the waves to foam around us. Our rescue mission has suddenly picked up speed. We're no longer looking for a vessel adrift on open sea with a young lifeboatman at the helm. We're hunting for a lone swimmer, fighting to keep his head above water.

5

Sam has tasks to complete before work, so he makes a quick exit to collect his mother's medication in time for visiting her tomorrow. It's a relief to escape his landlord's voice echoing up the stairwell while he makes endless phone calls. Moyle's loud tone comes from working on building sites, making himself heard over drills and concrete mixers. His statements often sound like taunts, which sets Sam's teeth on edge. He prefers peace and quiet since he gave up drugs and booze. Life is beginning to feel normal again, after years of exaggerated highs and lows, but he's a long way from calm. Last night's trip to the pub was his first since leaving prison. He still jumps out of his skin if a door slams, like someone's fired a starter gun.

He stops by the quay, wishing he had time to hunt for his phone. People are relaxing on benches while they wait for ferries to the off-islands, for picnics or to visit relatives. When he looks north, the lifeboat house's doors hang open. He'd love to know what's happening, but there will be no news until the crew return. Then accounts of their latest rescue will spread round the island like wildfire, their bravery growing as the stories pass from house to house. Jez was treated like a local hero for months after taking part in the year's most dangerous lifeboat mission. It seems unbelievable that he's the one in peril now.

Sam increases his pace as he marches uphill to the hospital. The duty doctor explains his mother's tablets to him as if she's addressing a slow-witted child. He would have reacted harshly to being patronised in the past, but his temper has improved. An anger management course in prison taught him how to deal with provocation; all he needs to do is count to ten under his breath to avoid a foolish mistake.

He's rewarded by far-reaching views when he goes out-side. English Island lies in the distance, the off-islands fading from black to grey. It seems strange that he once dreamed of escaping this landscape, even though it's hard-wired in his DNA. All he needs now is to stay on course, to put his life back together.

His next port of call is the library on Porthcressa beach. It's one of the few places where he never feels judged; he's enjoyed visiting it since his mother took him as a kid, to borrow picture books. Little has changed since then. It still lies on one of St Mary's prettiest bays, an unassuming build-ing full of treasures. The place looks empty when he walks inside, until he spots the head librarian, Linda Thomas, a lithe white-haired figure. She's in the distance, stacking books on shelves, giving him a cheery wave. If she judges him for his past, there's no sign of it.

He's about to head over for a chat when another woman enters the reception area. His breath catches in his chest as she takes her place behind the counter; it's Danielle Quick, the lifeboat coxswain's daughter. She's got wavy dark hair cut in a bob, and a pretty heart-shaped face that caught his attention years ago, when they were at school. He's seen more of her since she joined the lifeboat crew, which is one of the biggest perks of the role, but no one told him she'd found work at the library.

'Hi, Sam,' she says, smiling. 'Did you miss the shout?'

'By the skin of my teeth.'

'Me too, but it's just as well. Linda's teaching me the catalogue system this afternoon.'

'Did you hear that it's Jez who's missing?'

She looks shocked. 'That's awful news.'

'Your dad will bring him home safe, don't worry.' He watches her smile slowly revive. 'I didn't know you wanted to be a librarian.'

'It's my first week. I love it, especially the kids; they ask the funniest questions.' She looks embarrassed. 'Sorry, it's so new, I can't help gushing.'

'You'll be great here.'

'I got sick of slaving in a hotel kitchen. Are you looking for something today?'

'Just a couple of books I ordered.'

She checks under the counter, then pulls out a single volume. 'They only delivered this: *Accountancy Level Three*. That sounds like fun.'

He feels uncomfortable. 'It's for night school, so I can do my own bookkeeping. Maths is the one thing I did okay in at school, but it's pretty dry.'

'It's great you're studying. I admire people with ambition.'

'Don't hold your breath, I might flunk the exam.'

'Have faith in yourself, Sam. I bet you'll do great.'

Sam can feel colour rising in his cheeks when he carries the book over to a table, to put in some study time before work. It's so long since anyone except his mother or Father Mike gave him encouragement, he's not sure how to react. It's easier to focus on sums and calculations and avoid remembering Jez's absence.

When he glances up fifteen minutes later, Danielle is helping an old lady to choose a romantic novel, her face animated. He hopes she's never guessed that he sent her a Valentine's card fifteen years ago. The embarrassment would kill him, but he can't help watching her chat to the old woman, her smile gentle, like she's got all the time in the world.

6

We've been at sea for six hours, sailing at ten knots, which allows for precise observation. Eddie's been calling Sam Austell all morning for details about Jez, but he's still not answering. Liam Quick has passed the steering wheel to Paul Keast and is sitting on the prow with binoculars trained on the starboard horizon. My own eyes ache from the glare rebounding from the water's surface, its fierce whiteness searing my retinas. There's silence on deck, apart from the engine's grind and the seagulls shrieking overhead. On an ordinary day, the ride would be a pleasure. Grey seals are sunning themselves on Gunner Rock, and Bishop Rock lighthouse looks striking in the distance, its white walls shimmering. My eyes only linger there for a moment before returning to the sea, hoping to catch sight of a raised arm waving for help.

My binoculars are still pressed to my eyes when Isla taps my shoulder. We're doing lookout duty in half-hour shifts, to avoid fatigue. None of us would forgive ourselves if we missed a sign that Jez had swum this way after a freak accident carried him overboard. Isla looks keen to get to work; she's got a quiet, serious nature, her black hair cut in a no-nonsense crop. I've been impressed by the way she handles herself from the moment she joined the team two years ago. She seems just as dedicated to her work as a lifeboat volunteer. The young constable doesn't say a word before she slips into my place, raising her binoculars to the horizon.

Stuart Cardew has his phone pressed to his ear when I go down to the hold. Father Michael is standing close by, but Cardew still looks out of reach. His frown is etched deep into his skin, like a tattoo.

'The wife's not answering her bloody phone,' he mutters. 'She keeps it turned off at the weekend, the daft cow.'

'Have you called Jez's mates?'

'None of them can help, except Callum Moyle. He says Sam got back around ten last night. I warned Jez not to live with that psycho.'

'Is Jez still seeing Anna Dawlish? Maybe he's with her.' Asking the question feels awkward; Anna was my first serious girlfriend, until she ditched me at sixteen, after we'd been together for a year. It hurt at the time, but it was soon water under the bridge. We're on friendly terms now, although we haven't spoken for months.

'He ended that a while back, thank God. He's not ready to commit to someone ten years older with a kid.

He hasn't mentioned any other girls since.' Stuart rubs his hand across his brow, like he's trying to straighten out his thoughts. 'Eddie says Sam seemed edgy, he left the Turk's Head early. Jez only had a pint or two. He'd have been sober when he set off around eleven; he should have reached Hugh Town well before midnight.'

I'm certain Stuart could discuss possibilities for hours, but solid information is what we need, so I contact the police station by radio. Sergeant Lawrie Deane sounds like I've caught him napping; his speech is slower than usual when I ask him to check if Cardew's boat was seen in Hugh Town harbour late last night. I could be clutching at straws, but boats occasionally work loose from their moorings then drift into open water; or someone moves them to another harbour as a practical joke.

Stuart still looks dazed when I stand beside him again.

'Do you think one of Jez's mates could be behind this?' I ask. 'A stupid prank on a summer evening?'

'No way. They're grown-ups now, with jobs to do.' He hesitates. 'The only one mad enough is Sam Austell. Maybe he's behind all this.'

'I doubt it. He's cleaned up his act recently.'

'My son's a soft touch. Sam's other mates all dropped him when he went off the rails.'

'He joined the crew for a second chance.'

'Who else would cut my boat adrift?'

I could point out that there may simply have been a

tragic accident, but it's the wrong time. It only takes one mistake for things to escalate; Jez might have hit his head, then fallen overboard. The only other time I remember an unmanned boat being reported was years ago, after the 2008 financial crash. A local businessman with money worries sailed his yacht a mile out to sea, wound the anchor chain round his neck, then leapt overboard. His body was dragged to the surface the next morning by the lifeboat crew. It's possible Jez has done something similar, even though he gave no sign of despair.

I stand back while Stuart calls Sam Austell again for more details, but the frustration on his face deepens.

'The little shit's turned his phone off.'

There's a sudden yell from above. Isla is pointing due west as we rush on deck, and the boat veers in a new direction. She keeps both arms directed at the sight mark, giving the skipper a line to follow. My eyes chase the horizon but see only a distant freighter, beginning its two-thousand-mile journey to America.

There's a blemish on the water's sunlit surface when I lift my binoculars; a tiny patch of darkness. There's no way I'd have spotted it unless it was pointed out. The object is turning with each wave, and my stomach tightens. I was on a shout last winter when we found a missing yachtsman. His corpse twisted and rolled in just the same way. I blink my eyes shut, remembering my father's last journey on his fishing trawler to the Atlantic Strait. Paul Keast's dad was lost on the same voyage, twenty-five years ago. I hate the idea of finding one of our crewmen drowned, but if the worst has happened, it's the best outcome. No one grieves fully over an empty coffin. My mother never got the chance to stand by Dad's grave, her mourning so long and complex she never fully recovered.

We're close now, the lifeboat slowing. I stand by Stuart's side, aware that he might dive overboard if it's Jez's body in the water. He's whispering an invocation to the gods to keep his son alive. Father Michael is next to us, his face blank.

'It's him, isn't it?' Cardew mutters.

'I can't see yet, Stuart,' the priest replies. 'Let's pray he's safe and sound.'

My hopes plummet as we draw close. It's just a black piece of fabric, drifting on the water.

'Grab it for me,' Cardew yells out. 'Don't let it float away.'

Paul Keast hauls it on board with a boat hook. We all stand in a circle like we're protecting Stuart from a harsh wind as he holds the torn bomber jacket in his hands. He remains silent until he unzips one of the pockets; small change spills onto the deck with a gush of brine.

'That's Jez's key ring,' he mutters.

I take the jacket from his hands as gently as possible, but the other pocket's empty, so Jez's phone could be lying on the ocean floor. Stuart drops to his knees without warning as I fold the jacket into an empty kitbag.

Father Michael helps me carry him downstairs, and we wrap him in an emergency blanket. Despite the day's warmth, Stuart is shivering like he's been underwater far too long.

7

Sam is still at work when dusk falls, building kitchen units in a run-down house on Museum Street. The room looks chaotic. Lengths of oak are stacked on the floor, which is thick with sawdust and covered in half-made cabinets. It bothers him that he hasn't had a moment to retrace his steps and look for his phone, but nothing goes missing on the islands for long. Someone may find it and contact him, or he'll have to use some of his hard-earned savings to buy another if it doesn't turn up tomorrow.

Callum Moyle has been in a foul mood all afternoon, due to Jez's absence. He's releasing his fury by hammering nails into place with extra force. The second-home owners will arrive from London soon, to inspect their progress on the renovation of the property, and he hates being judged.

'Jez worked for a kitchen company in Penzance, but you'd never guess. His joinery's crap,' he says.

Sam glances at a cupboard assembled by his friend. 'It looks okay to me.'

Callum gives him a dead-eyed stare. 'Prison taught you to sit on the fence, did it?'

'It beats arguing all the time, like you and Jez.'

'He acts like he's God's gift, that's why. You two make an odd pair; he won't stop yapping and you never say a word.' Callum reaches for his nail gun. 'Where do you think he's gone?'

'How would I know?'

'He's pulled a fast one, hasn't he?'

'I told you, he's missing at sea.'

'You can't seriously believe that. He'll be bunked up with a woman somewhere.'

The two men work on despite the tense atmosphere, with only the radio's old-fashioned pop songs to dilute it. Sam feels certain Jez wouldn't stay out all night without telling him first, and he hasn't mentioned any girlfriend, but there's no point in arguing. He found out the hard way in prison about men like Callum. They lashed out for no good reason, never dropping their guard.

'We'll have to go flat-out to finish this job,' Callum snaps, 'while Jez is off enjoying himself.'

Sam carries on with his joinery in silence. It's a skill he learned in prison, and he enjoys the craftsmanship, even with Callum peering over his shoulder. He loves feeling the wood's grain in his hands and inhaling its musky, resinous smell. Every piece of furniture feels like an achievement.

'You need to speed up,' Callum says, 'but at least you're thorough.'

Sam acknowledges the half-compliment with a nod. He's still focused on his work when his RNLI buzzer sounds in the pocket of his jeans.

'I have to go,' he says, jumping to his feet. 'They'll need more crew.'

Callum blocks his exit. 'Stay here, or you're fired. I expect loyalty, all right? I don't give a shit about that lifeboat.'

Sam's instinct tells him to barge past and run to the harbour, but he can't afford to lose his job, even though his fears are rising. Jez has been secretive for months, but he's not the kind to land himself in danger. If the worst has happened, someone else must be to blame.

8

We return to St Mary's as night-time settles over the water. There's so little light pollution here, the stars dazzle like fireworks, but I've never felt less celebratory. Cardew's boat is trailing behind us on a towline, with Paul Keast and Isla steering it home. It feels wrong to go back with nothing to show for our day-long search except the empty vessel. The crew remain silent when Hugh Town's lights appear on the horizon. I keep picturing Jez clinging to a rock somewhere, and Stuart's posture reveals a similar state of mind. He's slumped in a corner of the hold, folded in on himself like a collapsed building. Father Michael sits beside him offering words of comfort.

The coxswain appears undeterred, despite our exhausting search. I can tell he's got no intention of giving up. He crouches beside Stuart to explain the next stage, but the man's eyes are empty, like blank sheets of glass. His expression worries me. There's an odd fixity in his gaze, like he's blinded himself by staring too long at the sun.

'Let someone else take over, Liam. You're exhausted,' I say.

'This is just the start,' Quick says, ignoring my comment. 'We'll refuel, then try again with a fresh crew.'

Stuart grabs his arm. 'Let me come along. I can't stay at home, knowing he's out there.'

'Not this time, mate, you're needed at home,' the cox replies. 'Ben's taking you, in the police van.'

'What do I tell the wife?' he whispers.

'Let Ben do the talking for now.'

Stuart turns in my direction. 'Delia will blame me for all this.'

'Of course she won't,' I say, shepherding him to a seat.

'I was mad to lend Jez our boat with that idiot on board.'

His face holds guilt as well as anger, even though no one will blame him for letting his grown-up son borrow his boat. Islanders make the same short journey thousands of times each year, in good weather and bad. Something else appears to be troubling him, but it's the wrong time for questions.

The whole team is focused on practicalities when we drop anchor near the quay, where a fresh set of volunteers will replace us. The coxswain shakes his head when I suggest again that an experienced crew member should skipper the boat in his place. His movements are rapid, masking his tiredness, even though my own head's pounding with eyestrain from staring at the water. The man's commitment is a double-edged sword; it strikes me as obsessive, but his tenacity's admirable, and I'm not his boss. I'm powerless to detain him on land.

The lifeboat house feels like paradise after so long at sea. It's not just warm and dry; support team volunteers are making us hot drinks and handing out food. They're led by Janet Fearnley whose commitment to her role seems to have doubled since becoming a widow. She reminds me of my godmother, Maggie, who loves supporting her community. I grab a sandwich from Janet's tray, telling her she's a lifesaver, then swig down my coffee. Everyone looks worn out, yet we're all unwilling to give up our search for Jez.

The new crew is assembling while the boat refuels. They're a mix of experienced and novice volunteers. Liam is keen to get back to work. Eddie is also staying on board for the next phase. I'd rather someone with fresh eyes took his place, but this is the cox's domain, not mine. His daughter Danielle is among the new crew, jogging down to the speedboat. She's in her late twenties, but looks younger, her eyes shiny with excitement.

Len and Molly Bligh are next to jump on board; the brother and sister are impossible to miss, with matching flame-red hair. They run a riding school and horse sanctuary near Hugh Town; they've been crew members for years, and understand the role completely because their father was a lifeboatman too. The pair look a hundred per cent focused on the challenge ahead. The boat departs at top speed, back to the same stretch of ocean we combed all day, but their task will be far harder in darkness. Soon the lifeboat is just a dot of light heading west, leaving human habitation behind. It looks more like a moonshot than a rescue mission, with stars clustered on the horizon.

Isla keeps Stuart company in the lifeboat house while I collect the van. I'll take her with me when we drive him home. The young constable lives in the next bay and has known the Cardew family since birth. Her gentle manner always calms people in distress, while my own bluntness has the opposite effect. I'm about to head for the police station, ten minutes' walk away, when a familiar noise reaches me. Shadow's howl of greeting sounds like a wolf baying in an Alaskan forest, and he bounds out of the darkness, his paws landing on my shoulders, desperate to lick my face.

'What's this?' I ask him. 'You should be at home.'

He whines repeatedly, like he's offering me a detailed explanation in dog language. I give his fur a hard rub, then he trots at my side down Quay Street, satisfied. I can't fault his loyalty. He's proved that he'd lay down his life for any member of my family, spending June recovering from a knife injury he received trying to defend us. It's a mystery how he figured out I was on the lifeboat and knew exactly where to wait. Either he's clairvoyant or he saw me jumping on board all those hours ago and stayed put until my return.

I pull out my phone to call Nina as I walk. Relief washes over me when she picks up; her voice is relaxed as she explains that she caught the ferry home to Bryher hours ago. Noah went down easily, after a big feed. I may have spent the day with a distraught father, but my own small family is safe and well. She teases me about using the lifeboat as an excuse to avoid wedding planning, then says she and Noah want me home soon, leaving me on a high.

My mind is clear as I drive back to collect Isla and Stuart, aware that my break from police duties has been cancelled now Jez is missing. Neither of my passengers comment on Shadow's presence. He often accompanies me when I'm patrolling the islands, and is smart enough to stay quiet on the back seat. The route east from Hugh Town is through complete darkness. Islanders complain if the council threatens to install more streetlights, so local kids have to walk home each winter afternoon guided only by starlight if they forget to carry a torch.

Stuart says little as we drive past fields, with the van's headlights bouncing off the dry-stone walls that line our roads in Scilly. Isla keeps up a murmur of conversation until we swing down the lane to Porth Hellick bay. It's a picturesque cove by daylight, with tall pillars of granite guarding the beach. It looks more ominous at night, when the rock formations loom above the water like the ghosts of dead smugglers.

The Cardews' house is the only one lit up when we

45

arrive. It stands above the bay, by a sign for the plant nursery Delia runs. Her large greenhouse shines in the darkness. My hands have been clenched around the wheel so tightly, they feel numb when I switch off the engine. There's no good way to tell a mother that her only son is missing at sea.

Stuart is staring at the ground; I'm not even sure he hears me curse when Shadow escapes from the van and shoots towards the Cardews' home like an arrow. The dog pays no attention to my calls, and I'm assuming he's found a rabbit to kill when Delia Cardew appears on the pathway. She's a tall, slender woman with grey hair clipped back from a face that usually looks serene. She reminds me of a gardener from one of those TV makeover programmes, where someone's messy back yard is transformed into an oasis in a couple of days with minimum fuss. She is famous for her horticultural knowledge and is most people's first port of call if their garden is ailing. Tonight she's wearing muddy jeans and a smock, like she's spent all day tending her plants.

'There you are, Ben,' she calls out, her expression anxious. 'Is Jez with you? A neighbour just told me he was missing.'

'Can we talk inside, please? I'll give you the details.'

'Thank God, I've been worried sick.' She leans down to pet Shadow, burying her hand in his fur. When she spots Stuart lingering by the van, she looks glad that her husband is back on dry ground, but then her smile fades. 'What on earth's happened? Stu's as white as a sheet.'

'I'll explain everything, I promise.'

I follow her down a hallway lined with pictures of gardens she's designed. A couple of Stuart's old guitars hang from the walls, relics of past gigs, but it's the photos of Jez that catch my attention. The latest ones show him in his RNLI uniform, holding the medal he received six months ago for bravery at sea. He looks like the archetypal Hollywood hero: tall, blond and rugged, with a raffish smile.

Stuart's footfall sounds heavy in the passageway, followed by Isla's lighter tread. I can tell from the state of the kitchen that the Cardew family love their home. The floor tiles are clean enough to sparkle, and the units look brand new.

'Shall I put the kettle on?' Delia asks.

'Let's sit down together first, please. Have you heard much about what's been going on, Delia?'

'Only bare details. I was alone here all day, working in the potting shed,' she says, her gaze searching her husband's face. 'I've been worried about you, Stu.'

'I tried calling earlier,' he says. 'Your bloody phone was off.'

'Now you're scaring me. Just tell me what's happened, for God's sake.' She stares at each of us in turn.

'We found your cabin cruiser drifting ten miles from shore.'

'How do you mean?' Her movements come to a sudden halt, like we're playing musical chairs.

'The boat was empty. No one's seen Jez since he

47

left St Agnes late last night. We found his jacket in the water.'

I'm about to give more details when Stuart produces the jacket from an RNLI carrier bag. Drops of brine splash on the tiles as he passes it to his wife. Her stunned expression reminds me of my mother's after she heard Dad's boat had gone missing. She puts the jacket in the sink, then turns away, shrugging off Stuart's attempt to touch her shoulder.

Delia keeps her back to us, her hands braced on the counter. Her eyes are a shade darker when she finally turns round, shiny with suppressed tears.

'The lifeboat will find him, don't worry. Jez is the strongest swimmer I know.' Her denial is loud enough to resonate from the walls.

Stuart collapses onto a bench as Delia busies herself making hot drinks. He seems spent after hunting for his son; his reaction is the opposite to his wife's. I can see terror in her eyes, but she's not letting it overwhelm her. There's nothing in the police manual to say that an officer should stay with the family when someone's missing at sea, but Isla volunteers to support her neighbours. Shadow positions himself at Stuart's side, as if he's sensed his vulnerability. Stuart's expression remains vacant, which isn't surprising. It's human nature to ignore unimaginable loss, until it slaps you in the face. I don't want the couple to suffer any more than necessary. If the worst has happened, I'll do everything in my power to bring their son's body home.

9

Shadow slinks under the Cardews' kitchen table. He seems determined to remain there, and the couple are too preoccupied to care. He gives a low snarl when I tug his collar. I can only apologise and ask Isla to bring him to the station with her tomorrow morning. Delia still seems calm, but her eyes have retained their odd gleam.

'Don't worry about us, Ben. No news is good news, isn't it?'

I wish them goodnight, then return to the van, my head full of questions. The biggest one is the need to find out what happened to Jez's phone; there's no way he'd have left it at home when he set out for the pub. But when I punch his number into my own phone, the answer's disappointing. The last time his network picked up a signal was just after eleven-thirty last night. The simplest answer is that he fell into the sea, during a solo voyage home, on a flat calm sea, yet the idea doesn't convince me.

I can't go home until another question is answered,

but when I park on Quay Street, Callum Moyle's house is in darkness. Sam Austell might be in the Ship pub, seeking company even though he claims to have stopped drinking. I hammer on the door anyway. I'm about to walk away when a slim figure appears in the doorway. Austell's dark hair is cut shorter than when I arrested him years ago; he's wearing a worn-out dressing gown, his feet bare. He looks stronger than when he returned to the islands, but still vulnerable. I can see suspicion on his face, something that's common among ex-cons. A stretch in prison leaves many of them with a lifetime fear of the authorities.

'We need to talk, Sam. Didn't you get my calls?'

'I've lost my phone.'

He takes a grudging step backwards, allowing me to enter. He's unwilling to maintain eye contact, but I know from experience that the guy's shyness is bone-deep. I arrested him for possession and hoped he'd turn over a new leaf, but he was prosecuted for drug dealing on the mainland, which put him away for three years. I've been impressed by his efforts to stay clean since his release. He's making better choices, and his volunteer role on the lifeboat seems to have improved his self-esteem. He leads me into the living room that's seen better days, with dark walls and battered furniture.

'Have you heard the news about Jez?' I ask.

'I found out this morning.'

'Talk me through last night's events, please, step by step.'

'He invited me to the Turk's Head, so I went along for the ride. We set off about seven thirty.'

'You both had your phones on you?'

He gives a rapid nod. 'Jez moored up on the jetty and I joined him in the pub for an hour. He stayed there after I left.'

'How come you went so early?'

'I was testing my willpower.' He looks uncomforta-ble. 'I was tempted to have a beer, so I got out, fast. I gave up booze months ago.'

'Where did you go after that?'

'For a stroll round the island.'

I've taken that walk myself after a night at the pub. You often see grey seals on the rocks, basking in the moonlight, and razorbills nesting among the outcrops, silent for once instead of releasing their piercing cries. St Agnes is so small, you can circle its perimeter in less than an hour.

'Then what?'

Sam looks away. 'I sat on the quay, hoping for a lift.'

'Why didn't you wait outside the pub for Jez?'

'He always comes home late. I hear the front door at two or three in the morning several times a week.'

'Is he seeing someone on St Agnes?'

'Jez hasn't told me. He's private about stuff like that.' Sam's gaze is steady now, I'm almost certain he's speak-ing the truth. 'A couple took me back to St Mary's; their yacht was moored in the harbour.'

'Who are they?'

'Retired holidaymakers, I've forgotten their names.'

'What's their boat called?'

'I didn't notice.'

I stare back at him. 'Some mystery couple took you home on a yacht with no name?'

'It was a ride back, that's all.'

I drag in a breath and hold it until calmness returns. Stuart Cardew might dislike Austell, but I remember him as a kid growing up on Bryher, with a mother some islanders treated as a social outcast.

'Listen to me, Sam. People will say you and Jez went drinking together on St Agnes, then had a fight. They won't believe you're on the wagon. You could have dumped his body, before setting his boat adrift. They'll blame you if anything's happened to him because of your past. I know it's wrong, but that's the way it is.'

'Why would I hurt my best mate?'

'Give me every detail you can about the couple who picked you up. I'll record it on my phone.'

He starts to babble. 'They were northerners, in their sixties, the friendly type. The boat was a newish twenty-five-foot motor yacht. It was their last night in Scilly; they're stopping in Penzance, then going up the coast in a week or two.'

'That's better. Now tell me when you lost your phone.'

'God knows. I didn't miss it till this morning.'

'So it's on Jez's boat, or at the pub on St Agnes?'

He looks uncertain. 'I might have dropped it on my walk. My whole life's on that fucking thing.'

'Someone'll find it. Come to the station tomorrow morning for a formal interview. Jez's family need information about the evening, and it'll stop people jumping to the wrong conclusion. Be there by ten, please.'

'Can I bring Father Mike? He's been supporting me since I got back.'

'Of course, but you're not under arrest, remember? I just need to record details.'

The tension on his face increases when footsteps thud on the path outside and the front door creaks open. Callum Moyle has been drinking; the hot reek of brandy reaches me the minute he enters, his movements twitchy. I don't know much about him, except for his reputation as a decent builder. My uncle almost employed him as a trainee in his boatyard ten years back, but Moyle rejected the low starting wage. He's shorter than Sam but looks more like an ex-con, with a thuggish face, razor-cut hair and bloodshot eyes. Something about his demeanour announces that he's spoiling for a fight.

'This is a rare pleasure, DI Kitto,' he says with a fake grin. 'Has my lodger been causing you trouble?'

'Not to my knowledge.'

'Good, or he'll be out on his ear.' He gives Austell a long stare. 'Is this about Jez? I can't believe anything bad's happened to him. He leads a charmed life. We call him lover boy round here.'

'How come?'

'He gets more women than he deserves.'

'That's no surprise, is it? Jez is seen as a hero since winning that lifeboat medal.'

'He's got flaws, like the rest of us. I bet he's buggered off to the mainland with some bird.'

'What are you talking about? It's possible he's drowned. Jez would never leave his dad's boat adrift.'

'Maybe he's got debts he can't pay.'

'Rent, you mean?'

'And the rest. He borrowed cash off me last month.'

I can't pinpoint my dislike for Callum Moyle, but he's always struck me as fake. His animosity towards his housemate seems strange, especially when he's Jez and Sam's employer, as well as their landlord. Maybe he enjoys the power. He carries himself like a boxer but can't disguise his refined public-school accent.

Sam looks uncomfortable as I prepare to leave, while Moyle scowls.

'Goodnight, both of you. See you tomorrow, Sam.'

Moyle sniggers, like he's heard a first-class joke but only he gets the punchline. The visit has given me little new information apart from proving that Callum Moyle likes to drink, his manner arrogant. Tomorrow I'll need to track down the yacht Sam mentioned, to check his story adds up.

It's almost 1 a.m. when I reach my bowrider speedboat, *Morvoren*, in Hugh Town harbour. Boats take the place of cars in Scilly; the waters between St Mary's and the off-islands are called the Street by locals, with the marine thoroughfare in constant use. Kids are ferried over to Five Islands school, and many of the islands' two thousand residents commute to work by sailing for twenty minutes each day.

I make the journey home at a slow pace, letting the warm air dispel my tension, but plenty of questions need answers. Why would an experienced sailor abandon a seaworthy boat? I've come to understand Sam Austell better over the past six months, by watching his attempts to reintegrate. I can't believe he'd jeopardise his progress by attacking a friend, then tossing his body to the waves. There's a big difference between a minor drug dealer and a cold-blooded killer. I try to picture Jez Cardew, his manner always friendly and relaxed. There was a party in his honour at the town hall back in January, after he won his lifeboat medal; I can't imagine a single islander disliking him, unless someone's keeping their resentment hidden.

I fix Bryher in my sights as the boat cuts through low waves. The island where I was born expands on the horizon, with the outline of Gweal Hill rising in the distance. There's nothing like a fruitless search at sea to make you grateful for home. The lights are out in the flat above the boatyard when I dock on Church Quay. My uncle will have smoked his last roll-up, drunk his regular nightcap of single malt, then gone to bed by eleven so he can rise obscenely early tomorrow.

A fresh surge of energy hits me suddenly, making me break into a jog as I follow the path home. I know it so intimately, every bump and rabbit hole is familiar. I'm sprinting by the time I reach Hell Bay, then hurry across the shingle to the stone cottage my grandfather built. All the lights are out, and silence engulfs me when I step inside. I spot the padded envelope on the kitchen table. When I glance at the postmark, I see it was sent from Hugh Town, St Mary's. There's a note inside that I didn't notice, along with a dozen RNLI badges. The hangman Eddie described is scrawled in the top corner, showing a fragile stickman dangling from a rope. There's a message below in wobbly block capitals:

'FULL FATHOM FIVE THY FATHER LIES,
OF HIS BONES ARE CORAL MADE.
THOSE ARE PEARLS THAT
WERE HIS EYES.'

It takes me a moment to decipher the words, then I drop the paper like it's hot enough to burn. Why would anyone send me a reminder that my dad drowned on his fishing trawler, his body lost fathoms under water, years ago? His whole crew had perished in a vicious storm before the lifeboat could reach it. I had nightmares for years about his remains drifting on the open sea, at the mercy of every tide. When I do a search on my phone, I discover it's a quote from a Shakespeare play, *The Tempest*. Some idiot's trying to be clever. I take a deep breath, then stuff the note back into the envelope. Instinct makes me lock the front door, and the windows, even though no one bothers with security out here.

Noah is fast asleep in his cot when I enter his small nursery, where moonlight pours through a gap in the curtains. He's flat on his back, hands raised above his head, his minute breaths too quiet to hear. I stand in the doorway until my anxiety ebbs away. I could stay here for hours, watching him shift in the darkness like a swimmer doing backstroke as he reaches for shore.

10

Panic sets in once Sam is alone. None of it makes sense. He sits on the edge of his bed with his hands clasped in his lap, trying to recall details. The pub's interior lingers in his memory. It was his first time in a boozer since leaving prison; the air smelled of wine, beer and home-cooked food. Jez melted into the crowd immediately, always at ease amongst people. Sam sat in a corner while Jez spoke first to his cousin, Eddie, then to the landlord, who looked angry for some reason. The place bored him after half an hour, even though bars had been his favourite environment before his life fell apart. He clenches his hands more tightly, glad that he stuck to his plan and never touched a drop. It felt safer to go outside into the fresh air and stroll round the island, like he did as a boy, with his mother reciting the names of every medicinal plant in the hedgerows: feverfew, witch hazel, samphire.

He falls asleep soon after he lies down, exhausted by the week's labour. Something wakes him hours later, and his system floods with relief. Jez is back home; he can hear him through the wall, preparing for bed. He rises to his feet, eyes bleary, but when he reaches the landing, he realises that something is wrong. His landlord is rooting though Jez's possessions, the overhead light glaring down.

'What the hell are you doing, Callum?'

Moyle jerks upright, dropping clothes on the floor. 'Jez owes me rent, plus five hundred quid. If he's done a runner, I need it back.'

'Why now? He could have drowned, for fuck's sake.'

He shrugs. 'It's my money, I've got materials to buy.'

'Why did you tell Kitto that Jez chases women? I don't even know if he's got a girlfriend right now.'

'Are you kidding? Blokes like him get them all, while the rest of us go begging.' Moyle's tone is caustic.

'How come you hate him all of a sudden?'

'He pretends to be a big hero, but his type always grab more than they deserve,' Moyle sneers. 'Now fuck off back to bed. I want more work out of you tomorrow.'

Sam turns away; it's not worth getting into a fistfight that could land him back in jail. He returns to his room, but the sound of Moyle rummaging through Jez's belongings continues to drift through the wall, and sleep takes a long time to arrive.

11

Sunday 27 August

Nina doesn't stir when I wake at 6 a.m. after too little rest. My mind remained at sea all night, hunting for Jez Cardew. I ease out of bed, then go into the kitchen and tune the radio to the RNLI's frequency but hear only a crackle of white noise.

My coffee's brewing when the radio finally spits out the information that the night-time search was fruitless. The lifeboat travelled far out into the Atlantic Strait, but with no success. The chances of anyone surviving in open water for over twenty-fours are almost non-existent. Even confident swimmers succumb to hypothermia or get dragged under by currents. Tension curdles in my gut. I've never heard of a rescue mission where someone's found safe and well after such a long interval.

I can hear Noah waking up as I move around the kitchen. He's not yelling, exactly, just welcoming the

60

new day. When I go into the nursery, he gazes up at me from the cot my uncle Ray built, arms outstretched, waiting for me to scoop him up. He's big for three months, a solid weight in the crook of my arm. He's a dreamer already; his green eyes are fixed on the middle distance when he offers me his first smile of the day. I don't fully understand why, but that grin has the power to dissolve my resentment about sleepless nights, endless filthy nappies and my reduced sex life.

'Life was easy before you, buster,' I tell him. 'I know you're hungry, but hold on, okay? Your mum wants her beauty sleep.'

He's too busy watching how I pour my coffee to complain, storing away information for future use. He's still heavy with sleep as I stand by the window with him on my shoulder. The sea is flat calm, the same mid blue as my wedding suit, with the sun dominating the eastern sky. Noah's energy is reviving as he claps his hands, excited by the ocean's hugeness. He's a typical Kitto, more at home in water than on land. I'd love to take him for a dip while the beach is empty, but that'll have to wait. His nappy needs changing, so I cart him to the bathroom and deal with the disgusting mess he's made overnight.

'How can anyone so small produce that much crap?'

Noah is unashamed, blowing raspberries at me while I wipe him down.

'Your personal hygiene needs work, my friend.'

He waves his legs in the air, carefree and supple. I'm

admiring the way he can clutch his toes with his hands when Nina calls out from the bedroom.

'Bring him here, can you?'

My fiancée looks gorgeous, her face still flushed with sleep, as I pass Noah over for the day's first feed then lean down to kiss her. She's taking a year's leave from her new job as a counsellor at St Mary's hospital, and seems to have no regrets. She's done the lion's share of daytime childcare since my paternity leave ended, yet she rarely complains.

'It's beautiful out there. Promise me you're not working today, Ben.'

'I've got no choice, sorry.'

'I heard about poor Jez going missing, but it's Sunday, and you're meant to be with us. Sorry if that sounds heartless, but Maggie needs us at the church tomorrow too. She wants answers about food, flowers and everything else.'

'I'll be there, I promise, but today's busy.'

'The wedding's next weekend and nothing's ready.'

'I have to find out what happened to Jez, for his family's sake.'

Her voice softens. 'God, his parents must be in bits.'

Nina has a calm disposition, but her eyes turn misty. The idea of Jez's mum and dad losing their only son hits a raw nerve for me too. I rest against the pillows while she nurses Noah, and count my blessings. We distract ourselves with chat about everyday stuff while Noah's belly swells with milk. Nina spoke to my older brother yesterday. Ian plans to fly his whole family over to Scilly, arriving just before our wedding, but seeing is believing. He ran off to America straight after his medical training, when I was twenty-five. If he gets here, it will be his first time on home soil since our mother's funeral years ago.

'I've almost persuaded Ray to give a speech,' Nina says.

'You must have magic powers.'

My uncle is quiet by nature. I've always enjoyed his company, but he's fonder of boats than human beings. Ray becomes gentler in Nina's company, and more inclined to laugh.

'Do you need any wedding stuff done today?' I ask.

'Loads, but most of it's covered,' she says. 'Ray picked up the serviettes and wine glasses yesterday. Just promise to get a haircut. You look like Tarzan, and not in a good way.'

'I'll sort it, don't worry.'

'Thank God, or the photos will be ruined. Can you take Noah while I jump in the shower?'

She dumps him on my lap, leaving me to rub his back, his small body squirming. After ten minutes, she emerges from the bathroom wearing shorts which reveal legs that go on for miles, and a white linen top, her dark hair almost touching her shoulders. She's still beautiful enough to twist my stomach into knots.

'You could have had any bloke you fancied, Nina. How come you picked me?'

She leans down to kiss my cheek. 'Idris Elba's taken, so I settled for you.'

'Too late now. Don't overdo it today, will you?'

'I'll take Noah for a paddle, then check the florist has our bouquets ready for the church. Maggie says three hundred people will come to the picnic.'

'We'll go bankrupt at this rate.'

'My parents will cover most of it.' Nina hefts our son over her shoulder. 'Zoe's still promising to sing, but she seems low. Can you go and see her today, if you get the chance?'

'I'll call by tonight.'

When I look north from our porch, Hell Bay Hotel is visible at the far end of the bay, its white walls gleaming in the early sunlight. My friend Zoe was born there and her family still own it. We used to communicate via semaphore and Morse code when we were kids, and she was my favourite partner in crime. She's flown back from India for my wedding, but finding out why she left her husband behind will have to wait. I need to visit the Turk's Head before interviewing Sam Austell again. I stuff the envelope containing the badges in my pocket before setting off.

It's only 7.30 when I cross Shipman Head Down, with Watch Hill ahead of me. Early morning is my favourite time on Bryher, when the landscape's empty and the air is clean enough to dazzle. There's evidence of prehistoric inhabitants everywhere I look, with Puckles Carn lying due south. No one knows why they piled rocks into towers that rise twelve or fifteen feet high, or how they managed to position huge slabs of granite over mass graves to protect ancestral spirits. The only thing missing is Shadow, but I've grown used to his independence. He worships my family, but enjoys trying other households on for size, especially if someone's in trouble. He seems to believe it's his duty to safeguard the whole population.

I'm not surprised to find my uncle working when I reach Church Quay, even on a Sunday. The doors to his boatyard hang open, with the sound of hammer blows ringing out. The noise makes me nostalgic. I loved spending summer holidays there, helping him turn raw wood into seaworthy vessels. Ray raises his hand in greeting when he spots me, but there's no time for a mug of his ultra-strong coffee today. If I'd agreed to be his apprentice twenty years ago, my life would be simpler, but I was desperate to see the world.

The sea is yellow with sunlight as I steer the bowrider Ray helped me build through New Grimsby Sound. St Agnes is twenty minutes away, but Samson appears first. The ghostly island has known plenty of sadness. It was home to a thriving community until two hundred years ago, when the well ran dry; the deserted homes still look habitable from this distance, even though their windows shattered a lifetime ago.

It's 8.30 a.m. when I moor below the Turk's Head on St Agnes. The pub's motor yacht, Seal Watcher, is already at harbour, and a familiar boat is approaching from the south. It's an old trawler, customised to hold two horseboxes on deck. Molly Bligh's vivid red hair shines in the sun, a wild cloud of ringlets flying in the breeze. She was on the second search mission last night, looking for Jez, and must be tired from the hunt. I wait on the jetty until she throws me her mooring rope. She's a tall, strong-looking woman, around thirty, with a serene air. Molly's a key member of our lifeboat crew and volunteers as a lifeguard each summer, but I've never seen her look so exhausted.

'Are you okay, Molly?' I call out. 'When did you get back?'

'Just now. I haven't slept yet, but we're looking after some ponies out here. I feed and check on them every day.'

'Couldn't someone else do it for you, just once?'

'I'm better keeping occupied, till there's news about Jez.'

I touch her shoulder. 'We've done all we can. You spent the whole night looking for him.'

'It may not be enough, that's the trouble.'

Molly hurries away without saying goodbye, clearly desperate for time alone, to process her time on the lifeboat. The look on her face was pure misery, her usual calmness absent. Maybe her feelings for Jez go beyond friendship. It's a reminder that many people in our community, not just his family, will be distraught if the worst has happened.

I walk up the steep slope to the Turk's Head once

she's gone. The pub is the focal point of the island's tiny community of less than a hundred permanent residents. It's often empty in winter, but is packed with holidaymakers all summer long. It's like the interior of an old whaling ship, with wood-lined walls and beams supporting the ceiling; I can imagine smugglers gathering round the inglenook fire centuries ago, bragging about their battles with the excise men, but today it's suffused with sunlight.

Debbie and Tommy Brookes have run the place for two years, renting out half a dozen rooms each summer. Their work requires them to rise early because most of their guests are birdwatchers, anglers or walkers. The couple are on the pub's terrace, laying tables for breakfast. They're native islanders, a good-looking middle-aged pair, well liked by the community. I see them out on the water occasionally, on their yacht, taking guests out to Norrard Rocks. Both are dressed for high summer as I climb the steps. Debbie is wearing flip-flops and a pale blue dress that flatters her slim build, with her dark curls framing her face.

Tommy looks relaxed too, in shorts and a T-shirt emblazoned with the Turk's Head logo, his salt-and-pepper hair in need of a comb. I know the guy's fit for his age because we're both members of the islands' wild swimming club. Tommy's a decade older than me, but he puts in a good performance every year in the island's ten-mile swimathon.

'Good to see you, Ben,' he calls out. 'Are you after a full English?'

'Just a bacon sandwich to go, please, and some information.'

'No problem, give me five minutes.'

He heads for the kitchen, leaving me with his wife. Debbie looks less carefree up close, with fine lines etched across her forehead. She listens attentively when I explain that Jez Cardew is still missing after last night's search.

'That's awful news, Ben. Everyone loves him here.'

'I'm afraid his chances are poor after so long.'

'We'll keep praying for him.' She touches the small gold crucifix that hangs at her throat.

Prayer isn't an option for me. I enjoyed the Sunday School stories I heard as a boy, but interpreted them as fairy tales, which puts me in the minority in Scilly. Many islanders are devout Christians. I've always believed that their faith is affected by our close relationship with the sea. We're surrounded by danger, from storms and rising tides; it's not surprising people long for guardian angels to protect them and their families.

'Tell me about Friday night, please, Debbie. Did you see Jez and Sam arrive?'

'I was in the kitchen most of the time, but I said hello.' She shifts her gaze to the sea. 'Sam's like a coiled spring, isn't he? The lad hardly spoke a word.'

'Was he on the booze?'

'Just orange juice. Jez had a few pints, then left around eleven.'

'Does he drink here often?'

'Several times a week, but he rarely stays the whole evening; he comes for darts, a drink or two, and the pub quiz. Everyone loves chatting to him.'

'Did you see him sail away?'

'Tommy might have, he often watches the boats leave. He says it's peaceful, seeing them disappear. He even takes our boat out sometimes late at night in summer; it's the only free time we get.' Debbie looks preoccupied, like she's struggling to concentrate.

'Tell me more about Jez, please. He's been on boats his whole life; I can't see him getting into difficulties.'

'I don't know about his personal life, but we chat sometimes if the place is quiet. He's such a nice lad.'

'Has he got a girlfriend over here?'

'I never ask intimate questions,' she says, looking away. 'I'm a landlady, not a shrink.'

Debbie seems so anxious, I feel almost certain Jez has burdened her with a secret she can't share. The landlady's gentle manner makes her an ideal confidante, her eyes full of sympathy. She's about to speak again when Tommy reappears, carrying my sandwich and a coffee. I suspect she was about to reveal something, but her closed expression stops me mid-question.

Tommy is full of bluster, talking about the gig-racing final and the island's football team, like he's determined to avoid the elephant in the room. If he's concerned that a young man may have drowned soon after visiting their pub, there's no sign. He avoids direct questions, saying he doesn't recall seeing Jez's boat arrive or leave.

'You know how it is, Ben. We run around keeping everyone happy. I hardly have time to take our boat out these days. Come back soon, won't you? Breakfast's on the house,' he adds, before hurrying away.

Debbie peers over her shoulder, watching her husband greet half a dozen guests as they arrive for breakfast, her face expressionless.

'You didn't find Sam Austell's phone here Friday night, did you?' I ask.

'He got Callum Moyle to call me about that just now. We haven't seen it, I'm afraid.'

'Is something wrong, Debbie? You don't seem yourself.'

'It's sad, that's all.' She pulls in a long breath. 'Jez was facing a big decision.'

'About what?'

'I don't know, but something was wrong behind that big smile. Life was getting him down. He didn't sail to St Agnes so often just for our beer.' Tommy is beckoning for help, and Debbie is already backing away. 'Sorry, I have to go. Our guests need serving.'

She rushes off to greet her customers. She hasn't provided any concrete facts, but it's the first time anyone's hinted that Jez may have been carrying secrets he never chose to share.

12

You can't avoid people in a place like Scilly, so it pays to stay on good terms with everyone, unless you hate their guts. I can't tell whether my first-ever girlfriend is glad to see me when I bump into her on Hugh Town quay; Anna Dawlish was always good at keeping her feelings hidden, especially during our year together. She's a petite blonde, pushing forty like me, yet from a distance she could be in her twenties. Her cool demeanour was part of her allure back then, but it's lost its appeal now I'm an adult. I prefer openness these days. Nina gives straight answers to every question, and her kindness is bone-deep. Anna let me down gently when she walked away, but I'm still convinced her backbone's made of steel.

'How are you, Ben? I haven't seen you in ages.'

'Pretty good, thanks.'

'Ready for your big day?'

'More or less. I had no idea it would swallow my entire bank balance.'

71

She smiles for the first time. 'It'll be worth it, I bet. Sorry to rush off, I've got a housekeeping job over on St Martin's.'

Anna's already backing away as the ferry pulls into harbour. It won't leave for ten minutes, but commuters still pile on board early. She seems glad of the excuse to part company, but I'm not done with her yet.

'Do you know much about Jez Cardew's movements these days? He's been going to St Agnes regularly, but no one can say why.'

'To see a woman, no doubt. Good luck finding him.'

Anna turns away before I can say goodbye, hurrying down the steps to board the open-topped boat. If she feels any regret about her ex going missing at sea, it's not on public display. I can tell she's still able to keep her feelings under wraps. I can't understand why such a bright woman has been reduced to cleaning for a living, but she's too proud to reveal any hardship at home.

It's nearly ten o'clock when I reach the police station in Garrison Lane on St Mary's. It's a small grey building with a three-storey apartment block behind and terraced houses crowding it from all sides, showing how the force operates in Scilly. We're regular citizens most of the time, and part of the community's fabric, which has its ups and downs. The five inhabited islands are mainly law-abiding, and few crimes are reported, so our relationship with the population of around two thousand is cordial. It's the crimes we don't hear about that concern me. Islanders are a tough breed, with a tradition of resolving their own grievances. Smuggling used to be the main trade, and lawlessness is still in our blood; no one welcomes external interference, even to fix long-standing disputes.

I stop to greet a retired fisherman who's making his way uphill at a snail's pace, even though I'm keen to get to work. Life revolves around courtesy here. I know for a fact that the police have less power than the islands' elders, who are held in much higher esteem, and you never know when you might have to call in a favour.

The station is unlocked but empty, apart from Shadow, who's waiting patiently by Lawrie Deane's desk. He must have tired of the Cardews' company and run here, hoping for a free meal. He knows that Deane always collects his breakfast from the Island Deli on the high street, five minutes away, and he's likely to benefit.

'You're all about food,' I tell him. 'Where's the love?'

He licks my hand in a casual manner, then returns to his position by Deane's chair. It's a far cry from my days in the Met, when lateness was a disciplinary offence; Deane's habit of rolling up ten minutes late most days rarely draws a rebuke from our boss. It took me a full year to readjust to the islands' slow pace, where nothing can be rushed.

I'm preparing to interview Sam Austell when DCI Madron's door creaks open. He's not on the duty roster, so it's a surprise to see him in full uniform, despite the heat. My boss is small and well groomed, his tie tightly knotted despite the day's warmth, his salt-and-pepper hair slicked into place.

'Step into my office, Kitto, I need a word. Tie that bloody animal up outside first.'

'I'll be right with you, sir.'

Madron is behind his desk when I enter. His office is a monument to obsessive tidiness, with no documents cluttering his in-tray, and everything alphabetically filed. I've learned to expect disapproval from him, even when nothing's wrong. His grey eyes have narrowed to slits as he orders me to sit down. I may be a foot taller, with a four-stone weight advantage, but it still feels like I'm facing the headmaster for a dressing-down.

'How many times have I told you to leave Shadow at home?'

'Plenty, sir, but he doesn't follow orders.'

'Just like his master. You're meant to be on leave, remember?'

'Jez Cardew's still missing. We need answers, for his parents' sake. I'll have to reschedule my holiday.'

He gives a curt nod. 'Tell me about yesterday's lifeboat operation.'

'I was on the first shout, with Isla and Eddie. Jez is still missing, so Eddie did a double shift.'

'Very heroic, I'm sure, but it can't happen again.'

'How do you mean, sir?'

'It's irresponsible in the extreme. What if you'd capsized? Scilly would lose half its police team in an instant, with no permanent replacements for months.'

'It's our duty to answer every shout, if we're free.'

'Did it even cross your mind that the Lifeboat

Festival needs policing? There was a party on Porthloo beach while you were all at sea. Luckily it passed without incident, but I had to call on volunteer stewards. Eddie and Isla should have been there, overseeing it.'

'Jez Cardew was our first priority.'

'Your biggest obligation is to the force. I won't allow more than one officer at a time on that boat in future, even if you're off duty. Do you understand?'

'I can't follow that order, sir.'

'Are you questioning my authority?' Madron's eyebrows shoot towards his hairline.

'The RNLI comes before standard police work, in my view, unless there's a crisis. There are crossovers between the roles. Our job is to protect people and save lives, isn't it?'

'Don't argue, Kitto. We police the land, they take care of the sea. I told you not to sign up, and yesterday proves why. We were badly short-staffed.'

'I need to investigate why Cardew's boat was found empty. He's a skilled navigator and knows the local waters like the back of his hand.'

'You think there was foul play?'

'I want to know exactly what happened on that boat. I'm interviewing Sam Austell here this morning to check if he saw changes in Jez's behaviour.' I pull the envelope from my pocket. 'Someone sent me this package in the post with RNLI badges inside. Eddie got one too, with a similar message. I want to find out if Jez received one too.'

'Show me the note.'

Madron peers at the scribbled drawing and the message. 'That line's from Shakespeare, isn't it? But it doesn't prove anything, Kitto. It must be some kind of joke.'

'I still need to find the source.'

'People drown every year in Scilly. It's a fact of life, especially when they sail after a drinking session,' the DCI snaps. 'The seas here are capricious, as you well know. I won't have you wasting police time.'

'You can't make me leave the RNLI.'

'I don't like your tone, Kitto, but you're excused this once. I know your family history. No child should lose their father, but you can't fight the sea, or save every single islander from drowning. Do you understand?'

I'm too irritated to reply politely, so I keep my mouth shut.

'Now get out there and police these islands, without that wretched dog.' He points at the door, banishing me, and there's no point in arguing.

Madron rarely accepts that he's wrong, which is a trait we share, although I hate to admit it. He loves the routine of domestic policing, but panics in a crisis, yet he's touched a raw nerve. I've had a love–hate relationship with the sea since my dad drowned. I joined the lifeboat crew to save other families from experiencing the same loss. The sight of Jez Cardew's boat adrift on the tide will stay with me until I learn what happened. Madron could be right about me resenting the sea's ability to steal people's lives, but that won't change. If it's not my duty to solve the mystery, who else will answer the Cardews' questions?

Lawrie Deane has arrived by the time I'm back in reception.

'Did you get the hairdryer treatment?' he whispers.

'More or less.'

'The bloke's an idiot. Manning that lifeboat trumps everything we do here.'

Deane will have heard my whole exchange with Madron because the walls are paper thin. He gives me a look of sympathy, then offers me a croissant from a large paper bag. He throws one to Shadow too, who retreats to a corner to enjoy his prize. The sergeant has grown on me over the years after a bumpy start. He may look like a stout red-haired curmudgeon, approaching sixty, his skin pockmarked by childhood acne, but appearances are deceiving. He's travelled all over the world and speaks three languages. He's covered for me many times when I've broken Madron's rules.

I'm still smarting when Sam Austell arrives, with Father Michael in tow. They could almost be father and son, with the same wiry build. The priest gives me an awkward smile, like he'd rather not be playing chaperone. The young man seems like a different character from the one I arrested years ago. He was so drug-addled then, he could barely string a sentence together, and his clothes were filthy and threadbare.

Now his hair is neater than mine, his shirt's been ironed and his jeans look brand new. Even his trainers are spotless. The only trait I recognise from the old days is his anxiety, his hand movements jittery when the interview starts.

'Thanks for coming, both of you. I hear you've been helping Sam since he got back, Father?'

'We meet for coffee each week, that's all.' The priest's voice is mild. 'I can't take any credit for Sam turning his life around. He did that for himself.'

'I'm glad to hear it,' I say, turning to Sam. 'But we need clear information about Jez. Have the two of you been getting on well recently?'

'Nothing's changed. We've always been close, ever since school.'

'Yet he doesn't share secrets with you. He's been spending a lot of time on St Agnes, so he's probably met someone there. Do you know who he's been seeing?'

Austell shifts in his chair. 'He hasn't said a word, but he might be keeping it private. Jez's split with Anna Dawlish at the start of the year was a nightmare.'

'Why's that?'

'Check his phone record. She bombarded him with messages and calls, even hassling him in the street.'

I stare back at him in surprise. The description doesn't match how Anna looked today, self-possessed and fully in control. She's the last person on these islands I'd expect to have a meltdown over a break-up.

'Had Jez fallen out with anyone else?'

'The only other ex he mentioned is Molly Bligh, but that ended years ago. They're still mates. I've never seen him argue with anyone.'

The news about Molly interests me. It chimes with my sense that she's been knocked sideways by Jez going missing, when we bumped into each other on St Agnes.

'Let's talk about life at home for a minute, Sam. How did you end up lodging with Callum Moyle?'

'Jez wrote to me in jail, saying he'd help.' His voice slows to a halt. 'Most people walked away, but he twisted Callum's arm to give me work and a place to stay.'

'Moyle acted like he can't stand Jez last night. How come they're sharing a house?'

'They rub each other up the wrong way, that's all. Callum's pissed off that Jez owes him rent. I saw him going through his things last night.'

'Looking for what?'

'Money, I suppose. That's always top of his list. Him and Jez were pally, until he started getting on Callum's nerves.'

I shake my head. Callum Moyle must be heartless if he went rooting through his lodger's belongings while the search continued at sea.

'Can you think of anyone else who dislikes Jez?'

He hesitates. 'No one, except Anna. Winning that lifeboat medal for bravery makes everyone else treat him with respect.'

I'm suddenly aware that Sam could have hidden on Jez's boat, then attacked him for reasons unknown, reverting to old form. 'Do you ever envy his popularity?'

'Of course not,' he says, swallowing a deep breath. 'Jez earned the whole community's respect, fair and square. Not many people would jump onto a sinking boat in a force nine gale.'

I nod to acknowledge his point. 'Have you found your phone yet?'

'I'll have to buy a new one today.'

'What time did you get home from St Agnes, exactly?'

'Tennish, I think. Callum was already there.'

'You saw him before going to bed?'

Sam shakes his head. 'I heard him playing music in his room.'

I can see his discomfort growing until Father Michael speaks again.

'Is there anything else, Ben? Sam went to a pub with a friend, then got a lift home from someone else. That's not a crime, is it?'

'I need to check everyone's actions on St Agnes, on Friday night, and timings matter. A man like Jez wouldn't fall overboard on a flat sea.' I reach across the desk to hand Sam my card. 'Get a new phone today and call me if you remember anything else.'

'Do you think he'll be found alive?' His gaze lingers on my face. It feels wrong to snuff out the hope flickering in his eyes, but the situation is bleaker than last night.

'I'm sorry, but his chances are falling all the time. People rarely survive this long in open water.'

I can see how badly the thought of losing his friend has affected him when he rises to his feet. His gait is so unsteady it looks like he's drunk vodka for breakfast, and the priest has to steer him towards the exit. I want to advise him to sit down again and take a few breaths, but the fresh air should help his recovery.

My job now is to make sure his alibi stacks up, because the islanders will already be making up stories to explain Jez's disappearance. If anyone believes Sam harmed Jez, it's possible they'll punish or ostracise him, even though he's trying to change his ways. I call the coastguard first, then the coxswain of the Penzance lifeboat, who agrees to check every boat in the harbour there to find out who gave Austell a lift between the islands.

Eddie Nickell rushes in before I have a chance to start ringing Jez's friends. His fresh-faced appearance has vanished overnight; I've never seen him unshaven until now, with bags under his eyes. He must have come straight from the lifeboat station.

'I've got new information, boss.' His voice is gruff with tiredness. 'A woman just rang me. She was sitting at a table outside the pub and saw Jez leave Perconger harbour on St Agnes just before last orders. According to her, he was alone. His boat sailed west at speed, making for open water.'

'That's useful, but we still need his phone record. It'll tell us who he called last night.'

'There's a problem. Apparently the network went down for almost the whole night; there's a problem with the mast on St Mary's.'

'Just what we need. Get them to send us anything they're got, okay?'

Technical failures are a fact of life in Scilly, but they always slow us down. Eddie's news is starting to register. Jez should have sailed due north to reach St Mary's; all that lies to the west of Scilly is the Atlantic Ocean at its most dangerous, with storms that boil up unannounced even in summer. The only solid land is treacherous outcrops with names like Hellweathers, and Bishop Rock lighthouse blinking out warnings. I can't believe that an experienced lifeboatman would make such a bad decision, unless he had a death wish.

13

Sam's nerves are shot as he walks to Hugh Town harbour, with the priest still at his side. Multicoloured bunting hangs between lamp posts and buildings on the quay, and he's never felt more out of step with his environment. There are signs everywhere for lifeboat festival events, with a band night at the church hall and a lifeboat-themed party for kids. The whole community seems determined to enjoy themselves. The quay is thronging with families waiting to catch ferries to the off-islands; kids are carrying buckets and spades, excited about the day ahead.

Father Michael's face is patient when he turns to say goodbye.

'Thanks for your help today, Father.'

'Don't go just yet. I've got something for you.' The priest reaches into the bag that's slung over his shoulder and brings out a package. 'I knew you'd want this.'

Sam looks inside: a brand-new phone. 'It's too much, I can't accept it.'

'Call it a reward, from one friend to another,' Father Michael says. 'You've made so much progress, I'm proud of you.'

'I'll pay you back, I promise.'

'No need, and remember, you can always talk to me. Your friend Jez did, several times this year. You know where I am.' He gives Sam's arm a light tap, then heads away into the sunshine.

Sam feels grateful but confused. Jez never mentioned visiting the priest, even though he knew that Sam was seeing him. He can't imagine someone so confident needing advice, and it seems strange that he wouldn't say anything. It takes effort to bring his mind back to the family duty that lies ahead.

He finds a seat on the boat to Tresco and Bryher. The open-topped ferry can carry fifty passengers, seated on benches nailed to the deck. It's filling with day trippers, and locals going to see relatives or birdwatch on Shipman Head Down. Sam is still processing the conversation at the police station. He's managed to steer clear of the building since being released; his only contact with the police has been when he bumps into DI Kitto. The bloke seems decent, and it's thanks to him that he won a place in the lifeboat crew, but his questions this morning made him feel vulnerable. There are plenty of islanders who could jump to the wrong conclusion about his presence on Jez's boat before he went missing, and use it to force him off the islands. His thoughts keep flitting back to his friend. Jez has never been in trouble until now. Girls love his relaxed banter, and blokes respect him too.

When he finally lifts his gaze, even the sight of Danielle Quick boarding the ferry fails to lighten his mood. As she squeezes into the one remaining seat beside him, it feels like something's blocking his throat; he inhales the citrus scent of her perfume, but he's too embarrassed to speak. She's one of the prettiest girls on the islands, in her summer dress covered in flowers, yet her smile is hesitant. It helps to see that she's shy too, and his courage slowly returns.

'Are you okay, Danielle? You look upset.'

'I was on the search for Jez last night. I didn't get much sleep.'

'Me neither. I won't relax till we know what happened.'

The ferry leaves the harbour, heading north to Tresco. They remain quiet as the boat ploughs through shallow waves into a warm breeze. Tresco is only a mile away, its hills already expanding to fill the horizon.

'Jez was such a golden boy, wasn't he?' Danielle says, breaking the silence. 'I remember how close you two were at school.'

Sam can tell her sympathy is genuine. 'He's the only mate who stuck by me when I was in prison.'

'Everyone deserves a second chance. That's still true, whatever happens to Jez. Lots of people are impressed by how well you've knuckled down.' Her voice is so gentle, it feels like she's throwing him a lifeline.

'Where are you off to today?' he asks.

'I visit my gran every weekend. You?'

'Just seeing Mum.'

'That's sweet, I bet she can't wait.' The boat is already docking on Tresco's New Grimsby quay, the fifteen-minute journey passing in a flash. 'I'll keep my fingers crossed for Jez.'

Sam is about to say goodbye when she drops a light kiss on his cheek, leaving him astonished. When she disappears into the gaggle of day trippers on the quay, it feels like he should pinch himself just to prove the gesture was real.

14

I'm sitting in the office I share with the rest of the police team, mulling over the new information. One of the regulars from the pub is sure that Jez Cardew's boat sailed west from St Agnes, and I trust her judgement. She's a local woman, with a good knowledge of the waters. It hits me for the first time that Jez might have taken his own life, even though his behaviour never signalled distress. Maybe it's hard to admit you're struggling psychologically if your whole community views you as a hero. Debbie Brookes implied he might be facing some sort of secret crisis, which could have been emotional or financial. It could have seemed easier to sail out to deep water and dive overboard than face his problems.

I'll have to pick my time to broach the subject with Eddie. He was close to his cousin; I'm almost certain he'd have guessed if Jez was seriously troubled. It can wait, though. I can tell he's running on empty. Yet even though he's gone twenty-four hours without sleep, he shows no sign of giving up. 'What should we do next, boss?'

'You need some rest. I'll check Jez's boat again, then visit your aunt and uncle.'

'They're my family, let me do it, please.'

I'm prepared to accept his request. I'm learning that Eddie can be as stubborn as a mule, and right now it would be churlish to refuse.

'Okay, but focus on finding out more about Callum Moyle first. He's always criticising Jez, and may have searched his room straight after he went missing.'

'I rang the Atlantic pub earlier. He was in there until around nine, then left without speaking to anyone.'

'Sam got back at ten. He heard music from Callum's room, but he could have left it playing.'

Eddie frowns. 'This isn't a murder investigation, boss. I'm still hoping Jez is alive.'

'Me too, but someone like Jez wouldn't just fall into the sea. We have to investigate what happened.' The exhaustion on his face looks even deeper than before, but I need his help. 'Tell me about Anna Dawlish first. How come Jez stopped seeing her?'

'Cold feet, I think. The ten-year age gap bothered him too. He felt bad about leaving her and Kylie, but he wasn't ready to commit.' Eddie gives me a side-long look. 'Didn't you and Anna have a fling, back in the day?'

'She chucked me for the captain of the football team. Bruised my ego, but there were no hard feelings.'

'She went psycho over the break-up with Jez, it sent her off the rails.'

'Maybe she was angry enough to find a way to attack Jez at sea.'

Eddie gives a slow nod. 'You think there was foul play?'

'We can't rule it out. He went to a pub, spent a relaxed night there, then sailed away on a boat with no technical issues. Why head in the wrong direction? Could he have been meeting someone at sea, or in one of the coves? It might have been a smuggling deal gone wrong.'

'Jez isn't that stupid, but your idea about Anna's got me thinking. She locks her feelings away, and that causes trouble, doesn't it? Things can fester.' His eyes look glassy.

'Eat something before you keel over.'

He grabs a croissant from the bag on Deane's desk, cramming it down in two bites. His stare proves that he's in no mood to wait, and I feel the same. Jez had secrets I need to understand, and the cabin cruiser is a good place to start.

'Let's take another look at Jez's boat,' I say.

My deputy appears glad to have something practical to do. I attempt to leave Shadow in Deane's care, but the dog leaps to his feet the moment we head for the door.

Two elderly women are selling teddy bears wearing knitted RNLI jumpers as we head down the high street towards the lifeboat house, with Shadow running ahead sniffing the sea air. I've learned to walk purposefully and not meet anyone's gaze if I need to get somewhere fast. People always stop me if it looks like I've got time to burn, and the locals will be keen to know about last night's search. Information travels fast here, with the local radio station issuing hourly bulletins and people travelling between islands carrying information as they go. The whole community will be aware that Eddie and I were both on the first shout. It's a miracle that we make it down the narrow pathway to the lifeboat house without being accosted.

Liam Quick is doubled over the table inside the office studying a sea chart. He's abandoned his sweltering kit, but the RNLI's crest is printed on his T-shirt, making me wonder if he ever forgets his role as coxswain when he's off duty. I sense that he's been under pressure since his divorce a few years back. We rely on him to lead almost every shout. He seems wired from excess adrenaline, with a muscle ticking in his cheek.

'I'm surprised you're still here, Hawkeye.'

He glances up at me. 'I need to check last night's coordinates again.'

'How come?' Eddie asks.

'To be sure I made the right decision. I sailed west, with the current, but the riptide could have dragged him south.'

'We covered that direction too.'

'Maybe we should have started there.' His voice is

flat with exhaustion. 'Jez has been on more shouts with me than any other crew member last year. The lad's a natural; I was planning to train him as a navigator so he could work here full-time.'

'Was he keen?'

'It was his idea. We were just waiting for headquarters to agree funding for the position.'

'He never said a word,' Eddie says.

'I told him not to jinx it before the RNLI finalised their decision.'

Liam seems relieved to hear that we're going to search Jez's boat again. His gaze returns to the map, his fingertips poring over the pale blue arrows that indicate tidal flow. He appears to be fighting a private battle about last night's search, which I can understand. There's always the nagging belief that acting differently on a mission could have kept everyone safe. I spent years replaying the day my father left on his last fishing trip, wishing I'd persuaded him to wait for calmer weather.

I turn to Eddie as we head down the slipway, where the Cardews' boat is moored.

'Has Jez been okay in himself lately, Eddie?'

'A bit quiet, maybe. Why do you ask?'

'I'm just gathering background information.'

He comes to a sudden halt. 'Jez wouldn't kill himself, if that's where you're going. He's the bravest man I know.'

'We have to consider all angles. Debbie Brookes thinks he's burdened by something.'

'He'd never hurt his parents like that,' he snaps. 'He's too decent.'

'Suicide's not a coward's choice. People do it because they're ill, or facing a crisis. We shouldn't condemn them for it.'

'I can form my own opinion, thanks. There's no fucking way he'd top himself.'

'Calm down, Eddie,' I say, staring back at him. 'If you can't handle intimate questions about Jez's life-style, I'll have to replace you with an officer from the mainland. There's no shame in standing down. But if you're working on the case, keep a clear head.'

'That won't be a problem.'

His tone is so sharp, I keep my thoughts private. The missing man is more like a brother to him than a cousin, and I'll have to tread carefully, but there's no avoiding hard questions. Eddie may know something vital without even realising it.

The cabin cruiser's name seems even more incongru-ous as we approach, the words *Happy Daze* flaking away from their white background. Most modern cruisers are made from fibreglass, but this one is clinker-built wood, like the ones Ray makes in his yard. I stand on the slip-way, taking in every detail of the twenty-foot vessel. The radio and VHF antennae project from the wheelhouse roof, both intact and operational. The outboard motor is in good working order too, like the propeller – the technical details were all checked last night. I pull on some sterile gloves, then pass a pair to Eddie.

'Go over the deck again, please. We need photos for the case file.'

He drops to a crouch immediately, and the obsessive look in his eye worries me. There's an edginess about him that I've never seen before. It's like he's prepared to examine every splinter in order to bring his cousin home. I leave him to it and enter the wheelhouse, noticing again the reek of petrol, or boat diesel. The walls carry nautical maps, a tide table, and a faded photograph of Jez on board with his parents. It must have been taken a decade or more ago. The teenage boy is giving a big thumbs-up, while his dad sunbathes on deck and his mother waves.

I run my hands over the panelled walls, then check inside a cupboard that only contains a first-aid kit. The cabin below deck is basic, to say the least. Two narrow bunks line the walls, leaving little floor space. The only thing I see is a padded envelope on the floor with Jez's name scrawled on it, bearing an island postmark. It contains a handful of RNLI badges, like the ones sent to me. Eddie has rung everyone on the crew and found out that most members received one or two of the packages. Janet Fearnley told us they didn't come from her, but any of the festival organisers could have mailed them out as a reminder to get involved, yet it still strikes me as strange that she had no idea about it.

I search the recesses under each bed but find only life jackets and a water ski. Frustration nags at me and I lower myself onto one of the bunks. It occurs to me again that I might be seeing complications where none exist. Jez Cardew's fate could have been ugly but simple. He may have fainted and fallen overboard, his life over in moments.

'There's nothing here, Eddie. Let's go back.'

I stand up before he can reply, and something flutters to my feet. It's a piece of white paper that must have been tucked under a cushion, folded into neat squares. The message is nothing like the one I received in the post. It's written in flowing, adult script, different from the childish block capitals on the note I received. I'm holding my breath as I study the words scribbled in black ink. The word 'love' is scrawled at the bottom, but the rest is so badly written, it's hard to decipher.

15

Sam doesn't have far to go when the ferry moors at Church Quay on Bryher. His childhood home lies five hundred metres south, in Green Bay. He made the same journey each day as a boy, when the ferry deposited him after school, and little has changed since. The bay is still an arc of pristine white sand, extending for half a mile. Tresco's rounded hills rise above New Grimsby Sound to his left. It's a larger version of Bryher, with a landscape that's carefully maintained, and twice as many inhabitants. He feels stronger now he's back on native soil. He'd love to return here one day, if the islanders ever forgive him, but he knows that may never happen.

Rose Austell's cabin looks dilapidated as he crosses the sand. It's the only building on the bay, a simple wooden structure raised on stilts that protect it from floods. The walls are painted a rainbow of colours because his mother maintains her home by using leftover paint donated by the other islanders. One of the steps up from the beach is broken. It needs fixing, before her Parkinson's causes her to have another fall.

Sam finds her in the small back garden she adores, gazing

at flowers that fill every corner: agapanthus, orchids and wild lilies. Her beehives are empty now; she's grown too frail to tend them, yet she still looks vibrant, like a gypsy queen. Dyed black hair tumbles over her shoulders, her outfit a clash of vivid colours. The necklace she's wearing is made from shells and small pieces of driftwood collected from the shore.

'There you are.' She grabs his hand and pulls him down for a kiss.

'You look thin, Mum. Still beautiful, though.'

'That's a sweet lie.' Rose beams at him. 'Come inside, love. I've made lunch.'

Sam watches her struggle indoors, clinging to the handrail. Parkinson's has slowed her down, but she prefers to manage alone, so he doesn't offer to help. She'd only reprimand him. Her cabin is full of herbs, drying in bundles, suspended from the ceiling and walls by string. They have to squeeze past to reach the kitchen table. The smell takes him back to his childhood: dried lavender, candle smoke, and the neat alcohol Rose uses in her herbal tinctures. He used to envy his friends' homes, built from bricks and mortar, but he understands now why she adores this place, even though the floors are uneven since last year's flood. Seagulls are her only neighbours, and the view is matchless: the beach unrolls into the distance, where the channel separating Bryher from its sister island is a vivid blue ribbon.

He puts Rose's medication on the table, knowing she hates to discuss her illness directly, but her movements are slowing. He's noticed on his weekly visits that walking is harder than before, and she struggles to lift dishes of food onto the table.

'How's life treating you, Mum?'

'Fine, sweetheart. The shop's still selling my herbal remedies, in exchange for groceries. They give me more than I need.'

Rose has always bartered for her living. It used to embarrass him as a boy, but he respects her for raising him alone, with no partner or extended family to help, even though they sometimes went hungry. He admires her lifestyle choices, and the fact that she rarely touches money. When she sits down opposite him, her eyes are circled by shadows; she seemed so powerful when he was young, but those days are over.

'I should thank you more often, for looking after me when I was sick,' he says.

'Any mother would do the same. I'll give you some echinacea tea to take home, to build your strength.' She reaches across the table to catch his hand. 'Has something upset you, love?'

'I should be living here, on Bryher, helping you.'

'There's something else. Tell me the truth, Sam.'

'Didn't you hear about Jez Cardew?'

'My radio's on the blink. What on earth's happened?'

'They think he drowned.'

'I can't believe it. That boy understood the sea's moods better than anyone.' She grips his hand. 'He was such a good friend to you, wasn't he?'

'The best.' Tears smart behind his eyes.

'Eat something, love. You need to stay strong, whatever's happened.'

The meal Rose provides is made from vegetables, rice and wild herbs, with a glass of bitter red wine. Even her food appeals to him more these days. He glances at the clock ticking loudly on the wall. It's 1 p.m. already, yet he's determined to mend the steps before catching the ferry back to St Mary's. He can't even give Callum a ring until he's charged his new phone. His boss will be furious if he misses the entire day, but his mother's safety matters more than Callum's temper.

16

Eddie is frowning with concentration; Shadow sits at his side like he's keen to help. The dog's whole attention appears focused on the sheet of paper. I feel sure he'd have finished *War and Peace* by now, if only he could read. All the note proves is that Jez was having a secret relationship, as I suspected. 'Looks like it was written in a hurry.' Eddie reads the message out loud, stumbling because the words are so unclear. 'Jez, come back after dark. I wish we didn't have to hide! I'll wait for you in the usual place, my love . . .'

'Can you make out the initial?'

He shakes his head. 'Is that an L, or a C?'

'It's just a squiggle, isn't it? Maybe it's an E.'

'Someone could have left it on the boat while Jez was in the pub.' I take an evidence bag from my pocket and drop the note inside. Eddie looks as confused as I feel. Jez was having a clandestine relationship with a local woman, who must be grief-stricken, yet no one has come forward.

'This might be linked to the notes we got, Eddie, but the writing's different. Do you remember what yours said?'

'It's a Shakespeare quote about having one foot on land and one in the sea. It was in pencil, a kid's uneven block capitals. There was a stick man hanging from a yardarm drawn in the top-right corner.'

'Mine's the same, but it's a different quote from *The Tempest*. We need to find out if Jez got one too, but this is a love letter.' I read it again. 'It explains why he sailed west, instead of north. I bet he doubled back to one of the coves to meet someone. Let's look at the map and see where he was heading.'

Eddie's fatigue is growing clearer by the minute. He could chat for Britain most days, but he trudges after me in abject silence as we walk back up the slipway. The lifeboat house stands empty. Liam Quick has gone home at last, leaving us to study the nautical map of Scilly that's spread across the office table. We're still peering at it when Len and Molly Bligh arrive, sending Shadow into a fit of ecstasy. Molly is one of his favourite humans. He jumps up to give her a boisterous greeting, and she crouches down to offer some treats from her pocket that she carries for her own dogs at home.

The Blighs often cross paths with us. They take turns as lifeguards on Porthcressa beach in summer, as well as their lifeboat duties. Molly looks stronger than when I saw her this morning on St Agnes, with more colour in her cheeks, wearing a light green dress that flatters her colouring. Her brother Len has a shyer manner, his red hair cut close to his skull, the colour matching his sister's wild curls. The guy is obsessively loyal to our region. His T-shirt bears the Cornish flag, a white cross on a black background, symbolising our mining history, with seams of tin hidden among the coal. Len's glasses give him a studious air, even though most of his time is spent outdoors, tending horses and ponies.

'Is there any news, Ben?' Molly asks. 'We came by to check.'

'Nothing, I'm afraid. The chopper's going out one last time this afternoon.'

She blinks rapidly. 'I was planning to resign from the crew, but this clinches it.'

'Don't rush your decision, Molly. We need you on board. You're a cool head when things are rough.'

'I've already told Liam. I felt bad, but he understood. I can't face another shout.' Tears glisten in her eyes. 'The sea gives nothing in return for the risks we take. Fishermen can't even make a living from it these days.'

Grief is a strange emotion; its flat sound resonates in her voice like a broken bell. I can't pressure her to stay in the crew while we're still discussing Jez going missing in the present tense.

'How well do you two know Jez?'

Len shunts his glasses back onto the bridge of his nose. 'We were all on the same darts team till he started going to St Agnes. Molly knows him better.'

'We've been pals since nursery school,' she says.

'They dated for a while too,' Len adds.

She gives him an arch look. 'That's ancient history, we were schoolkids.'

'Sorry, this must be awful for you both, and for Eddie.'

My deputy's face is blank when he glances at me, acknowledging my comment.

Molly steps back, her movements twitchy. 'We should go, kids are waiting for rides on the beach, to raise cash for the festival.'

'One more question first. Do either of you know if Jez was seeing someone on St Agnes?'

'I teased him about having a mystery girlfriend, but he denied it,' Molly says. 'People think Jez is this big extrovert, but he hated the gossip about him and Anna, so he was keeping things discreet this time.'

'He never confided in you?'

'Jez spoke to his grandad about important stuff like that. You should ask Denzel Jory.'

'Really? Most people keep out of his way.'

'Jez remembers him before he grew bitter. He respects Denzel more than anyone.' She hurries to the door. 'We need to get to work, Ben.'

I can see a pair of ponies on the beach, with teenage volunteers holding their leads. A queue of children trails across the sand, waiting for rides. It's a good way of raising funds for the RNLI, but Molly still has tears in her eyes and Len's face is ashen.

'We could cancel it, if you like,' I suggest.

'No way, the kids would be heartbroken,' Molly says. 'The ponies love it too.'

My dog howls in disappointment after she gives him a final stroke, then the Blighs disappear, as quietly as they arrived.

'I know you prefer girls, but she's busy,' I tell him, then turn to Eddie. 'Did you know about Molly and Jez dating?'

'It's nothing. They were about thirteen, I think.'

'First love cuts deep sometimes, doesn't it?'

'What are you saying, boss? Molly wouldn't hurt a fly.'

Shadow slinks off to a corner to doze, leaving me to reflect on Molly's announcement while Eddie continues forensically studying the map. The lifeboat crew will be a lot weaker if she resigns. Her serene manner balances everyone on board, and her presence encourages more women to get involved.

Eddie continues forensically studying the map. I'm still amazed that Denzel Jory might be the only islander that knows Jez's secret. He lives on Gugh, St Agnes's satellite island, one of Scilly's oldest residents. He used to be a community hero, spending decades as a lifeboat volunteer, but now the former stonemason rarely has a good word to say about anyone, including relatives. Jez may have been the only one able to stay close to him. There's an outside chance the old man knows the truth, so we'll need to pay him a visit.

I join Eddie for a final look over the nautical map. It's possible that Jez's boat sailed west from Perconger Quay because travelling east involves detouring around Gugh. He would have passed the island's wildest terrain, where the ground is so rocky, no houses have ever been built. St Agnes's properties all lie at its core, protected from Atlantic storms, but up there the ground is littered with granite boulders.

'He wanted to stay under the radar,' Eddie mutters.

'That makes sense if he was seeing a married woman, for instance.'

He nods his head. 'By the way, Janet Fearnley says Anna Dawlish and her daughter were at hers on Friday night while Jez was on St Agnes. They didn't leave till ten, so we can strike Anna off our list.'

I'm glad to know my old girlfriend has a firm alibi. I'm certain Jez Cardew's been having a clandestine relationship on St Agnes, judging by the breathless tone of the note, and Molly's suspicions. Adultery is nothing new in the quiet world of Scilly; long winters and isolation put a strain on all couples, when there are few distractions. It's easy to look elsewhere, even at the risk of being exposed. Molly could be right about a quieter personality lurking behind Jez's veneer of confidence, making him long for privacy.

I'm still running through possibilities when my phone rings; it's a voice message from Isla saying that Stuart and Delia Cardew are desperate for an update.

'At least we're gathering information,' I say to Eddie.

'We know Jez was secretly seeing a woman on St Agnes, and only eighty people live there full-time. Let's get back over there tomorrow. We can start collecting handwriting samples to try and get a match with the note. Now go home before you fall over. I'll go and see Stuart and Delia.'

He narrows his eyes. 'Not without me.'

'I'm in charge, remember? You're running yourself into the ground.'

His tone softens by a fraction. 'Just let me do this, please, boss. I can't let them down.'

'Then you're on the next ferry to Tresco.'

The change in Eddie's personality is striking. He's gone from being meek and obliging, to a man who always fights his corner. I can't tell whether his new-found confidence will hinder our work, or bring us a result, but the transition feels awkward. I hardly recognise who he's becoming, but it's more important to focus on finding out about Jez Cardew's relationship.

We hurry back to the station to collect the van. When I look down at Hugh Town beach, it's like a different world. Kids are enjoying the Blighs' dappled ponies, and the feeling appears to be mutual; the creatures prance across the sand, with Len and Molly holding their reins. They're decked out with ornate bridles and saddles, like they belong on a fairground carousel. The whole island seems to be enjoying the sun, a stark parallel to the investigation.

Eddie is frowning when we climb into the van, his

voice a low monotone. 'It'll hit Stu and Delia hard if he's gone, but it's best to be honest.'

'Of course, but there's not much to share yet.'

He gazes straight ahead as we set off, with Shadow in the back. It's already 5 p.m., the sunlight turning from white to gold. By the time we arrive ten minutes later, Eddie is fast asleep. I consider leaving him in the van, but he startles awake when my door opens, his movements uncoordinated as he staggers out.

Isla looks concerned when she opens the door. She's been with the couple since last night, and I can see she needs a break too. There's relief on her face when she tells us her mother is going to call by after her shift finishes at the hospital. Dr Ginny Tremayne is the islands' chief medic and a well-known community figure, trusted by everyone.

She leads us through to the kitchen, where Stuart is slumped over a mug of tea. His face brightens when he sees us, but that soon fades when he learns there's no news. Eddie puts an arm round his shoulders. I listen to Stuart pouring out his woes to his nephew, while Isla steps outside to answer her phone.

Shadow's piercing bark guides me to the greenhouse. It's sweltering inside, the air sweetened by pollen and decay. Delia is standing straight-backed at a potting table, doing something intricate with her hands, her grey hair drawn back from her face. When I look closer, I see that she's transplanting seedlings from a tray to individual pots of compost. I can tell it's a delicate procedure from the way she cradles each one in the palm of her hand.

'You look busy, Delia.'

'It's keeping me sane. I can't just sit around waiting.'

She repeats the same action over and over, nurturing the roots of each small plant before placing it in fresh soil.

'Have you had any rest?'

'Worry about Stuart, not me. He's the sensitive musician. I'm the practical one in our family.' Her gaze is empty. We're sharing the same overheated space, yet it feels like we're on different planets. I suspect she's using every fibre of her being just to stay upright. I'm about to speak again when Isla rushes through the door.

'Can I have a word, please, sir?'

Delia doesn't seem concerned by my sudden departure, and neither does Shadow. The dog normally hates hot environments, yet he remains curled at her feet, unwilling to leave.

Isla's face is tense when I get outside. 'Father Mike just called, from Bar Point. He's found something on the beach.'

'What exactly?'

'I don't know. He asked us to get there fast, then hung up.'

'Let's take the van. Eddie can stay here.'

My nerves are on edge as we set off. It's never good news when a witness finds something that's too ugly to name.

17

Sam is still on Bryher as the afternoon unfolds. The phone signal's down, so he couldn't call Callum Moyle from his mum's phone, but the steps outside her cabin have taken hours to fix. He's replaced each tread, and the handrail too, while Rose showers him with compliments.

'Lovely work, son. You're a real master craftsman.'

Sam smiles, but knows she's biased. There are plenty of carpenters with better skills on the islands. If he leaves Moyle, he'll need to take any work he can find to earn a living wage. His dream of building furniture in his own workshop and managing his own finances seems far out of reach.

'I have to go, Mum. I'm late for work, Callum was expecting me hours ago.'

'Sunday should be a day of rest.' Rose peers up at him. 'Don't let Callum Moyle push you around. Stay here with me if he gives you trouble.'

'I can handle him.'

'He seems like a bully to me.'

'Don't worry about it. I'll call you soon, I promise.'

Sam hurries back to Church Quay. He manages to board the 4 p.m. ferry back to St Mary's just as it's departing, and his mood has already soured. The sea is calm and featureless, a jade-green expanse with no end in sight; his eyes blink shut as he thinks of Jez, fighting to stay afloat. When they open again, Hugh Town harbour is straight ahead.

He's on autopilot as he jogs along the quay. It's past 4.30 when he finally reaches the house that Callum is renovating. He peers through the letter box because no one answers his knock, even though the hall is still full of tools. He's still crouching there when a hand grabs his shoulder, making him spin round, and he's slammed against the wall. Instinct makes him raise his fists. Prison taught him to fight off attackers, but Moyle looks amused.

'Think you're a tough guy, do you?'

'Don't push me around, all right?'

'Remember you owe me, big-time. You wouldn't last a minute in Scilly without my protection.'

Sam's anger is fading, but he doesn't reply.

'Where the fuck were you all afternoon?'

'My mother needed help on Bryher.'

'So you're a sweet little mummy's boy.' Moyle grips Sam's shoulder again, hard enough to burn. 'You can work all evening to make up for it. Let me down again, and you're history. Do you hear?'

Sam holds his gaze, but keeps his mouth shut. The house resonates with tension as he reaches for his tools.

18

The police van hurtles north with Isla at the wheel. It gives me time to call Nina and explain that I'm running late. She sounds concerned, while Noah coos in the background. I feel guilty for not being around all day with so much wedding stuff to do, yet she doesn't complain. I'll have to stop at the shop and buy her some chocolate, if the place is still open when I get back.

The island's lanes make speeding impossible, unless you want to plough into an unlit bicycle, a stray goat, or a crumbling dry-stone wall, but Isla's testing the limits. St Mary's is only five miles long, but it can take twenty minutes to drive from end to end. We have to slow down by the woods at Holy Vale to let a gaggle of birdwatchers cross the road. The sunlight is fading into dusk, so they'll hear the chiffchaffs and nightjars starting to call.

History dominates the landscape we're travelling through. When I look out of the window, I see Halangy Down, covered in standing stones and cairns; it's the remains of a Neolithic village that runs down to the sea. The island's military past greets us as at Bar Point. Bant's Carn Battery lies to the west, and there's a nineteenth-century pillbox on the beach to protect lookouts from invaders. There's no modern-day threat to the huge spit of sand except the encroaching tides. The sea is so far out, the beach looks endless, turning from gold to silver as the stars emerge. Despite the idyllic view, my sense of foreboding is rising all the time.

I see the priest's thin figure up ahead as we leave the car, his hand waving like a metronome set at top speed. I flash my torch a few times, then break into a jog, even though it's pointless. If Jez Cardew's body has washed up on the shore, it's too late to do anything except break his parents' hearts. There's shock on Michael's face, his hands trembling as he clutches his dog's lead. I'll need to send him home straight after he's answered basic questions. His black Labrador appears unaffected by the find, standing on her hind legs to greet us like she's loving the adventure.

'Thanks for phoning us, Mike. What time did you get here?'

'Half an hour ago. I often bring Sheba to this beach for a last stroll.'

'Can you show us what you found?' I can tell from the way his gaze slips from mine that he's reluctant to see it again.

'Sheba uncovered it, I had to drag her away.'

'Just point us in the right direction, please.'

'It's over there, under a plastic bag.' He drops his gaze like he's struggling to say something. 'I should have mentioned this sooner, but it didn't feel right on the lifeboat. Jez came to see me recently, to share his troubles.'

'Like what, Mike?'

'Some type of crisis. He seemed scared, but exhilarated too. I got the sense he was planning to leave Scilly. Jez hated the idea of letting people down.'

'Let's discuss it after we've checked the scene. Wait by the car, will you?'

The priest's pupils are dilated when my torch illuminates his face, but he's alert enough to nod in agreement.

Isla jogs at my side until we reach a blue carrier bag held in place by stones. When I crouch down to peel it back, I hear her gasp. A human hand lies palm down on the sand; the skin is bleached and waterlogged, a tangle of veins and arteries dangling from its severed wrist. I can't prove it's Jez Cardew's, but the theory makes sense. I shut my eyes and picture Jez Cardew's body smashing against the rocks beyond St Mary's Sound until it broke apart. When I open them again, I notice something is bound to the index finger: a gold disc, attached to a frayed blue ribbon. I use my torch to look more closely. It's an RNLI medallion, engraved with the figures of lifeboatmen on a raging sea, finely etched waves threatening to overwhelm their vessel. They seem unconcerned for their own safety, working together to pull a drowning boy from the water. I've never paid much attention to the words circling the edge, until now: *Let not the deep swallow me up.*

'It's from Jez, isn't it?' Isla's voice is a raw whisper.

'We'll need a DNA test to find out.'

'He was my age, boss. I've known him all my life.'

When I turn round, she's swaying on her feet. 'Take a breath, Isla. That's it, and another. Are you okay?'

'Sorry, it's just the shock. He was such a great bloke.'

'It may not be his, remember.'

'Do you think the badges we've been sent in the post are linked to this?'

'You've had some too?'

'They came by post this morning. The note had a Shakespeare quote, with a hangman drawn in the corner.'

'I got one, and so did Eddie. All crew members could be vulnerable. Call them, please, and find out who's had a note, with a packet full of badges. I want the envelopes analysed.'

The priest looks stricken when we return.

'Does this mean Jez is gone?' he asks.

'We need to confirm it, but it seems likely, I'm afraid. Please keep it to yourself until we make an announcement.' He looks so affected I reach out to touch his shoulder. 'Have you been sent any RNLI badges this week, with a written message?'

'Not so far.'

'That's good news, Mike. Just out of interest, do

you know where the quote on the RNLI medals comes from? *Let not the deep swallow me up.*

'It's biblical, Psalm 69, Verse 15. A prayer for salvation and forgiveness of sin.'

'Someone's got a sick mindset, to link such a pure idea to this.' I turn to call for Isla. 'Drive Father Mike and Sheba home, please. I'll wait here for Gareth Keillor.'

The young constable leaves as darkness thickens. Her voice echoes across the beach, carried by the breeze, calm and reassuring, as she leads the priest and his dog away. I pull in a breath before covering the hand again, then I ring the island's only consultant pathologist. I could put the grim find in an evidence bag and deliver it to the hospital, leaving it safe in the morgue's refrigerator until morning, but I want Keillor's opinion about it in situ. He may be past retirement age, but he never misses a trick.

I drop onto the sand to gaze at the sea ahead, littered with crags and outcrops. The lights of St Martin's and Tresco glitter in the distance; the night air is still warm, and my head is buzzing with questions. It's almost certain that the ugly remnant belonged to Jez Cardew, the rest of his body stolen by the waves. My curiosity goes into overdrive as I consider why he would pitch overboard from his dad's boat. Why would anyone bear a grudge against a young man who delighted in having fun while being brave enough to face the sea at its worst? I feel certain it's linked to the scrawled love letter I found on his boat.

I'm still obsessing about it when an arc of light sweeps the beach and Keillor's Audi crunches across the shingle. I've never understood why so many of St Mary's inhabitants buy expensive new cars when most places lie within walking distance, but I'm grateful he got here fast.

Gareth Keillor looks younger than his years as he trots towards me, medical bag in hand. It's only when he gets closer that the lines on his face show in my torch beam, his scant grey hair unsettled by the breeze. He peers at me through horn-rimmed spectacles.

'My wife's not thrilled, Ben. I've been doing an online cookery course; tonight's burnt offering was chicken madras.'

'This won't take long, I promise.'

'You've found Jez Cardew?'

'Part of him, maybe.'

He grimaces. 'This is a bleak bit of coast. Wreckers used to lure boats onto reefs here, in the old days of smuggling. Body parts washed up here for days, after a hard storm.'

'The rocks are that savage?'

'If you beat anything against granite for long enough, it won't survive.'

Keillor mumbles to himself when I point my torch at the sand. It sounds like he's whispering a prayer as he takes torchlit photographs with his phone, then pulls on sterile gloves. I've always admired his way of handling the dead, treating them like they're still alive, and tonight is no exception, even though it's just a fragment. Keillor manipulates each finger gently, like he's trying to avoid causing pain, then takes a photo with his phone before shaking his head in disgust.

'It's a male's left hand, judging by the size. No distinguishing features except a vascular birthmark and a historic scar on his palm. The recent wounds are more interesting. Can you see that red line crossing his wrist?'

I crouch beside him. The line is about a centimetre wide.

'That's a ligature bind. It was tight enough to slice through skin and soft tissue.'

'What are you saying, Gareth?'

'The victim could have been tied to a rock or the handrail of a boat with strong twine. I can't say yet whether the limb was hacked from his body by a propeller, or the tide smashing him against rocks. Someone attached that medallion to his finger with cheese wire, so tightly even the sea couldn't loosen it.'

'They wanted to see him drown.'

My thoughts shift into focus at last. I knew from the start that a skilled sailor like Jez wouldn't topple from his boat for no reason. Our hunt for a man missing at sea has become a murder investigation at last. The killer's amusing themself too, sending Shakespeare quotes and badges to members of the lifeboat crew.

'This isn't absolute proof that Jez is dead,' Keillor says. 'People survive traumatic amputations every day, but the blood loss would have been extreme without a tourniquet.'

I rock back on my heels. There's an outside chance that someone intervened to save his life after a murderous attack, but surely he'd be in hospital by now? My mind is blank when I study the hand again. 'Could Jez's parents identify this as their son's?'

'DNA testing would be kinder.'

'I'll offer them both options, after I take this to the hospital. Go home and finish your meal.'

'My wife's a sensible woman, Ben. She'll have chucked my curry out and opted for frozen pizza instead.' He gives a narrow smile. 'Tonight's find has killed my appetite anyway. Hop in the car, I'll give you a lift.'

Darkness has settled over the island so completely, we have to rely on my torch beam to reach Keillor's Audi, and its appeal registers once we're inside. The interior smells of leather, peppermints and safety. Keillor drives south through the island's winding lanes, while a young man's hand rests on my lap, with palm outstretched like it's begging for mercy.

19

Shadow must have read my mind. I'm about to set off home from Hugh Town when he races down the quay and leaps on board, clearly tired of the Cardews' company. My uncle Ray is awake when I get back to Bryher, with Shadow standing on the prow. Yellow light burns in his living-room window; chances are he's alone, watching some ancient documentary. I'd like to know whether his on–off relationship with the island's registrar is still going, but Ray would prefer flying to the moon than discussing his private life. That's why his flat over the boatyard was a sanctuary for me as a kid whenever I wanted peace and quiet. The man is so monosyllabic it was easy to spend time there without saying a word. But tonight I need information, not silence.

It's no surprise when Shadow runs up the steps to the flat, even though Ray expects one hundred per cent obedience from all canines, which my dog rarely achieves. I find my uncle sprawled in his favourite armchair in his sparsely furnished living room, while John Wayne fires at a moving target. Ray loves classic westerns, but this one can't be very entertaining. He looks relaxed in sleep, his hard-boned face serene, thick white hair in need of a trim. He startles awake when Shadow jumps up to greet him.

'You were snoring, Ray.'

He frowns first at me, then the dog. 'I was just resting my eyes. What time is it?'

'Midnight, but I could use your help.'

'With what, for God's sake?'

'Finding out what happened to Jez Cardew. It's pretty gory, I'm afraid.'

'Just spit it out, Ben.'

'Part of his body washed up on Bar Point tonight. Is there a chance we'll find the rest?'

He pauses, letting the information register. 'That's not easy. I'd need to study my charts.'

'If you do, I'll give you two days' free labour after the wedding.'

'I'll hold you to that. No one replied to my advert for an apprentice; most youngsters hate getting their hands dirty.'

It doesn't surprise me that Ray wastes little time agonising about the likelihood that Jez has drowned. He liked the young lifeboatman, but rarely expresses his emotions. He's already rooting through maps in the plan chest he built himself. Ray is an expert on local tides. He can predict the weather with greater accuracy than any meteorologist, just by observing sea conditions.

He hunches over a nautical chart of Scilly, which is covered in faint arrows illustrating tidal flow at different times of day. He scribbles numbers on a scrap of paper, then returns to his chart before making his pronouncement.

'There's a fierce southern current for the rest of this lunar month. The water moves in circles because of the eddies round Kettle Point. Most objects get carried down New Grimsby Strait at this time of year. His body may have travelled as far as St Agnes, or Bartholomew Ledges, but it's more likely to wash up near here.'

'How sure are you, Ray?'

'Fifty per cent, sixty at most. The sea's unpredictable.'

'Thanks for trying.' I hesitate before turning away. 'Nina tells me you're giving a speech at our wedding.'

'I haven't made a decision.'

'Her dad's saying a few words. It would be great if you did the same.'

'The situation's different, Ben. I'm not your father.'

'Aren't you?' I gaze back at him. 'It feels like I had two. I never realised at the time, but it's clear to me now. You stepped up after Dad died; Noah's lucky to have you as his grandfather.'

'We'll have to see about that.' He looks down at his gnarled hands. 'Don't forget you're helping me in the yard. I've got a bowrider to finish.'

'I promised you, didn't I?'

There are questions in Ray's eyes, but he never asks about my police work as a matter of principle. I'm about to leave when I spot a notebook open on his table, the word 'marriage' scribbled at the top of the page. Nina must have hypnotised him, if the island's quietest man really plans to address a crowd, but I'll believe it when I see it.

I'm dead on my feet when I leave the boatyard, with Shadow traipsing behind. I feel certain the hand Father Mike found belongs to Jez Cardew, because no other mariners have been reported missing. Madron won't be able to claim that it was a simple drowning, what with the ligature, and the medallion bound to his finger. I'd like to know how the killer managed to get hold of one, making me wonder if they own any more RNLI memorabilia.

I trudge across the island without switching on my torch. The shingle path is so familiar, I can follow it blind, while clouds race overhead obscuring the stars. I'm halfway down the path to Hell Bay when Shadow howls, then sets off like a rocket. A light is flickering from Hell Bay Hotel, and time is slipping backwards as I try to understand Zoe's message, just like when I was a boy. Her SOS keeps on repeating, and adrenaline gives me a sudden boost of energy. I set off fast, but my carthorse build works better in water than on land, and it takes me five minutes to cover the distance, then race up the fire escape to my friend's flat, where the front door is ajar. I'm looking for signs of blood or disaster, but all I see is Zoe clutching a flashlight. She's tall and statuesque, her blonde hair tousled, wearing an uncertain smile.

'What's the emergency?' I ask.

'I didn't want to ring and wake Noah. I just hoped you'd see the light. You're the only person who'll understand.'

'It's okay, Zoe. Tell me what's wrong.'

'Can you handle a complex story, big man?'

'They're the best kind, but feed me first. I'm starving.'

I haven't seen Zoe for months, but our friendship always clicks back into place, no matter how long we've been apart. She hugs me, then hurries into the kitchen, where she dumps her fridge's entire contents onto a tray. I get the chance to observe her while she completes the task. She still looks like a more robust version of Marilyn Monroe, with peroxide-blonde hair, but her looks are just part of the picture. She's got a gift for singing, which is how she met her husband, teaching music at one of the street schools he runs in India for homeless kids.

When we return to her living room, I load my plate with bread, ham and cheese, aware that I've skipped too many meals.

'Want some of this?' She holds up a bottle of Grey Goose vodka.

'More than life itself.'

She pours generous shots into two glasses, just like when we used to throw parties in her room while her parents worked in the bar downstairs, too busy to stop us raiding their drinks cabinet. We played music at top volume, and danced around like lunatics till the small hours.

'I saw Nina today,' Zoe says. 'She looks fighting fit, and your boy's a chip off the old block, isn't he?'

'How do you mean?'

Her hundred-mega-watt smile ignites at last. 'Noah's a big, handsome lad, laid-back too. I adore him already.'

'But that's not why I'm here, is it?'

'It's to give you an apology. I can't sing at your wedding. There's no way I could entertain anyone right now.' She takes a long breath. 'Dev isn't coming, I told him to stay in Mumbai, to give us some thinking time.'

'Why?'

'I've asked him for a divorce.'

I blink at her in disbelief. 'That's crazy. You're nuts about him, and he feels the same about you.'

'Things have changed, Ben. The schools keep him so busy, then there's the baby thing.' She takes another slug of vodka. 'The clinic won't give me any more IVF. There's no point; I've got a thousand-to-one chance of carrying a baby to term.'

I gather my thoughts before replying. 'Whatever happens won't change how Dev feels. Or have you fallen out of love with him?'

'I hate seeing him sad every day.' Her fists are clenched in her lap. 'He's always wanted kids. It's fairer to get the hell out and set him free.'

'What about adoption, or surrogacy?'

'It wouldn't work.'

'The kid has to carry your genes or nothing?'

'Dev could build a life with someone else, and I want someone who looks at me the way you look at Nina.'

'How's that, exactly?'

'Punch-drunk and stupid with love.'

'That makes me sound like an imbecile.' I lean forward to grab her hand. 'Don't be a fucking hero. You still love him, don't you? Let Dev make up his own mind.'

'It wouldn't be fair, Ben. His sense of honour won't let him walk away; he needs a get-out card.'

'At least wait a while, before you chuck it all away.'

She breathes out a long sigh. 'When did you get so bloody wise?'

'No one's ever called me that before.'

'You must be learning from Nina.' She pinches the bridge of her nose, trying not to cry.

'Let it out if you want, babe.'

'I've shed enough tears.' Her smile glitters again, bright enough to illuminate the room. 'I'd rather get rat-arsed and go out dancing.'

'No chance out here. Can you believe I've hardly touched a drop since Noah was born?'

'Let's make up for it now, sunshine.'

She pours a double shot of vodka into my glass, and I know it'll be a long night, so I send Nina another text. It's lucky my bride-to-be isn't the jealous type, but

123

she's got nothing to fear. I was madly in love with Zoe aged thirteen, but now she's just my biggest ally, with decades of shared history between us.

'Do me a favour before you get pissed, okay?'

'Anything, big man.'

'Cut my hair, so it's decent for the wedding.'

'No way. I haven't used my scissors for donkeys' years.'

'I trust you to get it right.'

'You crazy misguided fool.'

Zoe qualified as a hairdresser in her teens, before pursuing her vocation to become a singer. Soon I'm sitting by the mirror in her hall, with a towel round my shoulders, while she talks about shattered dreams. I've always admired her tough spirit, but her voice is thick with regret as she performs her magic tonight. After a while, she falls silent, concentrating on my hair. All I can hear is the waves' slow whisper. I think of Jez Cardew, terrified on the open sea. If he was murdered simply for being a lifeboatman, I'm looking for a bona fide lunatic. Only half of my mind listens when Zoe speaks again, the rest of my thoughts adrift on the ocean breeze. When I look in the mirror, my hair's shorter than it's been for years, and a younger, more vulnerable version of myself is staring back at me. My face still looks haunted, despite the booze.

20

Sam is powerless to help as Jez flails in the water. His friend is far from the lifeboat, hands outstretched, too weak to catch the rope he's thrown. Sam hangs from the side of the boat while the waves splash higher. Terror rises in his chest as he dives overboard, desperate to reach Jez, but it's too late ...

He startles awake, his eyes jacked wide. He's had the same vicious nightmare since Jez went missing, leaving him struggling for breath. He knows it will take ages for his thoughts to settle; his best bet is to go for a walk, so he rises to put on his clothes.

Sam hears a new sound as he dresses. Someone is talking in a murmur. It can't be his landlord, who always yells, but it's coming from downstairs. Curiosity makes him follow the sound, taking care not to make any noise.

Light spills from the living room as he stands in the hall, the door open a crack. When he peers inside, Moyle is almost unrecognisable. His chest is hunched over his knees, the look on his face tortured. He showed no regret when Jez went missing, but maybe that was just an act; his bravado has been wiped away, misery spilling out in a slow, anguished chant. Instinct stops Sam from barging in to ask what's wrong. The man would never give him an honest answer, so he lingers by the door, listening. When Moyle lurches to his feet suddenly, he backs away, then out of the front door, taking care to shut it quietly. His landlord would pick a fight immediately if he knew his moment of weakness had been observed.

Sam still feels wired when he reaches the street, like he did in prison. His only choice then was to march up and down his cell, three paces in each direction, until the panic faded. He walks through Hugh Town's quiet lane, the pubs and cafés all shut. It's only when he follows a narrow alley leading to the quay that he hears footsteps. Suddenly a shadow looms at him, and he's shouldered into a doorway. He catches sight of the man in the moonlight: it's Stuart Cardew, his face taut with anger.

'You attacked my son, didn't you? I bet you waited for him on my boat,' he hisses, his breath sour with booze. 'Leave these islands before I fucking kill you.'

'I'd never hurt Jez. He was my closest mate.'

'You lying bastard.'

Cardew slams him against the wall. He lands three hard punches on Sam's ribcage, then strides away. Sam doubles over, struggling to catch his breath, a spasm of pain making him so dizzy he drops to a crouch. His hands shake as the burning in his gut worsens, but he can't report the attack. Who would believe him over a popular man who's served on the lifeboat for twenty years?

Minutes pass before he's strong enough to rise to his feet

again. He cowers in the doorway, his bruised ribs still aching, then finds a bench on the quay, hoping that the harbour's calm will soothe the pain. As he sits there, he spots something odd in the distance. Callum Moyle is dragging his motorboat into the waves. The man curses as the outboard fails to start, then it finally grinds into life. Sam watches the unlit boat vanish through the harbour mouth, its outline soon hidden by the shifting waves.

21

Monday 28 August

I drive straight to Quay Street with Eddie this morning, hoping someone will be home at 8 a.m. Luckily it's Callum Moyle that answers the door, and yesterday's cockiness has faded. The bloke looks strung out, like he hasn't slept in weeks, already dressed in overalls. He only opens the door by a foot, his gaze flicking from my face to Eddie's. When he offers a shallow smile, his teeth are yellow with nicotine, hands twitching at his sides.

'What do you two want? It's a bank holiday.'

'We've got a case to solve, and it looks like you're off to work anyway. Are you all right, Callum? You seem jittery.' I'd like to explain that we believe Jez was killed, but we need definite proof first, or panic will spread like wildfire.

'I've never been fitter.' His voice is so firm, I know he's lying, but it's best to pick your battles.

'Can we come in? We need to search Jez's room.'

He hesitates before stepping back. 'Looking for anything in particular?'

'A package sent in the post.'

'I don't remember anything coming for him lately.'

The hallway still carries the bachelor pad stink of cigarettes, beer and dirty laundry. The carpet on the stairs is stained, the whole place in need of an overhaul. Moyle points at a closed door, then waits on the landing. Eddie gives a low whistle of disbelief when he sees Jez's room.

'Jez never keeps it this tidy,' Eddie says.

He didn't strike me as the kind of guy to hang clothes neatly in his wardrobe, make his bed, and arrange his shoes in pairs. The air stinks of furniture polish and bleach. When I glance through the doorway, Moyle remains on the landing, his arms folded tight across his chest.

'Did you clean up in here, Callum?'

'That'll be Sam. I always respect my housemates' privacy.'

'Really? I heard you were in rooting around in here, the night Jez went missing. Did you tidy up then or after?'

He tosses his head. 'I'd had a few drinks. It makes me forget about details.'

'Someone's been busy, that's for sure. Tell me again how you spent Friday evening?'

'I popped out for a beer at the Atlantic, came home by ten. I was knackered from work.'

I'm almost certain he's lying, his gaze furtive. It's possible he sailed out to St Agnes, to kill the housemate he'd begun to loathe. 'You own a two-berth boat, don't you, Callum?'

'The motor's buggered right now.'

'You've got a speedboat too,' Eddie says. 'I've seen you on it.'

'That's just for fishing, in my spare time.'

'How do you pay your employees, Callum?' I ask.

'Their wage goes direct to their banks. It's paid from a time sheet, then they give me their rent. Ask my accountant, if you like. She keeps the records.'

'Text me her number, please.'

I give him my card, and he pulls out his phone, obviously reluctant to follow my request.

'There you go. Now if you'll excuse me, I've got work to do. Shut the door behind you when you leave.'

'Arsehole,' Eddie hisses the word after Moyle trots downstairs, then slams the front door. 'He pays minimum wage to skilled craftsmen because there's so little work here. It's modern-day slavery.'

'What else do you know about him?'

'Callum's parents moved here when he was small. His family scattered, his sister's some big lawyer in the States. Only he stayed behind.'

'To make his fortune?'

He gives a snort of laughter. 'The bloke's so arrogant, most people steer clear. Only second-homers give him work.'

'Do you think he could have hurt Jez?'

'I've run him through our system. His record's clean, on the mainland and here, but he still gives me the creeps.'

'He's twitchy too. The bloke couldn't keep still.'

'Cocaine, or a guilty conscience, maybe. He's definitely a person of interest. Let's see what we find.'

I'm soon too busy checking every item in Jez's room to consider Moyle's lifestyle. Liz Gannick will be furious that we're wading through primary evidence, but I've got no choice. If we can find Jez's phone or another package full of badges and a note, we'll have something to work on, so we wear plastic gloves and try to get the job done fast. Eddie riffles through his chest of drawers, while I search his clothes. There's nothing hidden under his bed or mattress. His phone is nowhere to be seen, and there's no package either. I'm willing to bet it was Moyle who scoured the room, keen to rent it out to someone else. Only a few details give me access to Jez's behaviour. I find two dog-eared twenty-pound notes in his denim jacket, saved for a night out, a packet of condoms in the pocket of his Superdry jeans. It looks like he was having fun, in a place where excitement can be hard to find. I find what I'm looking for in the other pocket: it's a familiar padded envelope, just like the one sent to my home, and the one on his boat. Eddie appears at my side as I'm reading the message.

'ONE FOOT IN SEA AND ONE ON SHORE, TO ONE THING CONSTANT NEVER.'

'My note's the same,' Eddie mutters. 'The quote's from *The Tempest*, but what does it mean?'

'I think it's an accusation, about never committing yourself to anything. The killer sent Jez two packs, didn't he? The rest of us have only had one.'

'The words don't apply to Jez's life. He believed a hundred per cent in everything he did.'

'Someone disagrees, Eddie, or they're out to confuse us. That hangman figure is just like the one on mine. We need a police graphologist to check this, and all the other notes. Can you sort that back at the station?'

He places the package in an evidence bag, clearly glad to have a concrete task to complete. There's no sign of Jez's RNLI medal, even though pictures of him receiving it are plastered all over his parents' hall. We'll have to contact headquarters to see if they can identify if the one attached to the hand was his.

'His tablet's gone and his camera,' Eddie says. 'Sam probably nicked them. Moyle doesn't need to fence second-hand goods, does he? He's got his own business.'

'Maybe he's greedy. But tell me more about Jez. He liked a drink, didn't he? Was he into drugs as well?'

'Just the odd joint, now and then, in his teens.'

'I need the truth, Eddie.'

'Why would I lie, boss? There's nothing left to defend.' He sounds exhausted. 'I don't understand why anyone would kill a bloke who risked his life for others, so many times.'

'Perhaps someone dislikes heroes. The message is accusing him of being scared to make decisions.'

'Sick in the head then, aren't they?'

There's fury in Eddie's voice, but it's the wrong time to advise him to calm down. I step onto the landing to give him breathing space, then call Father Mike. I could stroll across the street to his flat, beside the church, but we're needed at the hospital soon. I need to hear more about his conversations with Jez Cardew, but the man's not answering, and Eddie looks ready to kick the wall, to release some adrenalin. There's no comfort available in this sterile room.

Eddie looks even worse by the time we reach the hospital mortuary, where the air smells of formaldehyde and decay. The Cardews haven't arrived yet, but Gareth Keillor looks relaxed in his empire. I'm surprised that Delia and Stuart have asked to see our find, rather than relying on DNA to identify the hand.

At ten o'clock, Eddie leads his aunt and uncle inside. My deputy seems calm, but Delia appears frailer than before. Her skin is flushed, eyes glinting with panic as she clutches Stuart's hand. He looks numb with misery, and the smell of booze he drank last night lingers on the air, like he's exuding neat whisky from his pores.

'You can still change your minds,' I say. 'A DNA test would give us answers within twenty-four hours.'

'Let us see it, Ben.' Stuart's voice is a low drone. 'We've made our decision.'

'You're sure?'

'Positive,' Delia replies. 'Or we'll never accept it.'

'Try to prepare yourselves. The hand was severed at the wrist; there are some cuts and lacerations too.'

Eddie positions himself next to his aunt, like he's expecting her to fall, and I draw back the sheet that is keeping the mangled wrist concealed. Delia remains steady, her gaze unblinking, while Stuart reels backwards. Eddie helps him out to the corridor for fresh air, but his wife is rooted to the spot.

'Jez got that scar from falling on broken glass on the beach when he was small. He's had that birthmark since he was born.' She presses her fingers to her mouth for almost a minute before speaking again. 'What the hell happened to him, Ben?'

'I'm afraid he was attacked. We're looking for evidence to prove exactly what happened.'

'Who'd hurt him, for God's sake?' Her eyes widen. 'Are you saying a killer tore him limb from limb?'

'We can't give any more details yet, but you know the ocean's savage, Delia. The rocks damage anything in the water. We found a RNLI medal attached to his hand, but there was no point showing it to you. It may not have been his, the name's been scratched from the back.'

I can tell she's stopped listening. When she touches her son's shrivelled fingertips, her calmness appears restored. She caresses her son's broken hand for another minute then replaces the sheet. There are no tears in her eyes when she lifts her gaze to mine. 'People thought Jez was fearless, but he was just like the rest of us. He was afraid he'd never find love, that's the saddest thing.' She continues before I can reply. 'Find out who did this, please, before Stuart loses his mind. Some evil bastard killed our son for no reason.'

Her stare is so direct, there's nowhere to hide.

'We'll pull out all the stops, I promise.'

'Start with his housemates. Callum's a bully and Sam's screwed up. Either of them could have done it.'

'We'll interview them, don't worry.' I hold her gaze. 'How did you get on with Anna Dawlish when she was with Jez?'

She looks surprised. 'You think she's involved?'

'No, I just need to understand everything, that's all.'

'We liked her at first, and her daughter's a sweetheart, but Anna held on so tight. Jez felt smothered, until he had to get away.'

'I'm trying to think of people he'd confide in. Would he speak about his relationships to your father? Molly Bligh says they were close.'

Delia frowns. 'Dad's a toxic force these days. Everyone knows it, but Jez still adored him. Age has made him spiteful. He only accepted Jez after he joined the lifeboat crew.'

'I need to pay him a visit.'

'Don't expect a welcome. When I took him a food parcel last week, he sent me packing without so much as a thank you.'

'One more thing, Delia. Do you know if Stuart got

an envelope through the post recently, with RNLI badges inside?'

She shakes her head. 'I collect the post each morning. He's had nothing like that. Why do you ask?'

'Some of the other crew members got one, including Jez. We think he had two.'

I'm about to leave when she grabs my arm.

'Keep me involved, please. Don't lock us out.'

'You'll get regular updates, I promise.'

'I hope you never have to feel like this, Ben. My world's broken, now Jez is gone.'

She turns away, leaving me shaken.

Gareth Keillor enters the room again, after waiting outside to give the Cardews privacy. I can tell he's glad that his job involves corpses and tissue samples rather than the chaos of human emotions. I watch him examine the hand again. The stark morning light shows extensive damage, with deep bruises and several broken fingers, but it's the ligature marks that hold my gaze. Someone tied a twenty-nine-year-old man to a rock, or the handrail of a boat, intent on seeing him drown. The sea's rocky outcrops may have done the rest, currents smashed his body against razor-sharp granite until his arm gave way.

I'm about to leave when Keillor drops a transparent evidence bag into my hand. It contains the medal that was tied to Jez's finger. It's a delicate gold circle, and the familiar words inscribed on it describes exactly what Jez must have felt as he drowned: *Let not the deep swallow me up.* The ribbon is badly frayed, but the medal itself is so glossy, it could be brand new. I'll need to find out if there's any way to check if it belonged to Jez from the RNLI. It's nothing like the crude badges I received in the post, in ugly dayglow orange, but it proves the killer enjoys any form of symbolism linking his crimes to the lifeboat service. I drop the bag into my pocket, then meet Keillor's eye again.

'Remind me how it was attached to his hand exactly?'

'With cheese wire. It's unbreakable without a knife or scissors,' Keillor says, assessing me over the top of his glasses. 'Someone looped it round his finger, then twisted it so tight it bit deep into his skin, but that was the least of his worries. If Jez was thrown into the sea, a cut finger would barely register. I'll get my pathology report done today, Ben. Call me if I can do anything else.'

'Thanks for your help, Gareth.'

I return to the empty corridor. There's no sign of Eddie, but Delia's floral scent hangs on the air, the fragrance too sweet for the occasion. I hope I'm never in her shoes. No one should have to identify their only child by a single limb under the clinical lights of a hospital mortuary.

The police van stands empty outside. I spot Eddie, hunched on the ground by the hospital wall, in a spot that's hidden from the car park. It crosses my mind to leave him in peace. It's normally him who comforts people in distress, while I stand back, too big and brusque to put anyone at ease. But there's no way I can desert him today. He averts his face when he sees me coming. He's crying so hard, his breath sounds jagged, tears dripping onto the ground like water from a faulty tap. I crouch beside him, but keep my distance. I get the sense he'd fall apart at the lightest touch. I crouch beside him, my hand on his shoulder. 'It's okay, mate. Better out than in.'

He wipes his hand across his face. 'Who the fuck would hurt a bloke like Jez?'

'We'll know soon enough.'

He almost manages a smile. 'It's normally me that's upbeat.'

'Jez was one of ours, Eddie. We won't stop till we get a result.'

'You're right.' He stumbles to his feet. 'Sorry I've been acting like a prat. I can't get my head round it, that's all.'

'I'd be the same in your shoes.'

Eddie gives a rapid nod. 'Give me a minute. I'll go inside, wash my face.'

He hurries towards the hospital's main entrance, his work ethic revived. I keep remembering the look in Delia Cardew's eyes when she begged me to find Jez's killer. We're going to need expert help. No one answers when I ring the police forensics lab in Penzance, forcing me to leave a message.

'This is for Professor Liz Gannick. It's DI Ben Kitto here. Can you fly over, pronto, please? Don't send me a junior. I need the best this time, our victim's a local hero.'

Eddie is already jogging back to the van, and it dawns on me that he's no longer a raw recruit. He's an experienced police officer, who never does things by halves. I don't know why seeing him cry seems like a rite of passage, rendering him fully grown up at last. He wasn't afraid to release his misery, and deal with it head on, while I've always buried mine.

'I'm not happy about you investigating Jez's murder, Eddie. I want to get officers over from the mainland, so you can stand down.'

'The islanders would never open up to a stranger, and there's no way I'm waiting at home.'

'If you're staying, you're going to be busy. We need to find out if this medal belonged to Jez.' I pull the evidence bag from my pocket. 'Someone erased the name for a reason. The symbolism's beyond me right now.'

Eddie takes a picture with his phone, before climbing into the van. His mood must be improving. He always records whatever he finds, even the smallest clues, like they might disappear into thin air.

22

My deputy is still too preoccupied to speak on our walk to the harbour. He doesn't even question why we're heading for St Agnes, but the pub's landlady seemed to know more than she admitted last time, so I want to question the couple again. The twenty-minute boat ride appears to lift Eddie's spirits. Regular sea crossings are a perk of life for most people in Scilly, including me. Being able to put a mile of clear blue water between work and home keeps me on an even keel.

I can feel my curiosity rising as we moor below the Turk's Head, then climb the slipway. We're retracing Jez Cardew's last steps. People saw him arrive with Sam Austell at around 8 p.m., then leave at closing time, sailing west into the night.

It's 10.30 a.m. by the time we enter the bar. I can still smell eggs and bacon, but the breakfast tables have been cleared and the place is empty, until Debbie Brookes appears behind the bar. Her smile vanishes abruptly, like someone hit a light switch.

'Can we talk for a minute, Debbie?'

'Let me bring you both a coffee first.'

'That sounds great, thanks. Is Tommy about?'

'He's taken the yacht out. Some guests wanted to go seal-watching.'

'They've picked a good day for it.'

She disappears into the kitchen. I'd rather be admiring fat grey seals, sunning themselves on Norrard Rocks, instead of asking uncomfortable questions. She doesn't take long to return with a loaded coffee tray.

'Is this about Jez?' Her gaze darts from Eddie's face to mine.

'We'd like to hear anything you can remember about Friday evening, please, Debbie. We know he sailed west from here, but not where he was heading.'

She shifts in her seat. 'I barely spoke to him that night.'

'You chatted other times though, didn't you? We're certain Jez was meeting a woman, after leaving here.'

'He seemed preoccupied, that's all.'

'Why, exactly?'

'Like I said, he was at a crossroads.' Her face tenses. 'He mentioned his thirtieth birthday coming up, like it was this big scary turning point.'

'Try to remember specific details from Friday, if you can. You may have been one of the last people he saw. You were fond of him, weren't you?'

She looks away. 'My loyalties were divided, to be honest. Anna Dawlish is a close friend of mine. He

141

treated her and Kylie terribly. I thought he must be in emotional trouble to desert them after making all those promises. He seemed too sweet-natured to act like that, without any reason.'

'I never heard much about their break-up. What happened exactly?'

'They were together six months. It was serious, until he dumped her, out of the blue. No explanation whatsoever.'

'That doesn't sound like him.'

'I suggested he talk to Father Mike if he was struggling. It's helped me a lot in the past.' She pushes her hair back from her face. 'Jez said he was facing a life-changing decision. He asked whether I'd walk away, or follow my instinct, in his shoes.'

'What did you say?'

'Nothing, I just listened. Something that big had to be his choice alone.'

'Can you think of anyone he liked especially, on the island?'

'Not really, it's mostly retired couples and young families out here . . .' Her voice trails away.

'But you've got suspicions.'

'His grandad's the best one to ask about personal stuff, Jez worshipped him.'

'Molly Bligh said the same, but he's switched off his phone. The woman Jez was seeing must be here on St Agnes, Debbie.'

Her hands jitter on the table. 'I've seen him chatting

to Sharon Cosgrove, here and at the shop, but only when her husband's away. If they were having a fling, it would cause one hell of a mess.'

'How about mates he saw recently?'

'I think he was friendly with Lewis Marling, the guy who bought the old pottery last year. He keeps himself busy. I haven't seen him all week.'

'That's a long time on a small island.'

'Lewis prefers making pots to human company, by all accounts.' Her gaze searches my face again, checking I'm trustworthy. 'Don't quote me about Sharon, please. I can't afford enemies.'

'We'll be subtle, don't worry,' Eddie says. 'Thanks for the coffee.'

I'm feeling better when we get back outside; we've uncovered our first scraps of useful information. There must be a reason why Jez sailed here so often in the past year, and a young woman with an absent husband sounds like a fair place to start.

We head for the Cosgroves' house first. It lies at the western edge of Lower Town, the same direction Jez sailed in, the night he vanished. Damian Cosgrove is a local boy, around thirty. His wife is Scottish; I rarely see her out and about, unless they're together. We pass the lighthouse that still dominates the island from its central position, even though it was decommissioned years ago. The tower is part of a private residence now, but the couple who own it are generous. They invite kids from Five Islands school to visit their home each year, explaining how the keepers tended the light twenty-four hours a day. We leave the tall white building behind us, then it's five more minutes to Lower Town. The settlement is a cluster of typical Scillonian cottages, built simply from grey stone, their backs turned to the north wind that ravages the islands each winter. The Cosgroves' place is a hundred metres further down the lane, in Perigilis.

'I've met Sharon a few times at the pub. Want me to question her, boss?' Eddie says.

'Go ahead. You're better at wheedling information out of people.'

My partnership with Eddie amuses some of the islanders. They see us patrolling the islands together, a blonde choirboy with his hulking minder, but the reality is more complex. I'm less taciturn than I seem, and he's quick-witted, which works to our advantage. I'm keen to hear Sharon Cosgrove's view of Jez, but there's no easy way to ask someone if they've been having an affair.

The cottage lies in an enviable location, close to Blanket Bay, where the beach gleams with sunlight. It has a direct view of Burnt Island's rocky peninsula and Bergecooth Carns spearing up from the Atlantic.

Sharon Cosgrove answers our knock in seconds, as if she's been waiting all morning for visitors. The young woman gives no sign of panic, her smile welcoming. The house looks orderly, but it's clear she hasn't yet absorbed the island's traditions: visitors are always offered tea and refreshments. Instead she stands in her kitchen gazing at us with curiosity. She's got an attractive oval face, with dark hair tucked neatly behind her ears. I only notice she's pregnant because she's resting one hand on her abdomen, like she's protecting her unborn child from invasive questions, but it's the wrong moment for congratulations.

Her stare is so forthright, I feel obliged to justify our visit straight away, even though Eddie's meant to be leading the interview.

'We're here about Jez Cardew. Is it okay to ask you a few questions?'

'The sea's vicious, this time of year.' Her voice has a soft Scottish lilt, tinged with sadness.

'There are some things we don't understand,' Eddie says. 'Did you know him at all?'

'Just as an acquaintance.'

'We're trying to understand why he'd been visiting St Agnes. How long have you lived here, Sharon?'

'Almost a year.'

'You've settled in okay?' Eddie gives his best smile.

'It's going well, thanks. I grew up on Orkney, so the lifestyle's similar, but the weather's kinder. I like working at the Post Office half the week.'

'Did you meet Damian on Orkney?'

'He stayed in my family's B&B while he was on the rigs. He's a mechanic at Newquay airport now, week on, week off. We see more of each other than we ever did back home.'

'It's important to get a decent work–life balance, isn't it?' Eddie leans back in his seat, clearly ill at ease. 'Sorry, but I have to ask, Sharon. Were you and Jez close? He sailed towards your house, rather than St Mary's, after the pub closed.'

Her face blanks. 'What do you mean?'

'You've been seen talking to him recently.'

'And a few conversations mean we're having a fling?' The warmth has left her voice. 'You're way off track. I can't even chat to a stranger out here without people jumping to conclusions.'

Eddie's normally great on interpersonal skills, but losing Jez seems to have blunted his empathy. I'll have to intervene before he makes matters worse.

'We just need to know where you were on Friday night, Sharon,' I say. 'There's nothing more to it.'

'I went to the pub for an hour, to stretch my legs. Jez was there, but I never spoke to him. My husband was visiting someone on Gugh.'

'Who's that?'

'Denzel Jory. He plays chess with the old man sometimes.'

'He must be brave,' I say, smiling. 'Did you know Denzel is Jez's grandfather?'

'I had no idea.' She takes a breath. 'Why are you bothering me? You can't just march into my home and accuse me of having an affair.'

'No one said that, Sharon. We just need his friends to share information, to help us find out why he died. We found a note on his boat. He was definitely seeing someone on St Agnes. It's important we find out who.'

'And I'm top of your list?' she snaps. 'Is that because I'm pregnant, or a newcomer?'

'We're obliged to investigate Jez's death. It's our job.'

'I never sent him a note or laid one finger on him. Okay?'

'We'll be calling at every household on St Agnes; you're not being singled out. Jez didn't just fall into the sea; we know there was foul play.'

She gives a brittle laugh. 'Who'd hurt him, in a place like this?'

'People feel jealous, the world over, and life can be hard on a small island, where everyone knows your business. We think he was seeing a married woman. I'm sorry if our questions felt invasive, but we need to take a handwriting sample from you, please.'

The woman says nothing when I produce some blank paper and a biro. I dictate a few words in a jumbled sentence, making sure to include the ones used in the note found on Jez's boat. Once she's finished, she thrusts the paper back at me, her expression hostile.

'The locals sent you, didn't they? They took against me, the minute I arrived.'

'This isn't about you, Sharon.'

'They'll be chatting about your visit, passing the word round.'

'Forgive me, but you sound a bit paranoid. We're

investigating a man's death, not your standing in the community.'

'You're accusing me of sleeping with a man I barely knew,' she says, rising to her feet. 'Get out, before my husband finds you here.'

'Call us, please, if you think of anything else.' I hold out my card, but she ignores it, so I leave it on her kitchen table. 'Thanks for your time.'

The front door snaps shut at our heels. Eddie waits until we reach the lane before giving a low whistle of disbelief. The young woman hasn't done herself any favours by acting so defensive. Her rudeness could be a form of grief, but we'll need to do more digging before making assumptions. Sharon knows how life operates on a small island, having come from Orkney; once a reputation's made, the stain is likely to be permanent. When I glance back at her house she's standing in the picture window, arms folded, clearly willing us to leave.

23

Sam isn't at his best this morning. Last night's attack has left a rainbow of bruises on his torso, but he can't rest in bed. He looks into Jez's room before leaving for work, noticing that his valuables have gone: his camera, laptop and tablet. Moyle must have taken them to sell. He should report the theft to Ben Kitto, but he knows he'll end up homeless if he blows the whistle.

When he arrives at the property Callum's been renovating he doesn't waste time, even though his landlord hasn't arrived. Prison taught him that work carries its own rewards, helping him forget his troubles. He's almost finished hanging the kitchen cabinets by mid-morning, which gives him a sense of pride; soon he can start cutting new skirting boards for the hall. He's busy screwing handles to cupboard doors when Moyle finally arrives, but something's changed. There's none of his usual bluster, his hands shaky as he sorts through tools.

'How come you're late?' Sam asks.

'Deliveries to chase, and wood's doubled in price.' Moyle

pulls a hammer from his tool-bag, then turns to him. 'Jesus, you look rough. What happened to you?'

'Someone attacked me last night, for no reason.' Sam straightens his back. 'How come you took Jez's stuff? It belongs to his family.'

'Keep out of it, I'm warning you.'

Sam counts to ten inside his head. It's a strategy learned in prison, to manage his anger, but it's not working today. Instinct tells him not to argue, even though Moyle's behaviour disgusts him. How could anyone pick over a dead man's possessions, like a vulture? His ribs are still burning from last night's attack, but he can't let Moyle's actions pass. He must stand up for Jez, no matter how much trouble it creates.

'What are you up to, Callum? I saw you leaving on your speedboat last night.'

Moyle crosses the room in a few strides, standing so close, their faces are almost touching. 'Are you spying on me, you little runt?'

'I couldn't sleep, that all.'

'Keep your nose out of my business.'

'You scoured Jez's room and took his stuff. What else have you done?'

'Shut up and work, for fuck's sake.'

Moyle finally steps back, but Sam's already seen his dilated pupils, and the tremor in his hands. The situation makes sense at last; his landlord's hair-trigger temper comes from cocaine use, or MDMA. He's seen it too many times. It shows in his rapid speech and his restless energy. Callum may have sailed off in his boat last night for a fix, if none was available on St Mary's.

Sam wants to confront him about it, but he'd come off worse in a fist fight, with the injuries he's carrying, so he concentrates on work, hammering another nail into place. The prison doctor told him to steer clear of users if he wanted to stay clean, but he needs to remain close to Moyle. There are questions that need answering. How come he's so angry since Jez went missing? Sam needs to find the truth, not just for Jez's sake, but also to clear his name.

24

My day is a string of frustrations. When I call Denzel Jory's home, one of the island nurses answers the phone. The old man is ill with stomach trouble, too sick to talk, so our visit will have to wait. I contact the RNLI headquarters next. They say it will be tricky to prove who owned the medal attached to Jez Cardew's hand. The officer gives me a lecture, explaining that the first ones went to Cromer's lifeboat crew in 1917, for gallantry at sea, after rescuing dozens of sailors from certain death in a gruelling fourteen-hour shift. The only way to identify the recipient is from the name engraved on the back of each medal, because dozens lie in the hands of collectors.

I want to know why the killer bothered scraping it away with a file. That act of erasure means something to the killer, just like the quotes from *The Tempest*, yet I can't pin it down. The officer sounds disgruntled when I request a list of everyone in Scilly who's been awarded a medal, since records began. It could yield valuable information, and reveal who to protect, but the man's tone is sullen when he finally agrees to email it to me tomorrow.

I knock on several doors on St Agnes, still trying to discover who Jez Cardew visited after the pub. An elderly widow saw his cabin cruiser moving west at a slow speed, as she closed her bedroom curtains. It barely marked the water, so the engine must have been idling, or the boat was adrift. I'm starting to wonder if Damian Cosgrove could have carried out the attack after seeing Jory, if he believed his wife was unfaithful, but Eddie appears unconvinced. He's certain Jez would have confided in him if he was troubled about seeing a married woman. We've tried calling Lewis Marling, to see if he has information to share, but there's still no answer from the potter's mobile. I can tell that frustration is nagging at Eddie, a muscle ticking in his cheek.

'Stay positive,' I tell him. 'We'll find the truth on St Agnes. We know Jez had fallen for someone out here. All we have to do is keep digging.'

Eddie's watching messages scroll across his phone, like the truth's concealed behind a million texts. 'What if Jez did something daft, to make cash?'

'Like what?'

'He dreamed of buying his own place one day, but you know how it goes here. People get stuck on minimum wage and the lifeboat job wasn't guaranteed. The cox had applied for funds to cover it, but it's never easy wringing money from a charity.' Eddie catches my gaze.

'Maybe he made extra cash from a few smuggling deals.'

'You think he'd stoop that low?'

'Sam Austell was a drug runner for years; he could be back to his old tricks. People are blaming him for Jez's death, especially Stu.'

'We've got no proof, Eddie. I keep telling you, there's no way he'd deal again, right under our noses, and Sam wasn't on the boat when Jez disappeared. I got an email from the harbour master in Penzance this morning. He told the truth about getting a ride home to St Mary's.'

'He's still the obvious suspect.'

'Prison works sometimes, Eddie. Over sixty per cent of male offenders never go back inside. Some go on to lead normal lives. You can tell from looking at Sam that he's clean, unlike Callum. He's still a person of interest.'

'We'll have to agree to differ.'

'Father Mike's convinced Sam's gone straight.'

'Priests see the good in everyone, don't they?' he snaps. 'It goes with the job.'

'If you can't be objective, stand down, Eddie.'

'No way.' His blue eyes fizz with anger. 'I'll stay professional, don't worry.'

Eddie's voice rings with anger. I know he wants quick answers, but they won't come from aiming at low hanging fruit. When my phone bleeps in my pocket, the first message is from Liz Gannick. It's a garbled speech about being on her way, after delays at the airport. The next is from Nina, reminding me I'm due at the church on Bryher in half an hour, to see Maggie about wedding arrangements. I'll have to put personal interests above policing for the first time in days. Eddie looks daunted when I explain that he'll have to welcome Liz Gannick by himself when she arrives. The forensics chief is notoriously hard to please. It's her job to scan the handwriting sample Sharon Cosgrove provided and get a police graphologist to compare it with the note from Jez's boat. There must be a reason for Sharon's defensiveness, but we can't question her again without evidence.

Nina fills my mind when I hurry down to the harbour and persuade a fisherman to ferry me over to Bryher, in exchange for cash. I've known most of the fishing community all my life, so the old man soon agrees when he hears I've got urgent wedding planning to do. He steers his skiff into a wall of sunshine. The water glistens like molten gold, and the twenty-minute journey gives me time to reflect. Nina's handled everything for our wedding since Jez went missing. Maggie and Ray are giving her support, but I've been negligent. I look out at Samson as we pass the island's deserted village, where ruined houses stare at me in blank-eyed judgement, through windows that shattered decades ago.

I thank the fisherman when he moors on Bryher. He protests when I press a tenner into his hand, insisting on paying for his diesel, but there's no time to argue. I jog uphill from the quay, to find Shadow waiting on the path. My dog offers his usual frenzied greeting, planting his paws on my chest, showering me with canine affection. It's a different story when I enter the church ten minutes late. Noah is crying at top volume, and Nina scowls at me while he waves his fists in the air, screaming in protest.

'What's upset him?' I ask.

'Colic, or your constant absence,' she replies coolly. 'He's been yelling his head off all morning.'

'Let me take him.'

'Gladly.'

She looks thrilled to dump him in my arms. Our son's still bawling, his face sticky with tears.

'No one likes a screamer,' I tell him, then hum 'Someone to Watch Over Me' in his ear, until his cries reduce to a murmur.

'That pisses me off so much,' Nina says. 'He's been inconsolable for hours, then you rock up late and he's putty in your hands.'

'Sorry, I—'

'Listen to me, Ben. You promised to help, then you vanished. Your work always comes first.'

'That's not true.'

'Don't bullshit me. I'm sick of it.'

We're still glaring at each other when my godmother breezes inside. Maggie Nancarrow has run Bryher's only pub all her working life; she's in her sixties but unwilling to slow down. The woman is small but indomitable. I can tell she's assessing the situation when she dumps a picnic bag on the church's stone floor, then seizes Noah from my arms. Maggie jiggles him on her hip, coaxing a smile; I can see him relaxing at last, now that he's in expert hands. She grins back at him in delight, even when he yanks at her cloud of grey ringlets.

'I brought your sample menu,' Maggie says. 'Go outside and taste each dish for me, can you? If it's okay, we'll run with it at the picnic. There's still time for a few small tweaks.'

'You're amazing,' Nina says. 'I was about to murder Ben.'

'Wedding stress hits everyone, sweetheart. Find some sunshine outside. I'll show Noah this old place, then we'll chat about flowers.'

We leave her pointing at the stained-glass windows, while our son reaches for the tinted sunlight, like he could grasp it in his hand.

Nina remains silent as we settle on a church bench, with Shadow close by. He's acting as referee, or just hoping that good behaviour will result in food. The cemetery is tranquil enough to calm any disturbed mind, with blue agapanthus spilling over gravestones, bees droning, and the square-walled church providing shade from the sun. We peer at the menu Maggie's dreamed up, printed on a card: barbecued salmon, miniature Cornish pasties, potato salad, couscous with local tomatoes and herbs, followed by strawberry tart, made with fruit straight from St Martin's fields. Shadow's delighted reaction to the pasty I throw him proves that the food will suit him fine. It's Nina who speaks first, her voice quiet.

'Noah got upset because of me. He senses whenever I'm stressed.'

'About the wedding?'

'Of course. Are you certain we're doing the right thing, Ben?'

'You know we are.'

Nina swallows a deep breath. 'You're amazing with Noah. It's always you that gets up in the middle of the night, but don't you ever feel doubt?'

'Loads of times, but never about you, or Noah.'

'How come you're so sure?'

'You're what I need. I knew from day one, and he's the icing on the cake. Nothing else matters now I've got you two. I'm the luckiest man alive.'

Nina stares at me, open-mouthed. 'God almighty, Ben. Where did that come from?'

'I wouldn't be marrying you if I felt different.'

'Days pass without you expressing your emotions, then I get your whole manifesto. I know you've been making an effort, but life would be so much easier if you shared your feelings more often.'

'I thought I'd nailed it by now.'

She smiles at last. 'You're getting there, and I love hearing it from you, each time. It's a change of mindset, that's all.'

'It cuts both ways, Nina. I need reassurance too sometimes.'

'Don't I give it to you?'

'Not that often.'

'I'll do better, sorry.' She rests her head on my shoulder, her dark hair glossy in the sunlight.

'It's too late for questions. We're a family already, the wedding's just a formality.'

'Sharing you's the toughest part. You've been married to your job for years, and now there's the lifeboat too. Your sense of duty's off the scale. I know that won't change, but I need more of your time, and so does Noah. I worry about him growing up without you around.'

'That won't ever happen.' I put my arm round her shoulders and squeeze her close. I still have nightmares about her getting caught in the crossfire on a case last year. The scar on her temple is almost invisible now, but she nearly lost the sight in one eye. I considered resigning for months afterwards, to keep her safe.

'Promise to spend the rest of today with us, Ben.'

'Nothing can stop me. Now, let's try the rest of this food.'

It's a luxury to steal time alone together. I can see her rallying as we regain our balance, and enjoy Maggie's delicacies. Fifteen minutes pass before we go back into the church, where my godmother is sitting in a front pew, with Noah asleep on her lap. My thoughts drift as Nina discusses how the aisles should be decorated, with Maggie scribbling a diagram. We're having local wildflowers, instead of hothouse roses. My brother and

I used to pluck them from the hedgerows to placate our mother, whenever we were in trouble. Wild lilies are far better than florists' bouquets, full of identical blooms, smothered in cellophane. I like knowing that my dad got married in this church, and his father before him, long before weddings turned into an industry.

We follow the coastal path to my godmother's pub, the Rock, which has stood on Bryher's eastern shore for two hundred years. It's the ideal place for a celebration, with Tresco's outline rising from the narrow strait between the islands. Maggie's partner Billy Reese is in the kitchen with old-school rock music blaring from his sound system as usual, his long beard more white than grey. I don't say much while the three of them discuss food, speeches and the bonfire for our beach party. The islanders have spent hours gathering driftwood and piling it on the shore, getting everything ready, but my mind keeps drifting to Jez Cardew. He'll never get the chance to marry or have kids, and survivor guilt nags at me.

'Any nearer finding out what happened to Jez?' Maggie asks.

'Not as close as I'd like.'

'It's Liam Quick I pity,' she replies. 'He's changed so much. He used to be so relaxed, and every shout was an adventure. The poor man seems burdened by it now.'

'You think he's a tortured soul?'

'Liam's been a great dad to Danielle, but his wife clearing off to the mainland with her fancy-man happened out of the blue. The poor man aged ten years overnight. He's always cared about his job, but now the lifeboat's his obsession. Haven't you noticed? You're cut from the same cloth, Ben. You'll have to take care.'

'Nina tells me that on a regular basis.'

'Your boy's restless again,' Maggie says, smiling. 'You should take him for a swim so he sleeps well tonight.'

'Good plan,' Nina replies. 'Fancy a dip, Ben? Or is that against your workaholic principles?'

'I'll grab some towels.'

It's early evening by the time we reach Hell Bay. The beach is deserted, even though it's high summer. Bryher's seclusion suits me far better now than it did as a boy. There's a limit to how large our population can swell, with hotel guests pushing it to two hundred in holiday season, but there's always room to breathe. Nina and I stand together in the water, our hands under Noah's belly while he thrashes his arms and legs. He's gurgling with laughter as Nina leaves him with me then swims out deeper.

My son is draped over my shoulder as the stars emerge. I've always loved the way nightfall arrives unannounced in Scilly, with little streetlight to soften the transition. I float on my back with Noah spread-eagled on my chest. The view above us is humbling, the Milky Way a thin swathe of chalk drawn across the sky. I swim for the shore, with my son enjoying the ride. I could watch the stars glimmer for hours, but Jez Cardew's death enters my mind again, making me shiver as we reach dry land.

25

I lay Noah in his cot, his night light glowing in the corner. Nina is playing a lullaby on her violin in the living room, which works its magic as always, and he only protests briefly. The music continues when I close the nursery door, Nina's body swaying to the rhythm. My self-taught piano skills could never match her talent, so I stretch out on the sofa to listen. She's taught me about classical music since we've been together, and I'm almost certain tonight's piece is a Schubert lullaby, slow and lilting.

Nina is normally relaxed after she finishes practising, but tonight her expression is sombre when she finally puts her violin away.

'Still fretting about the wedding?' I ask.

'Just thinking about the past.' She curls up beside me, her feet on my lap. 'The first time I got married, I was twenty-one and I wore a second-hand dress. It was a blistering June day and everything seemed perfect. But then Simon got sick, and things changed overnight. I sometimes feel guilty about life moving on so fast. Here I am, marrying again, with a new baby.'

'What do you think Simon would say?'

'Go for it, probably. He loved seeing me happy.' Her smile returns. 'The thing is, I've got some requests to make.'

'How many, exactly?'

'Two big ones.' Her gaze searches my face. 'Give up your lifeboat duties, please. I hate the idea of losing you.'

'I can't step down. Someone has to face the sea, all year round.'

'How come it's always you, when danger's involved? It's tragic that your dad drowned, but that wasn't your fault.'

I suppress a flicker of anger, because her words echo Madron's so directly. 'The lifeboat matters to me. I hear what you're saying, and I'll consider it, but my answer may not be to your liking.' I lean back in my seat. 'Can you help me with something on the case? There's some emotional stuff I don't understand.'

'What about my second request?'

'I'll grant whatever it is, if you help me.'

'That's a rash promise. Remember I'm a counsellor, not a forensic psychologist.'

'You know plenty compared to me. Why would Jez Cardew's killer send him some RNLI badges, with a quote from *The Tempest*, before drowning him deliberately?'

She looks surprised. 'Do you know what happens in the play?'

'I never read it at school. It starts with a storm at sea, doesn't it?'

'The rest takes place on Prospero's island. He's an exiled nobleman, desperate to regain his power. All sorts of magic takes place there. It's like a fairy-tale, with sea monsters and spells.'

'The island's a fantasy world then, unlike ours.'

'Maybe the killer sees a parallel. There's an epic battle against the sea, then the shipwreck's survivors jockey for power.' Her gaze levels with mine. 'Those RNLI badges are a direct link to the ocean too.'

'A gallantry medal was tied to Jez's body as well, with the name erased. What do you think that means?'

Nina considers the idea. 'A defaced medal sounds like symbolic sarcasm. It's saying, you're not such a hero now, are you? You can't even defend yourself. There are plenty of reasons why someone might resent a local hero. Jealousy, for a start.'

'I know men commit ninety-five per cent of violent crime in the UK, but this could be an exception, couldn't it?'

'Women only tend to attack when mental illness is involved, or after years of abuse. But anything's possible.'

'So it could be someone who hates anyone that's treated like a hero. It could explain why most of the lifeboat crew got sent badges, and messages telling us we're flawed.'

'Please don't tell me you're in danger. I can't handle any more worry, on top of the wedding.' She suddenly looks tired.

'You had two requests, Nina. What's the other?'

'Remember, you promised to say yes.' She leans forwards, touching my hand. 'I'd like another baby, soon.'

'Why take the risk?'

'I did three years' medical training, remember? I'll need close monitoring in my final trimester, that's all.'

'You almost died the first time. It scared the shit out of me.'

Her tone softens. 'That's natural, but I hated being an only child. Noah deserves a sibling, near his age.'

'He'll have all the islands' kids as playmates.'

'It's a gamble worth taking.'

'You must be crazy.'

'We have to make a decision together, but it's my body. Noah deserves a bigger family.'

'Blood doesn't mean anything. My brother lives three thousand miles away, and only visits for weddings and funerals. Zoe's more like a sister to me than a friend.'

'That was pure luck.'

'Noah has our undivided attention. Most kids yearn for that, don't they?'

'Let's talk about it after the wedding. It matters, more than anything else we do for him.'

'We should leave it till we're closer to agreeing.'

'I won't let you forget, don't worry.'

'How could I, when you keep circling back to it?'

'Forget it for now.' She's on her feet, tugging at my hands. 'Come to bed. Noah's asleep, and we're due an early night.'

Moonlight filters through the curtains in our bedroom. It casts a pale glow on Nina's skin as she undresses, which fits her image. She's like quicksilver, slipping through my hands. It's not just her looks that draw me, it's her independence, and the challenges she throws down. There are questions in her eyes when she steps into my arms, each of us haunted by different needs, but still prepared to meet in the middle. Her touch is gentle when she touches my face then kisses me. Need for her soon empties my mind of every other thought. She looks beautiful when she rises over me, her head tipped back, the tension inside me finally releasing. There's triumph on her face when I lose control, like she's proved her point once and for all.

Nina falls asleep fast, with her head on my shoulder, but my mind's still buzzing. An hour passes before sleep claims me, then I struggle to surface when my phone rings in the middle of the night. I stumble into the hall to answer it. The male voice is unfamiliar at first, the sound of waves murmuring in the distance.

'It's Liam Quick, Ben. Get over to Hangman Island fast, can you? I need help.' The line crackles then breaks down, which often happens in Scilly, usually at the worst possible time.

'I'm on my way, Hawkeye,' I reply, but there's only a hiss of static.

Shadow seems desperate to get outside once I'm dressed. He bounds ahead too fast for me to keep up as I cross the island, with my torch beam trained on the path. It's 3.30a.m., dawn won't arrive for another two hours. The lights are out in Ray's flat when I reach my boat. I make a vain attempt to leave Shadow on the quay, but he leaps on board as I depart, with my outboard motor churning the brine into foam.

We've only got a short distance to travel; Hangman Island stands in the middle of New Grimsby Strait, the narrow channel separating Bryher and Tresco. It's picturesque in high summer when you can walk out to explore it at neap tide, but tonight the island looks haunted. Black rocks stand high at its core, with a yardarm raised on the summit. Oliver Cromwell executed hundreds of traitors here, applauding each death from his castle on Tresco's western coast, during the English Civil War. Kids dared each other to swim out here at midnight when I was a boy, certain the island was haunted, and we may have been right. The air feels a few degrees colder as we approach.

Quick is in the distance, wearing his yellow RNLI oilskin, with his powerful motorboat moored in the shallows. I drop anchor and wade over submerged rocks. Shadow is standing on the prow when I look back, determined not to miss anything. The misery on Liam Quick's face announces that he's found Jez Cardew.

'Where is he?'

167

'We'll have to scramble to the other side,' the coxswain says. 'I've been sailing between here and Samson looking for him.'

'Why, for God's sake?'

'Ray thought the body might come this way, on currents travelling west. He knows the tides better than anyone.' Quick looks down at his soaked trainers. 'Prepare yourself, Ben. He's not a pretty sight.'

I follow him across the rocks, my feet slipping on wet seaweed. There's a white outline up ahead, against granite boulders. The sea has stripped away Jez Cardew's clothes. He lies face down on a crag, his body so broken I want to look away, his left arm ending in a ragged stump. His legs are so misshapen, the bones must each have shattered. My first reaction is anger, against whoever caused so much pain to a young man everyone admired. The body must be hidden before sun rises, or the islanders will be traumatised.

Quick stands close by when I call first DCI Madron then Gareth Keillor and Liz Gannick. It's only when I shove my phone back into my pocket that I notice the coxswain's angular face is pale with shock.

'Were you and Danielle sent RNLI badges in the post recently, Liam?'

'We each got a packet yesterday, with a weird note inside. I chucked mine away. Why?'

'Try and find them both, then bring them to the station today, please. Someone's targeting the crew. We all need to watch our backs till we find out who did this.'

'Why would anyone come after us?'

'It must be some kind of grievance. Don't worry, we'll find out.'

'The killer's in danger too.' Quick's fury is unmistakeable when he points at the yardarm above us. 'Some bastard ended Jez's life for no reason. He deserves to hang. I'll do it myself, if you like.'

'It's our job to solve it, Liam. Don't put yourself at risk.'

His face crumples. 'Jez wasn't just a volunteer, he was like a son to me. I thought he'd take over, when I retire.'

'I'm sorry. This must be terrible for you.'

Quick grits his teeth. I can see he's fighting the urge to cry about the murder of his best crew member, unwilling to break down in public. He's shaking with anger when I place my hand on his shoulder, and I know how he feels. I've never believed in capital punishment, but tonight's discovery is making me question my position.

PART 2

*The man who has experienced shipwreck
shudders at even a calm sea.*

OVID

26

Tuesday 29 August

The sky is slowly lightening from the east. I've covered
Jez's body with a tarpaulin, to hide it from view as
dawn arrives. It's a relief to avoid those gaping wounds.
His face is almost unrecognisable, the skin blue and
waxy, so swollen his eyes are just thin black lines. The
coxswain is keeping me company, even though back-
up will arrive soon. Liam Quick is one of the toughest
men I know, but he looks broken now his anger has
faded. We huddle together on a granite boulder, while
he keeps his eyes trained on the horizon.

'You did well finding him, Hawkeye. If you hadn't,
he'd have been carried west on the next tide.'

'That won't comfort Stu and Delia, will it?'

'It'll give them closure at least. My mother had nothing to bury; she never got over Dad drowning.'

'It was the same for all the families. My own mental
health suffered for a bit, to be honest.'

'How do you mean?'

'Those blokes were friends of mine, the same age. I carried it with me for years.'

'You were on the lifeboat when Dad's trawler went down?'

My words make him flinch. 'It was my first shout. We sailed out to the Atlantic Strait in the worst conditions I'd seen, but got there too late.'

'The RNLI would give you PTSD counselling these days.'

'What's the point? Nothing can bring those men back.'

'You did your best, Liam. We all do, on every shout.'

'I'm glad you signed up.' He forces a smile. 'It took guts for you and Paul Keast to join us, after losing your dads at sea.' Quick's gaze scans my face again, monitoring my reactions.

'I'd hate my own kid to go through the same. Nina wants me to resign.'

Quick looks shocked. 'And you're considering it?'

'I don't want to stop, but I'll have to consider it. Her health's not a hundred per cent, she doesn't need any stress.'

'We'd all miss your input, Ben, but I'd understand. You have to do what's right for your family.' His voice is bleak when he faces the sea again. 'I think about the ones we lost at times like this.'

'Me too, but let's focus on the present. Can you think of anyone who'd target the whole lifeboat crew?'

'It doesn't make sense. Dozens of volunteers give their free time to run the festival each year, just to support the RNLI.'

'Someone's nursing a grudge. You'll have to watch your back, Hawkeye. Stay safe, and Danielle too. If the killer's targeting crew, you're both obvious targets.'

'I won't let her out of my sight.'

'The lifeboat wasn't to blame for my dad's trawler sinking. No one's at fault, it was the ocean that took their lives.'

'Some people struggle to accept that, after losing a relative.'

'How do you mean?'

'Janet Fearnley's husband had a heart attack, alone on his boat last year, a mile out to sea. Trevor managed to ring us, but he died before we got there. I did everything in my power, but the boat's engine failed. It cost us fifteen minutes. We tried CPR on him all the way back to shore. Janet was furious, she said we should have taken the D class boat, to reach him in time. I've had to live with my decision ever since. It's my fault we took so long to arrive.'

'But she's still running the volunteer team.'

'She's apologised to me since, but she could be right. I was afraid to risk everyone's lives on the D Class, in a rising storm.'

'You were right about that,' I tell him. 'Find those envelopes for me today, please.'

'I'll do it straight away.'

Quick frowns at the sea, as if the returning tide carries blame, for each life it's stolen. The coxswain seems to be waging a battle with his conscience. All lifeboat volunteers pledge to save lives, yet hundreds of mariners still die on the water, and no skipper's record remains clean forever. The sea has no mercy if you're unprepared, or on the wrong side of a storm. Quick sets off on his motorboat as the police launch arrives, grim-faced as he heads back to St Mary's.

Eddie is steering the policeboat closer, even though I asked Madron to send Isla instead. It could damage him to see his cousin's body torn to shreds, but the DCI has ignored my request, as usual. Gareth Keillor and Liz Gannick are on board too, and their landing will be tricky. The boat is already so covered in scrapes and dents, most of its dayglow stripes have vanished, the police crest faded from black to grey. Eddie attempts to pull closer, but Hangman Island is just a pile of granite spikes. He could easily break the propellor shaft, so our experts are forced to scramble ashore.

Dr Liz Gannick's thick northern accent reaches me before she appears; her complaints are as loud as a foghorn, which doesn't match her image. She's an elfin figure as she raises herself onto the gunwale. The pathologist offers to help, but she bats him away with a grunt of annoyance. Gannick sometimes uses a wheelchair, but she prefers crutches, her pace faster than most people can walk. She reaches the shore before her male companions, cursing as she splashes over wet rocks. She's dressed in a leather jacket and vintage Levis, with a few locks of her short black hair dyed a vivid pink. The scowl on her face is so deep it appears to have been carved into her skin.

'This had better be fucking worth it,' she hisses. 'These boots cost a fortune.'

'Thanks for coming over so fast, Liz.'

'You begged; I had no bloody choice.'

'I'm still grateful.'

'Save it for someone who gives a shit. Let's work, shall we? I'm soaked to the skin.'

Gannick falls silent when Keillor stumbles ashore. The party each react differently to seeing Jez's body, but Eddie's response bothers me most. There's cold fury on his face, as if he plans to deliver natural justice to whoever killed his cousin with such violence. Gannick mutters a string of expletives, while Keillor works in silence, keeping personal feelings at bay. It takes us ten minutes to cover the body with a tent made of sterilised plastic. The sky has turned a brilliant pink, stippled with dots of cloud. The Eastern Isles look like they're on fire. I've watched sunrise transform this low-slung landscape many times, since Noah began waking early, but there's no time to appreciate it today.

Keillor is already speaking into his Dictaphone, making notes for the coroner's report. Gannick's face is tense with resentment at having to wait her turn. I've never met anyone with such a powerful work ethic, except Liam Quick. The county's forensics chief may be hard to please, but she's prepared to toil round the clock for a result.

'What's that twisted round his neck?' she asks.

I spot a thin wire under his jaw. Another RNLI medal is attached to it, like the one found on his hand. Something shifts inside my chest. The lifeboat crew are revered in Scilly, with every shout reported on the local radio. I can't think of anyone stupid enough to attack us, yet someone resents this man's heroism enough to drown him, and the rest of us could be next in line. The moment Gareth Keillor steps back, Liz Gannick drops to her knees, surveying the body for cuts, bruises and swellings. I've trained myself to remain calm at crime scenes and autopsies over the years, but it's always worse when it's someone you know. Jez Cardew's body was a blank page, with no tattoos or distinguishing features except his strong physique. I can tell he worked out, or did plenty of press-ups at home, but now his skin's ragged.

'The sea hasn't been kind,' Keillor says. 'He's been in the water forty-eight hours, judging by the bloating. The abrasions all travel in one direction, the epidermis dragged from soft tissue, but there's only stage one rigor mortis. I can't be more specific about time of death. The rules change when a corpse is immersed in saline water. It slows the process of decay.'

Liz Gannick rises to her feet. 'The modus operandi's all you need, isn't it, Ben?'

'Anything you see could help us.'

'It looks like he was tied by his left wrist, using metal twine sheathed in plastic, then dragged at speed, over the ocean floor,' she says. 'The cuts and scrapes all travel vertically down his body, like Gareth said. Submerged rocks tore away his clothes. Either the boat's propellor or sharp objects on the ocean floor severed his hand.'

Keillor nods in agreement. 'I can't judge if he went into the water dead or alive. I'll have to measure how much liquid his lungs contain. They'll be full if he was still breathing.'

'It's one hell of a punishment, like when sailors were keel-hauled.'

'What's that?' Eddie asks, staring at me.

'Sailors would be tied up after a mutiny in the old days, then dragged under the boat's keel. They were often maimed by barnacles scraping their skin. Many of them drowned.'

My thoughts stay with Cardew, choking as he was hauled through the sea, while the inhabitants of St Mary's danced on Porthloo beach. I follow Eddie out of the tent, then call Jez's parents, to give them the news that the rest of their son's body has been found. I hear Stuart's gruff voice first when the call connects, then a sharp cry as his son's death finally registers. The sound is high and endless, like a fox screaming when it's caught in a trap.

27

Sam is replacing old floorboards at work when his radio picks up the 11 a.m. local news. The announcer says that the weather will continue fair in Scilly, ideal for barbecues, with an outside chance of rain. Then his voice turns serious.

'The body of missing lifeboatman Jeremy Cardew has been found after a prolonged search at sea. The whole community will miss the popular twenty-nine-year-old, who lived on St Mary's all his life. There will be a police meeting at one o'clock today in St Andrew's Church Hall for anyone with information to share.'

Sam turns the radio off, suddenly in need of silence. His ribs still hurt from last night's attack, but this pain is worse. It feels like a part of him has been cut away. When he turns round, Callum Moyle is watching; there's a smear of oil on his cheek, like he's applied war paint.

'I heard the news, mate,' he says, his tone conciliatory for once. 'Sorry, I know you were close.'

'I need to be at that meeting.'

'Okay, but don't be long. We're falling behind.'

'Who cares? Jez's death matters more.'

Moyle's anger erupts again. 'How come you worshipped the bloke? He was a prick most of the time.'

'That's bullshit, and you know it.'

'His fake charm opened doors, but the reality was different.'

'What do you mean?'

'Look how he treated Anna Dawlish. He knew I fancied her. I'd almost won her over, but once he came on the scene, I didn't stand a prayer. Six months later he dumps her, just to prove his point.'

'It wasn't about you, Callum.' Sam stares back at him unblinking. 'But if you really think that, you must be glad he's dead.'

'You're blaming me for it?' Moyle releases a high burst of laughter. 'He pissed me off, that's all.'

'Coke makes people violent, I saw it in prison. How much are you using?'

'I never touch drugs.'

'But they've touched you. Keep that shit away from me, I've been clean all year.'

Moyle's eyes darken. 'Lifestyle advice from a loser like you sounds pathetic.' He waves his nail gun at Sam's face like he's planning to shoot him between the eyes, then marches back down the corridor.

28

The first thing Eddie and I do back at the station is phone every lifeboat volunteer to inform them they're in danger, whether or not they've received a pack full of RNLI badges with a note inside. We all need to stay vigilant and not spend time alone. Most react with surprise, but no sign of panic. So far the only ones to receive the packs are Eddie and I, Isla, Sam Austell, Jez, Molly Bligh, and Liam and Danielle Quick. I can't prove it yet, but the killer's approach is so loaded with symbolism, I'm concerned they'll try again.

Madron calls us all into his office once the calls are complete. There's irritation in his eyes when he glances at me, like I'm to blame for Jez Cardew's death. He taps his biro on the arm of his chair, while the rest of us squirm on hard plastic stools.

'This case is overshadowing the lifeboat festival. We need it solved fast, for the sake of the Cardew family. I want it wrapped up before your wedding, Kitto.'

'So do I, sir, obviously.'

'Professor Gannick, I'm grateful you've joined us, and congratulations on your promotion. I hear you're now a forensic lead at Scotland Yard, as well as running the Cornish team?'

'Thanks, but I was mad to accept. My workload's doubled.' Gannick gives him a narrow smile. She hates sycophancy, but the DCI ploughs on regardless.

'I'll lead the public meeting at 1 p.m., with you as SIO, Kitto. I want to hear from each of you in turn. You first, Eddie. I'm aware how hard it must be, losing your cousin. You can take compassionate leave, and there's online trauma counselling available. I felt it was important to let you see Jez's body in situ this morning, so you know the truth about his death.'

'Therapy won't help, sir. I just want the killer found.'

'Can you give us some background on Jez's recent behaviour?' the DCI asks.

'We hardly met up in the past few weeks, apart from a quick chat in the pub, the night he went missing,' Eddie says. 'We used to play football together, till life got busy. Jez was always easy-going, but I could tell something was nagging at him.'

'About his work situation?'

'I think it was something bigger. Jez said living at Callum Moyles's place started out fine, then went sour. Liam Quick was trying to get him a full-time job as navigator on the lifeboat. It's what he wanted, apparently, but he never said a word. It's not like him to be so secretive. I can't see any reason for the attack. The whole island turned out to celebrate when he got that medal last year.'

'Some people resent heroes, don't they?' I ask.

Madron's voice sounds compassionate when he speaks again. 'Everyone in this community will miss such a fine young man, Eddie.' The warmth in his eyes vanishes when he turns to me. 'When was the last sighting of Jez, Kitto? I want every detail.'

'He left the Turk's Head around 11 p.m. on his parents' cabin cruiser. It was seen rounding the island's western coast. Jez sailed to St Agnes often; something lured him there on a regular basis.'

'You're certain Jez was heading west?'

'One of the punters from the pub saw his boat leave, with just him on board. Someone could have hidden in the hold, after dark, but it's likely they'd have been spotted. It was a warm evening with people milling around by the quay. Liz is doing forensic checks on the boat today.'

'What about primary evidence?'

I place the scrawled note from the cabin cruiser on the table, inside a clear evidence bag. 'The writing's hard to decipher, but we've scanned it, and a police graphologist's report just arrived. The writing doesn't match the threats half the crew have had in the post, including Jez. She'll check again once we get samples from the female residents of St Agnes.'

'Let me work on the original notes,' Gannick says. 'Substances or fibres on that paper could lead us to the killer.'

I produce the package I was sent, containing the badges, plus the note, in a separate evidence bag. 'Members of the lifeboat crew have been getting these, sir, with quotes from *The Tempest*. Jez got one postmarked two days before his death.'

'Where was it posted?'

'The box outside the Post Office here in Hugh Town.'

Madron stares at me. 'The killer's bold, and well read, but that looks like a child's handwriting.'

'They could be disguising their style.'

I put another evidence bag beside the note, containing the medals found on Jez's body. 'One of these was attached to his left hand, the other round his neck. They're given by the RNLI for gallantry at sea. This could be Jez's medal, which is missing, but the name's been erased. We need to find out if someone broke into Moyle's, or it was taken by a housemate. The old ones are hard to find, but you see them occasionally online.'

'Do we have reason to believe the killer will strike again?' Madron's gaze is laser-sharp.

'It's possible, sir. Jez's first pack of RNLI badges arrived two days before he was attacked, then another the following day. We've alerted the whole crew not to spend time alone. We know the killer's highly motivated.'

Eddie catches my gaze. 'Janet Fearnley says none of the festival volunteers are admitting to taking those badges from her flat, but her door's never locked. Anyone could have gone in while she was out.'

Hearing Janet's name reminds me about Liam Quick saying she was furious after her husband died, alone on his boat, yet she's carried on supporting the lifeboat crew. The picture doesn't add up, but she doesn't meet my image of a vicious killer. I'm not surprised by Janet's lack of security at home. There's so little burglary in Scilly, most islanders don't bother with a lock and key.

Madron peers at me again. 'What about suspects?'

'Callum Moyle disliked Jez, despite renting him a room. I think he's got a drug habit which could make him more prone to violence, so he's a person of interest. I want to know more about Sharon Cosgrove too. She was too prickly about being questioned. Jez's ex, Anna Dawlish, was angry about their relationship breaking down, too, but she has a solid alibi. I'll be questioning her again, though.'

'I doubt a woman could carry out such a vicious attack, but you've made a start, at least,' DCI says, his tone as cool as permafrost. 'Professor Gannick, I'd like a private word, please. The rest of you can get back to work.'

I'm first to leave, irritated to be banned from the meeting, despite being the SIO. Eddie looks so shaken, I'm glad he doesn't have to hear a forensic discussion of his cousin's death. No officer would be asked to investigate a relative's murder on the mainland, but out here the rules operate differently, in such a minute team.

I send Isla and Lawrie Deane down to the church hall to prepare for the meeting in less than an hour's time, leaving me and Eddie to record operational details. He's sorting through images on his computer, including photos of Jez, and his parents' boat. Eddie still looks so shell-shocked, I hand him a packet of biscuits, which he leaves on his desk.

'We need to visit Denzel Jory later, if he's fit enough. He might know Jez's secrets. What did you and Jez get up to, last time you met?'

He scrolls through the calendar on his phone. 'We had some beer and watched football at mine. He mentioned something about big life changes coming up, but he was always a dreamer. I should have listened more carefully.'

'Stop blaming yourself, Eddie. It wasn't your fault.' I wait to catch his eye. 'I know this is left field, but do you think Sharon Cosgrove could be carrying his child? If her husband found out, he'd have a strong motive.'

Eddie looks shocked. 'Jez hardly mentioned her. He found her interesting because she went to art school, but he wasn't stupid enough to chase a married woman. He was more bothered about Anna Dawlish texting him months after they split up.'

'Saying come back, all is forgiven?'

'More like I still hate your guts.'

'Janet Fearnley says she took Kylie to hers the night Jez died, but let's see Anna after the meeting. She may have suspicions about Jez's last fling, if we can get her to open up.'

Eddie's eyebrows shoot towards his hairline. 'He was

six feet tall, with a solid build. Whoever killed him would need strength to fight him down, tie him up, then shove him overboard.'

'Not if the attack came as a surprise. Rejection's one of the top motives for murder, alongside adultery. It's too soon to rule out ex-girlfriends.'

I spend the next half hour inputting information to the case file. Record-keeping isn't my favourite task, but experience has taught me to keep up to date, or facts get lost. Eddie is working flat-out, his fingers fly across his keyboard, his face rigid with concentration. He's still staring at his screen when I remind him we're needed at the church hall.

Hugh Town is bustling when we leave the station. It's the size of a small village on the mainland, but it's the islands' thriving capital, and packed with day-trippers every summer. Four hundred passengers take the ferry ride from Land's End each morning, travelling home again at 4p.m. Many of them remain in Hugh Town for the duration, visiting its gift shops, pubs, small art galleries, and the museum. They all look carefree, clearly oblivious to a young lifeboatman's violent death.

Eddie and I are walking down the High Street at a brisk pace when a man lurches out from an alleyway. A fist flies in my direction, forcing me to duck. Eddie and I grab his arms before he can lash out again. He's tall and solid with muscle, his blond hair like straw thatch, eyes sparking with outrage. It's Damian Cosgrove, his face a livid red; he shouts out curses when we march him back down the alleyway, to avoid the curiosity of passers-by.

'Get your fucking hands off me.'

'What's wrong, Damian? Tell us now, or we'll arrest you for assault.'

He drags in a deep breath. 'You bastards accused my wife of shagging around. That baby's mine, all right?'

'No one questioned it, we're just doing our jobs.'

Cosgrove's eyes are too close together, like a bull mastiff that's been inbred. 'Sharon's sick of all the gossip. Some local tart was screwing that dead bloke on the sly, but you came after my wife.'

'It's not personal, we're investigating a vicious murder. Be grateful I'm letting you go, instead of chucking you in a holding cell. I expect more co-operation next time we meet.'

Cosgrove still looks braced to attack. I can't tell if he's absorbed my message, but he knows the consequences of further misbehaviour. He doesn't speak when I tell him our investigation will be based on St Agnes from this afternoon. The bloke marches away, soon vanishing among the crowd of day-trippers.

Eddie and I exchange looks of disbelief, then finish our journey to St Andrew's Church Hall. The venue is used for every type of event in Hugh Town: yoga classes, girl guide meetings, stand-up comedy nights, Scilly's Got Talent, and Alcoholics Anonymous sessions. It's neat and tidy today, with a hundred chairs laid out in ranks. There's no sign of Lawrie Deane, but

Isla is on the stage, attaching a microphone to a stand. Her quiet industry is something I take for granted, and Nina's reminder about openness comes back to me. I often think of speeches to deliver, but keep my mouth shut. The habit probably stems from having an older brother who's far more articulate. I feel awkward when I climb the steps onto the stage, but the conversation's long overdue.

'Did Lawrie help you get this place ready, Isla?'

She shakes her head. 'A woman outside lost her ferry ticket home; he's taken her to the travel office for another.'

'Stop for a minute, can you?'

'Is something wrong, sir?' She looks confused. 'If you want more chairs there are plenty in the back, I can get them out.'

'I've noticed how hard you work, that's all. You've done your job brilliantly, from day one. The whole team agrees you've never put a foot wrong. We'd be a lot weaker without your input. Don't go leaving us anytime soon, will you?'

Isla gapes at me in amazement. 'Never, sir. I love my job.'

'Why are you shocked?'

'You don't often give praise. It's like Paul Hollywood shaking my hand on *Bake Off*; I don't know whether to laugh or cry.'

'No tears, please. I'm sick of them.'

'Me too. I never cry, unless Plymouth lose a cup match at home.'

When she grins at me, my words seem to have hit the mark, proving Nina's point. If I voice my opinions more often than my uncle Ray, everyone wins. There's a new spring in Isla's step when she hurries away to greet the islanders spilling through the doors. Most of the faces are familiar, which is the beauty of policing a small community. We're all interconnected, in a pool of less than two thousand souls. Some have sailed over from the off-islands after hearing our announcement an hour ago. Nina is standing at the back of the crowd, with Noah strapped to her chest, and Shadow at her feet.

Madron arrives on time for the meeting. He normally lets me take the flak if a complex case arrives, but this time there's no evading responsibility. The murder of a young lifeboatman cuts to the quick of island values; everyone will be watching us, until the culprit's found. When I scan the crowd again, there are plenty of supportive smiles. Janet Fearnley is in the front row, with some female friends, all beaming at us. It's only when I look more closely that I spot anxiety on many of the faces. Sam Austell is circled by a ring of vacant chairs. That's the downside of a close-knit community: forgiveness can take a long time, if you make a mistake. He'll need to stay on the straight and narrow for years before he's deemed fully trustworthy.

The whole police team lines up behind Madron when he struts on stage, a small, dapper man, his hair slick with Brylcreem. I resent being forced to stand behind him like a backing singer. Madron promises to leave no stone unturned, even though he will remain behind his desk, leaving us to do the work. There's a quake in his voice when he talks about Jez Cardew being a role model for the islands' children. Madron describes the mystery of his boat being set adrift. He states that the inquiry will take place on St Agnes from today, because Jez spent his free time there, and may have been in a secret relationship. Murmurs rise from the crowd as more details emerge. Life is so peaceful in Scilly most of the time, people are always fascinated when something goes wrong, even in the bleakest circumstances.

'We're certain Jez was murdered, so you all need to keep safe, especially at night. That applies to lifeboat crew members in particular. Jez's killer appears negative about the heroic work you do, for some bizarre reason. If any of you have received a package containing RNLI badges through the post, it's essential you bring it to the station today.' Madron pauses for dramatic effect, loving the spotlight. 'I want you all to cast your minds back to what you were doing last Friday night. If you know anything about Jez's movements, or spent time with him recently, please share your information with us straight after the meeting.'

Madron's last gesture is to display one of the RNLI medals, projected on the wall, then ask if any have been stolen, but no hands rise. I'm not surprised when the DCI disappears via the back exit after his speech, to avoid contact with the general public. He prefers to remain in control, instead of fielding questions which may not have answers. I'm surprised that a cluster of people remain behind, queuing to pass on information. The island community is often close-lipped, but Jez Cardew's death has broken old habits.

The first person to approach me is my old friend, Paul Keast, who owns a farm above Porthloo beach; he's run it single-handed since his brother left for the mainland, to marry a woman he met online. Paul has carried plenty of dust indoors from the dry fields; it's all over his faded jeans and walking boots. He always seems relaxed, a man who enjoys a beer and a game of darts in the Atlantic pub, but appearances are deceiving. Paul's a hundred per cent committed to his farm, rising at dawn to milk his flock of cows, determined to nurture the land that's been in his family for generations. He's only my age, but his face is prematurely lined, and burnished to the colour of old leather. His smile falters when I ask what he knows about Jez Cardew.

'It may be nothing, Ben, but I was at the Turk's Head Friday night.'

'Why? The Atlantic's your local, isn't it?'

'Six of us travelled over on my boat for a darts match. We came back together after last orders.' He shifts his weight from foot to foot, clearly uncomfortable. 'I saw something round the back, when I went outside for a fag, about ten o'clock.'

'Go on.'

'Jez was arguing with Tommy Brookes. It sounded

pretty heated. I thought they'd end up punching each other, but Tommy stormed back inside.'

'Did Jez stay out there?'

'He looked angry, so I kept out of it. I never get involved in rows, if I can avoid it.'

'Could you tell me what it was about?'

'Jez called Tommy a liar and a fake, that's all I heard.'

'That's interesting, thanks.'

'Call anytime, if I can help. Whoever killed Jez is the scum of the earth.'

'That's for sure. Can you make a list of people you saw at the Turk's Head before you go? I'm asking all the punters to do the same, to give us the full picture. Leave it with Isla when you're done.' I hold his gaze. 'Did you go straight home on Friday night, Paul?'

He looks uncomfortable. 'I dropped by somewhere else, just for an hour.'

'Where did you go?'

'Anna Dawlish's place. We've been seeing each other a few weeks; she hasn't told Kylie yet.'

'It's okay, Paul. Dating her isn't a crime.'

'It feels weird, that's all. You went out together at school, then there was Jez. She's only had a few relationships, but two were with friends of mine.'

'That's life, isn't it? If you stay in Scilly, you end up dating pretty much everyone.'

He barks out a laugh. 'I haven't been that lucky, till now.'

'I hope it works out, but let's focus on Jez for now. Did you get sent any badges in the post?'

He shakes his head. 'Not yet. Want me to call you, if I do?'

'Bring the packet straight to the station, but stay safe anyway. All right?'

'I'll give you those names before I go.'

I hand him paper and a biro, then greet the next face in the queue. When I look up again, ten minutes later, Paul Keast is leaving at a rapid march, like he can't wait to return to his livestock.

29

The hall is almost empty by mid-afternoon, giving me time to look for Nina. There's no sign of her outside, but a dog's piercing bark sounds in the distance. Shadow treats the islands as his own private kingdom, even though his independence has won him injuries. He's older than me in dog years but unlikely to turn docile overnight. He seems happy to follow my pace as I walk along Hugh Town's northern edge. I'm determined to see Anna Dawlish before my investigation shifts to St Agnes. I was hoping Isla or Eddie would accompany me, but they're busy taking statements from the last few islanders. It feels uncomfortable going to see an ex-girlfriend about something so intimate, but there's no choice.

I haven't set foot inside her house since I was a lumbering teenager. Anna lives in a part of Hugh Town that day-trippers rarely see, hidden behind its shops, cafés and well-preserved fishermen's cottages. The council house where she grew up stands in a cul-de-sac of unloved bungalows covered in grey pebble dash. Many people assume that Scilly is dripping with money, but there's plenty of rural poverty; life is challenging for single-parent families in an economy dominated by low-paid tourism jobs. She used to have big ambitions when we were at school. It seems a pity that her income's still so low she's unable to rent somewhere better. Tiles are slipping from the roof, the front garden is a tangle of knee-high weeds, and the windows need double-glazing.

A seagull screams overhead when I press the doorbell, sending Shadow into a frenzy. Chasing gulls is his favourite activity, but his bark falls silent when the door finally opens. Anna is wearing a white sundress that accentuates her tan, blonde hair flowing over her shoulders. It's clear she's not thrilled to see me. She stands in the doorway with arms folded.

'I'm working right now, Ben. Can you come back tomorrow?'

'This is urgent, I'm afraid.'

She nods, just once. 'I can't be long, but bring your dog inside, if he's house-trained.'

Charcoal shadows under Anna's eyes reveal that she's not been sleeping properly, but the main change since we last met is in her expression. She looks concerned, as if she's waiting for the next hammer blow. Shadow appears devoted to her already. He's glued to her side as she leads me to a kitchen that looks unchanged since I used to come here after school, hoping her mum and dad would be out. I won't forget both of us losing our virginity in her small room upstairs, while they were visiting relatives on the mainland. I was overjoyed at the time, oblivious to the decor. The house appears lacklustre now. The council should decorate it from top to bottom, but its budget shrinks every year, leaving tenants to fend for themselves. Anna offers me a forced smile; Scilly's rules of hospitality die hard, even when a guest's unwelcome. Silence carries more weight than a rush of questions, so I keep my mouth shut when she places a mug of coffee in front of me, then provides Shadow with a bowl of water.

'What breed is he?' she asks.

'Czechoslovakian wolfdog: clever but stubborn.'

'Kylie's got a thing about dogs with blue eyes. She'd love him.'

'Bring her to the station any time. He's there most days, and he's great with kids.'

'You've changed, Ben,' Anna says suddenly, her shoulders relaxing a fraction. 'More chatty these days, aren't you? I had to ask you out, I seem to remember, not the other way round.'

'Then you dumped me for Darren Tilney, which pissed me off for a whole term. The bloke's an idiot.'

'You're right. What was I thinking?'

The years roll back when she laughs. Just for a second she looks like a teenager again, sweet and fun-loving, until adult wariness returns. She rubs Shadow's fur as he sprawls at her feet, clearly loving the attention.

I glance at her photo board, which is covered in selfies with her daughter.

'How's Kylie doing these days?'

'Fine, thanks, she aced her SATs tests, if that's what you mean.'

'It wasn't a loaded question. I just wondered how it affected her when you split with Jez?'

'She barely noticed.'

'Come on, Anna. Drop your guard for a minute, please. How did she react to him clearing off?'

'Badly, of course.' Anna takes the seat opposite, her face softening at last. 'He was the first bloke I'd dated for years. She adored him, but he stonewalled her too, after the break-up.'

'That's a cruel blow for any kid.'

'His mum never accepted me either. Maybe it was her doing.'

'That surprises me. Delia likes most people, doesn't she?'

'She thought Jez deserved better, but he was a real bastard. One minute he's acting like a devoted dad to Kylie, then he's gone. You can't ghost someone in a place this small.'

'I can imagine how bad that felt.'

'Can you, really?' she says, her voice cool. 'You've got a well-paid job, a house and a fiancée. I survive on benefits, and crappy part-time work, to fit around school hours. I should be making cold calls right now, flogging life insurance. I'm lucky if one person in a hundred picks up.'

'That must be frustrating, on top of the relationship ending.'

'Why act like that, after all those promises?' She covers her mouth with her fingers, but words spill out anyway. 'This isn't the life I wanted. Do you remember our teachers saying I should go to uni? I didn't have the confidence, but Kylie's turned out to be a blessing. I want to give her all the opportunities I missed.'

'She's lucky her mum cares so much. Sweet-looking too, isn't she?' I glance at photos of the young girl clambering over rocks on Porthloo beach. 'Tell me more about Jez, Anna. I know it's hard, but there must be a reason why your relationship ended so suddenly.'

'It started out great, although I took some persuading. He was a decade younger than me, for a start. I saw him as this hero who could do no wrong. He was great to be around, and he seemed principled too, but that was only half the picture.'

'You think he lied to you?'

'Judge for yourself, Ben. We spent this perfect Christmas together, as a family. He bought loads of presents for Kylie, we decorated the tree together and put up decorations, but everything changed at New Year. He suddenly ran off to Callum Moyle's, and started sailing to St Agnes every night. He never spoke to me honestly again.' She rises to her feet and scrabbles around in a kitchen drawer before producing a small velvet box. 'He gave me this, days before he left.'

The box contains an engagement ring, with three

diamonds glinting in the light. It would have taken Jez months to save for it on his low wage, if she's telling the truth.

'He proposed, then walked away?'

'Jez walked me down to the harbour on Boxing Day to pop the question. He even went down on one knee.'

'How come you've still got the ring?'

'Jez wouldn't accept it back; he could hardly meet my eye, it was like he wanted the ground to swallow him up. The worst thing was the aftermath for Kylie. All I wanted was the truth, for her sake. He made his house-mates pretend he was out all the time. I sent him texts, letters, you name it. He told people I was stalking him.'

'Can you think of anyone else who was angry at him?'

'Callum Moyle, probably.' She looks embarrassed. 'He asked me out a few times, but the bloke's too pushy. I don't trust him.'

'When was the last time you contacted Jez?'

She keeps her head high. 'Last week. I know it sounds mad, but his behaviour was wrong, on so many levels. I deserve an explanation. If he was here, I'd still be asking why he treated me and Kylie like dirt.'

'He's gone, Anna. You won't get answers now.'

Her eyes are suddenly glossy with tears. 'I can't grieve for someone who hurt Kylie so much.'

'Where were you on Friday night?'

'At Janet Fearnley's with Kylie, watching a Disney film.'

'You don't own a boat these days, do you?'

She looks startled by my sudden change of direction. 'The maintenance cost too much. I take the ferry now, or use Janet's.'

'It sounds like she's a close friend.'

'Janet's been brilliant from day one. She's always happy to babysit Kylie, and gives me great advice, because she's been through much worse.'

'Losing her husband, you mean?'

'It made her bitter for a while. The lifeboat's engine failed; they took twenty minutes to launch, while Trevor was dying. She's over it now, thank God.'

'It sounds like she confides in you too. What time did you get home?'

'About ten o'clock.'

'Did Paul Keast come round that night? He mentioned you're a couple now.'

She hesitates for a moment. 'It's still early days. Paul's way kinder than Jez, thank God. He stayed here less than an hour.'

'When did he arrive?'

'About eleven, after Kylie went to sleep. We had a drink, then said goodnight. I don't want another man in her life unless he's planning to stay.' Her gaze catches mine. 'I didn't hurt Jez, if that's what you're asking.'

'You've admitted to hating him. I bet you wanted him dead, didn't you?'

Her eyes widen. 'We go way back, Ben, you and me. Have you ever seen me harm someone deliberately?'

'No, but that was a long time ago.'

'You know I don't lie.'

Anna seems different from the girl I dated, her manner more intense, anger closer to the surface, but she's got a solid alibi. It's a pity Jez isn't here to defend himself. If she'd wanted him dead, wouldn't she have struck while the iron was hot? Her daughter deserved more respect, and so did she. When I scan the kitchen again I see shelves full of books in the corner, including a collection of Shakespeare's plays.

'I see you still enjoy reading. You've got plenty of books.'

'I buy them at jumble sales, for Kylie. She'll read them all one day; she's always hungry for knowledge.' Anna's gaze is glassy, like she's retreated into memories, but her voice suddenly turns fierce. 'Jez knew how to fool people, Ben. Maybe he treated another woman just as badly. Someone finally got even for his shitty behaviour, didn't they?'

The glitter of victory in Anna's eyes shakes my belief in her innocence. Any regret about Jez's death is hidden by a fog of anger, even though she's found a new relationship. She makes an unlikely killer, at five feet tall with a petite build, yet she can't be ruled out. She's smart enough for complex psychological manipulation. I can imagine her sailing to St Agnes after putting Kylie to bed. She had just enough time to commit murder, then return home for a nightcap with her new boyfriend, implausible as it might seem.

30

Sam's head is buzzing after the meeting. He's never liked the police, but the conviction on their faces lifted his spirits. Ben Kitto seems determined to find out who killed Jez, just like him, but he's not prepared to wait. It's a relief that he didn't bump into Stuart Cardew again. The wounds from his attack still feel raw; he hates knowing that Jez's family believe him capable of murder. Tension churns in his gut when he thinks of the killer, still on the islands, hidden from view. Sam knows it would be a mistake to go back to work yet. One more criticism from Moyle would unleash his anger. It's best to steer clear, until he's calmed down.

It's half past two when he reaches Porthcressa beach. The horseshoe bay is lined with golden sand, and holidaymakers sit on benches with their feet up, gazing at the sea. The water is polished aquamarine, a shade darker than the sky, with barely a ripple. The only sounds he hears are a child begging for ice cream and the mew of storm petrels drifting inland. He needs to talk to someone he trusts, but his choices are limited. The only locals who welcome his company are his mother and

Father Michael. His gaze drifts along the seafront to the library, set back from the walkway.

He marches there without questioning his decision. He doesn't know exactly what he's going to say, but the impulse is too strong to resist. The library is quiet when he steps inside, the air cool, and Danielle appears to be alone. She's sticking labels onto the spines of books, but when she catches sight of him, the volume in her hands clatters onto the counter.

'Sorry, I didn't mean to scare you.'

She looks embarrassed. 'I was concentrating, that's all.'

'Can you take a break? I need to ask you something.'

They stand together on the promenade while the sea rolls closer. Her gaze is calm as she waits for him to speak.

'I have to know why Jez died, Danielle. I can't just wait for news from the police.'

'I feel the same.'

'Jez's dad thinks I killed him. I have to clear my name, or I can't stay here.'

'That's crazy, you two were like brothers.'

'Will you help me find out what happened?'

She looks anxious, but nods anyway. 'Where do we start?'

'How about St Agnes tonight? We can retrace his steps.'

'I could meet you on the quay, about eight.'

'I'll find a boat for the ride. Will your dad mind you coming out with me?'

'He's been edgy for weeks. It's been worse since he heard the lifeboat crew are vulnerable, if we've had packs of RNLI badges in the post. Me and dad both got one.'

'Me too. Last week. Look Danielle, I shouldn't get you in trouble if Liam wants you to stay safe at home.'

'I can manage my life without his permission. See you at eight.'

Danielle smiles again then hurries back to work. He can imagine the rumour mill churning out gossip about the island's sweetheart hanging out with an ex-con, but needs all the help he can get. Jez protected him so often he deserves loyalty. The least he can do is fight for justice, for both their sakes.

31

Eddie is alone when I return to the church hall, tidying up to make room for tonight's yoga class. My job with the local force involves more mundane tasks than I could ever have predicted, but I help him stack chairs until the room empties. All that's left is the lingering smell of suncream and barbecue smoke. Shadow has seized his chance to rest. He's curled up in a corner, his snout resting on his front paws. My deputy looks less relaxed as I describe my conversation with Anna Dawlish. She may have a reputation as a tricky customer, but the distress in her eyes would have been hard to fake, even though she can't be ruled out. I can tell Eddie is reserving judgement, like me.

'Jez asked her to marry him then ghosted her. He seemed to care about Kylie too, but never said goodbye. Janet Fearnley's given Anna an alibi for the night Jez died, and Paul Keast's confirmed it.'

'Maybe he's covering for her,' Eddie says. 'We've got

no concrete proof, have we? It's people like her who end up murdering their exes.'

'How do you mean?'

'Anna chucked stuff at Jez's window back in January: stones, bottles, you name it. The broken glass went all over his bed. She could have blinded him.'

'Why didn't he report it?'

'Pity, I suppose. That's classic stalking, isn't it?'

'Anna still has the engagement ring.'

'No way,' Eddie says, gaping at me. 'Jez would have told me.'

'What's happening with his phone records?'

'The provider needs another twenty-four hours.'

'Seriously? Those bastards only have to push a button.'

'Tell me about it. The Crown Prosecution Service aren't playing ball either. The warrant I requested for a complete search of Callum Moyle's property still hasn't arrived.'

'That can wait till tomorrow. Let's catch up with Liz, then get back to St Agnes. I want a conversation with Tommy Kernow too. Apparently he had a flaming row with Jez the night he disappeared. And we need to see Denzel Jory. Have you spoken to him?'

'He says he's still too sick for visitors.'

'Let's go anyway. He may have been the only person Jez told about that secret relationship.'

The atmosphere shifts as we follow Museum Street to the centre of town. It's a beautiful August afternoon, day-trippers mingling with locals. Our visitors look carefree, while islanders stand in gaggles, discussing the meeting. High summer seems an odd time for a brutal murder. Violence has erupted here before, but most often in winter, when people are forced indoors by storms, and the islands often get cut off. If something's wrong at home, the situation becomes a tinderbox, ready to blow. Yet Jez Cardew's death has happened at our most relaxed time of year, when there's plenty of seasonal work, and long, sunny evenings to enjoy.

A small crowd is observing the scientific side of our investigation when we reach the lifeboat house, where the Cardews' cabin cruiser is still moored. Gannick is visible from the pathway, kitted out in white overalls, like a SOCO in *Silent Witness*. I ask the bystanders to move along, but they're bound to return once our backs are turned. The forensics chief seems oblivious to external forces. She's picking bottles of chemicals from a metal box she brought over from her lab. I tell Eddie to chat with the onlookers, to see if anyone has information about the murder, then head down the slipway. Gannick looks calmer, as if hard work has sweetened her temperament. I need to strike while the iron's hot.

'How's it going, Liz?' I call out.

'Fine, till you pitched up.'

'Do you need anything, before I go to St Agnes?'

'Two hours more daylight.' When I try to join her on the vessel, she shoos me away. 'There's been enough contamination, but one thing's clear at least.'

'What's that?'

'Someone scoured this boat clean.' She holds up a test tube containing a scrap of yellow paper. 'Know what this is?'

'Litmus paper?'

'It's a reactivant. Touch any surface and it changes colour: ammonia makes it go lilac, nitro-compounds turn it blue.' She holds up another test tube, which contains a green scrap of paper. 'I found paraffin all over the deck and cabin.'

'Meaning what exactly?'

She stares at me like I'm a numbskull. 'Paraffin is one of the most powerful solvents around. It removes glue from glass surfaces, and strips grease from steel. Fingerprints don't stand a chance.'

'That's why the hold stank of petrol.'

'There was no detergent on board, just a can of paraffin, so the killer made do. They soaked a rag, then ran it over everything in sight, leaving a residue. All they had to do then was chuck the rag overboard.'

'So they might be thorough by nature, or a smart opportunist?'

'Psychology is pointless beside cold hard facts.' Her frown deepens, until the line between her eyebrows looks immovable. 'I've found some dust or chalk, on the cushions in the hold.'

'Is that significant?'

'Only if it's from the killer's clothes. I need to analyse it first.'

'And you'll check the notes we found?'

'I'll see what I can do. Clear off, Ben, you're wasting my time.'

'Let's meet for breakfast early tomorrow at your hotel. You can update me on what you find.'

She mutters something caustic under her breath, which is the closest I'll get to acceptance. I mutter goodbye then hurry away. Gannick can be an entertaining on a good day, with a love of red wine, blue jokes, and gossip about the top brass. I've learned to take the rough with the smooth, since she admitted that a back operation to correct her spina bifida causes her agony every day. At least she's given me a better picture of the killer. It's someone methodical enough to clear away every trace, but my picture of Jez's death remains hazy. What happened on that boat, and how did the killer get on board?

Janet Fearnley is sweeping the lifeboat house's floor as I walk inside. She normally bustles around at a rapid pace, but today her movements are laboured. When I get closer, it's clear she's been crying, her face puffy with tears. Instinct makes me remove the broom from her hands and lead her to a chair.

'Feeling powerless is the worst bit, isn't it? It reminds me of losing Trevor.' Her eyes screw shut. 'I always hated him sailing alone, but the old fool insisted it was safe. He'd only been at sea for an hour when his heart gave out.'

'That must have been hard to accept.'

She blots her tears away. 'I said terrible things to poor

Liam, and even sent a formal complaint to the RNLI. I couldn't accept the crew taking so long to reach him, after he served that boat for years. Trevor was right as rain when he set out, but he was dead before the lifeboat arrived. I thought they should have gone straight away, on the smaller one. It leaves you with so many unanswered questions.'

'I'm sorry, this must raise painful memories.'

'I should never have criticised the cox, it was unforgivable. He has to live with his decisions.' More tears form in her eyes but she blinks them away. 'Jez's parents are the ones suffering now, the poor souls.'

'The community's supporting them, like you helping Anna. I hear you lend her your boat sometimes.'

'I can't look at it since Trevor went, so she's welcome to it. Anna keeps it moored by Watermill Cove. That girl's got no one else. Her parents hardly bother with her or Kylie since they moved to the mainland. Her dad's got a well-paid job but never sends her a penny.'

'Anna brought Kylie to yours on Friday night, didn't she?'

She nods rapidly. 'They came about seven, we made popcorn and watched a movie.'

'What time did they leave?'

She hesitates for a beat too long. 'I can't remember exactly; around nine, I think.'

'Anna said ten.'

'I could be misremembering. It was a treat for Kylie, staying up past bedtime.'

I sense that she's feeling cornered, forcing me to shift focus.

'I know Eddie asked you about the RNLI badges the crew keep getting. Can you think of anyone who might steal them from your flat?'

'I've asked all the committee members, but no one's putting their hand up.'

'We've checked the postcodes. They were all mailed from the box outside the Post Office in Hugh Town; anyone could have posted them at night without being seen. Who else is on the committee?'

'Father Michael, Maggie, and the Cardews. Debbie and Tommy Brookes joined last year.'

She mentions a few more names, but they're all pensioners, and unlikely to harm a fly. I can't imagine a Catholic priest like Father Mike committing murder. My godmother and the Brookes are publicans with no record of any crime, and the Cardews would never target their own son. Janet is already back on her feet, seizing her broom. It's a reminder that everyone in Scilly is affected by the sea. The relationship is casual most days, but the ocean sends frequent reminders that it's in control. I tell Janet to go home and rest, but she's already sweeping again, insisting she's fine.

Eddie is still chatting to onlookers when I get back to the road. He normally loves passing the time of day with the general public, always good-humoured and polite, but now he seems keen to leave. When we head for the quay together, he tells me his conversations yielded no fresh information, then falls into a gloomy silence as we board the police boat. Eddie's normal politeness has returned, but he still seems troubled.

I steer the boat while he huddles in the bow, despite the sun's warmth. Our journey west takes us past Garrison Point, where Star Castle stands on its hill, still guarding the island after four centuries. It's even more impressive from the sky. The castle's star-shaped perimeter walls were built at acute angles, so guards could watch all four points of the compass from a single building.

St Mary's Sound is busy as we head for St Agnes, studded with dinghies and skiffs, drifting with the tide. A speedboat is dragging a water-skier along at frantic speed. Most people in Scilly love and hate the sea in equal measure. It's pale turquoise today, glinting with sunlight, like nothing could ever go wrong. The determination on Eddie's face returns when we pass Gugh, St Agnes's tiny satellite island, connected by a sandbar which vanishes with each high tide. Gugh is home to only a dozen permanent dwellings; the residents value peace and quiet more than the inconvenience of being cut off from the rest of humanity twice a day. The houses near the peak of Gugh Hill have a direct view of the Turk's Head.

We'll need to interview all Gugh's residents, but Denzel Jory is at the top of my list, despite his refusal to play ball. I'd like to sail straight there, but our boat might get stuck on the sandbar, leaving us stranded for hours, so I moor by the Turk's Head. I need to check out Paul Keast's story that the landlord had an argument with Jez on the night he died.

The pub appears pristine in the late afternoon sunlight, its gleaming white walls proving that Tommy and Debbie are proud of their business. The inn's terraced gardens have neatly mown grass, with picnic tables protected by parasols. I'm about to head for the building when a familiar figure appears. Damian Cosgrove's square body shape is easy to identify; it's so bulked up he must spend all his free time pumping iron. He scowls down at me, but doesn't bother with a new confrontation. I'd like to know why he's made a solitary visit to the pub, in the lull between sittings. It doesn't seem to have sweetened his mood. Cosgrove throws me an angry stare, before marching away. The bloke's carrying so much rage, I still question if he thinks his wife's unfaithful, leaving him to raise another man's child. Having a short fuse doesn't make him a killer, but it certainly keeps him at the front of my mind.

32

The pub is quiet when we step inside, with Shadow at our heels. I can only see a lone bartender, gathering beer glasses from empty tables. When I ask for Tommy he points to the back corridor, so I go in search of the landlord while Eddie questions the man about Jez Cardew's last visit. Shadow remains near them, clearly in his element, sniffing around, hoping for food.

I find a door that's slightly ajar and peer through the gap. Tommy Brookes is hunched over his computer, hands buried in his greying hair. He looks startled by my knock, his smile running at half-strength.

'Come in, Ben, please. I need distraction; these accounts are killing me.'

'It's not your favourite job?'

He gestures for me to sit down. 'I hate it, to be honest. People-facing stuff is my forte. I imagined we'd get time on our boat, but I haven't taken her out under sail since we reopened. It's a pity to just motor guests around like a taxi service, showing them the sights. I should pay a bookkeeper, but it's cheaper this way.'

'You want to save money?'

'This place is empty all winter.' He gives a slow shrug. 'It's a juggling act to keep going.'

'I'm sorry to hear it. Can I ask you a few questions about Jez Cardew?'

'Of course, go ahead.'

'How did you two get along?'

'Fine, most of the time.' He shifts in his seat, his face thoughtful. 'He was a nice lad, popular too, but he never found his groove.'

'What do you mean?'

'Jez was good-looking, charismatic, young, but he wanted more from life than the islands could give him.' The sadness on his face appears heartfelt.

'What did you two argue about the night he died?'

He rocks back in his seat. 'Been listening to gossip, have you?'

'You know how it works, nothing goes unnoticed out here.'

'Debbie and I let our punters run up tabs, provided they pay us regularly. It saves dealing with credit cards, but the system operates on trust. Jez owed us three hundred quid. I was sick of his excuses.'

'Why did he call you a liar?'

Brookes's voice quakes with emotion. 'We both said stuff we didn't mean that night; it's given me night-mares. What if my anger was the last thing he heard?'

'You weren't to know, Tommy. Why was he so short of cash?'

'I can't say. It's a mistake to get involved in punters' finances. God knows how Maggie stays afloat.'

The landlords in Scilly are on good terms because each has their own clientele, but only my godmother acts like a bank. She's the selling agent for the fishermen on Bryher, haggling hard to get high prices for each catch. Maggie provides handouts each winter too if families struggle.

'I need to understand the run-up to his death. Give me every detail you remember, please, Tommy.'

'Jez kept claiming he was skint, and something in me snapped.' There's so much misery on Brookes's face, I can tell he's been replaying the conversation. 'I'd heard it all before. He was verbally abusive first, but I shouldn't have retaliated.'

Brookes strikes me as a decent bloke, and this conversation proves it. There's guilt on his face, for raising his voice at a young man with only a few hours left to live.

'How do you and Debbie share the running of this place?'

'I used to do the bar while she stayed in the kitchen, but we've had to adjust,' he says, dropping his gaze. 'Debbie has ME, but we haven't told people yet, so please keep it quiet. It leaves her exhausted, mentally and physically. She worries about stuff that never bothered her before.'

'I'm sorry to hear it. Does she know Jez owed you money?'

He shakes his head vigorously. 'I shield her from negative stuff these days. If she's stressed, the fatigue gets worse.'

'I'm not here to pick over your personal life, Tommy. Do you have any idea who Jez was flirting with over here?'

He looks puzzled. 'You know our community; it's mainly long-established couples and families. Jez sailed over here with Molly Bligh a few times, but they're just pals. The only girlfriend he brought over was Anna Dawlish last year.'

'No married women were interested?'

'I didn't see him flirting with anyone. Affairs are tricky when the whole island knows your business.'

'Did you ever wonder if Jez fancied your wife? I know he confided in Debbie sometimes.'

Tommy bursts into sudden laughter. 'She's nice to everyone, it's her way. He probably saw her as a second mum.'

'She's still an attractive woman.'

'Debbie's a churchgoer, she's not the kind to cheat.'

'So jealousy had nothing to do with your argument?'

'God, no, it was about cold hard cash. If our income dips, we struggle big time. Jez was no different to anyone else. He used to come over for a pint after work, to relax. I'd see his boat leaving the quay sometimes, late at night, when I was locking up.'

'Where did he spend the time in between?'

'He might have called on a mate like Lewis Marling, I suppose. I saw them playing pool a few times. He seems pretty solitary, but Jez could get under anyone's defences.' His smile slips away. 'I'll keep listening for news. The whole community drinks here, and secrets slip out now and then.'

'Debbie mentioned you take your boat out late at night in summer sometimes. Why's that, exactly?'

'For a taste of freedom. We do long hours indoors, I grab any chance to swim or sail.' He glances down at his pile of papers. 'Anything else I can help with today?'

'We've moved the investigation to St Agnes. Have you got any free space?'

Tommy nods rapidly. 'The snooker room upstairs is empty.' He pokes around in his desk drawer, then produces a key. 'Help yourself. I keep meaning to spruce it up, but I can't spare the time.'

'I appreciate it, thanks.'

I leave with his key in my pocket, glancing back just once before shutting the door. Tommy Brookes looks baffled, like he still can't accept that one of his youngest punters is dead. He may be right about his wife's loyalty, but stranger things have happened than a young man falling for a pretty older woman. I walk back down the corridor shaking my head. I must be seriously adrift to suspect a middle-aged churchgoer, in fragile health, of being involved in a murder. Debbie Brookes has never put a foot wrong, yet someone killed a young man who confided in her, and most of the island community appear equally unlikely. I can tell Shadow's had no luck either, when I return to the bar. He's curled up in the corner, muzzle to the wall, sulking about being ignored.

33

Sam's on edge, even though his boss is in high spirits when they get home from work. Moyle offers him a beer, which he refuses.

'Off booze for good, are you?' Callum says, laughing.

'That's my plan.'

'Good luck, mate. I tried it myself, but it never sticks.'

'It gets easier. Come to AA with me, if you want.'

'No way. I don't have a problem, like you.'

'Is that right?' Sam studies his landlord's face. 'You're risking everything by using coke.'

'Work's my only addiction.' Moyle takes a long swig of beer. 'My sister owns in a villa in California, with an eternity pool and sunshine all year round. I want to leave this shithole too, but it takes serious money.'

Sam looks out of the window as night falls over Hugh Town harbour; lights glow in the windows of stone cottages, as the tide turns. He can't imagine anywhere more beautiful. Memories of this simple landscape kept him sane in jail. It helped to block out the yelling from neighbouring cells, then close his eyes and dream. He pictured the islands' white beaches, granite carns and hills, lulling himself to sleep.

'Can I borrow your boat tonight, Callum?'

His landlord's gaze sharpens. 'Why?'

'I need to make a trip to St Agnes.'

'For business or romance?'

'Just seeing a friend.'

'Tell me her name.'

'Forget it, I'll ask someone else.'

'Jesus, you're touchy. Go ahead, but bring it back by eleven o'clock sharp.'

'I will, thanks.'

Sam goes to the kitchen, where the boat key hangs from a hook on the wall. He's pocketing it when Moyle appears in the doorway. His manner's changed when he speaks again, his expression hostile.

'You know I could put you straight back in jail, don't you?'

'What do you mean, Callum?'

'Nothing. It's just a statement of fact.'

Sam keeps quiet, unwilling to play mind games. Moyle's smile has returned now that he's back in control, the air humming with mistrust.

34

The only way we'll find Jez's killer is through bloody-minded persistence. If we stay on St Agnes round the clock, facts will start to click into place. We could be missing something obvious, but the main motives I can see for a young man visiting a place so frequently are love or money. Maybe he was infatuated, or trying to raise cash to repay a debt, or help a friend. It's 7 p.m. already, the whole day spent gathering handwriting samples and phoning crew members, making sure everyone's safe. I need to make one more house call before heading home. The prospect doesn't fill me with joy; the next man on my list is the island's worst curmudgeon.

'It's time to see Denzel Jory, Eddie.'

'He's still claiming to be ill.'

'Tough luck, he's put us off for days. We're going anyway. If he's feeling talkative, we might end up stuck on Gugh for hours. But who cares, if we get something useful?'

My deputy walks fast as we leave the Turk's Head to cross the sandbar, with Shadow running ahead. The pathway to Gugh is still a foot above water, but in a few hours' time it will be submerged, making the return trip impossible until the waves recede. Denzel's two-hundred-year-old house stands by the shore, directly opposite the pub. Similar cottages sell for a fortune now, but his looks unmodernised, with low windows. The name West View Cottage has been carved into a slate sign by the doorbell, but his career as a stone-mason ended long ago.

The front door is ajar, propped open by a lump of driftwood. Eddie calls out a greeting, but there's no reply as I stoop under the lintel. Denzel is in a rocking chair in the back room, with a blanket over his knees, while a radio blares a report from the latest Test match. Despite the heat, every window is sealed, the air suffocating. Denzel Jory's fellow islanders bring him food and supplies out of decency, not for the pleasure of his company. He's the most opinionated man in Scilly, his milky eyes full of disdain.

'I can't have visitors, with stomach trouble like mine.' His features look like they've been chipped from the granite he once carved into gravestones. 'Clear off and leave me alone, and take that bloody dog with you. They make me sneeze.'

'We'll put him outside. We only need a quick chat, Denzel.'

'I've got nothing to say, except the cricket's a bloody

disaster,' he announces. 'Those batsmen are spineless idiots.'

'The spin bowlers are worse,' Eddie replies.

Denzel gripes about the national team while the radio blasts out news of the latest innings. I liked rugby and boxing at school, and can't understand why anyone would play a game that lasts five days. Jory is wearing navy chinos and a short-sleeved shirt, his sparse white hair neatly combed, but his skin reveals his age. It's as thin as tracing paper, the veins in his hands dark blue, like a river's tributaries. If his grandson's death has left a mark, the old man is too macho to show any regret.

'We're sorry for your loss, Denzel. Can you tell us about Jez's visits?'

He switches his radio off at last. 'That boy was a disappointment to me. He only came here once in a blue moon.'

'Nonsense, Denzel,' Eddie says. 'Everyone knows he visited you once a week.'

'Calling me a liar, are you?'

Rage sparks in the old man's eyes. I'm sure he'd love to throw us out, but he's barely got the strength to stand. I remember admiring him when I was at school after he gave a talk to my class about his life as a stonemason. He was full of jokes and good humour, which expired years ago.

'Jez got his love of the sea from me, but he wasn't loyal.' His gaze lifts to a photo on his mantelpiece, of himself in his RNLI kit, the image bleached pale with age. 'I served that lifeboat fifty years. I thought it would make a man of him, but it never did.'

'How do you mean?'

His expression suddenly grows confused. 'Smuggling was easy in my day, if cash ran dry. Are you here to arrest me?'

'Not yet, Denzel. What did you trade in back then?' I know from experience that the old man needs humouring.

'Booze, cigarettes, silk. Anything people wanted.'

'I could still lock you up.'

'The evidence is long gone.' His laughter is a low rasp, like a creaking gate, in need of oil.

'Did Jez ever mention a new girlfriend?'

'He made bad choices.' Jory points at the window, his hand shaky. 'I saw his boat come and go all the time. Why make those journeys unless he was chasing a woman, or looking to profit?'

'You think he was smuggling?'

His frail hands wave in the air. 'Punishment was fierce for men like him in my day; if the others knew, they'd cast you overboard. No one cared if you sank or swam.'

The old man's words carry some truth. If Jez Cardew was running drugs for smugglers on the Atlantic Strait, his death may have been a warning to other small-time operators to toe the line. The love letter we found on his boat might not be connected with his death at all.

'Do you know if Jez had enemies, Denzel?'

'More than likely.'

'How do you mean?'

'His ex hated his guts, for a start.' He leans forward, wagging his finger in my face. 'She came here one time. I thought she was a pretty little thing until the dam broke. She came here to curse Jez, like she wanted him dead.'

'Anna's a strong character. What made her so angry?'

'He'd messed her around, she yelled about the damage he'd done. But none of that matters now.' The old man's voice cracks, but his grief is soon disguised. He's losing interest, fiddling with the radio's aerial. 'You boys can fetch me a cup of tea before you go. It's all my guts can handle.'

'Tell us about Damian Cosgrove first. He came by on Friday night, didn't he?'

'That's the type of man I admire. Damian understands hard work from his time on the rigs, in bad conditions far from home.'

'What time did he leave?'

'Stop nagging me, Benesek Kitto. We played chess. That's all I remember.'

'Eddie'll bring you that tea, then we'll leave, to beat the tide.'

'Why should I care? No one invited you.'

When I find Eddie in the kitchen, his expression's triumphant.

'Anna Dawlish never told you about confronting Jez here, did she? She had time to sail here, before seeing Paul Keast. Maybe he's lying too, to cover her back.'

'Jez left her high and dry, and her kid was heart-broken, but it doesn't make her a killer.'

Instinct tells me that Anna is innocent, but no one will forget her obsessive behaviour when her relationship ended. I'm more interested in Jory's scorn for his grandson right now. He's drifting into sleep, but his eyes snap open when I produce an RNLI medallion, still wrapped in an evidence bag.

'Do you recognise this, Denzel?'

He peers at it through eyes cloudy with age. 'They gave me one as a lad. You'll find it in a bowl on the dresser.'

'Why did you get a medal?'

'For rescuing a surfer in rough conditions.'

'So bravery runs in the family?'

'Stop flattering me, for God's sake. I hate that non-sense.' His voices rises to a shout, but when I look inside the terracotta bowl on his dresser, the medal looks different to the ones found on Jez's body. The words Royal Life Saving Society are embossed on one side.

'I've never seen this type before,' I say, passing it to him.

'I was a lifeguard the summer before I started my apprenticeship, sixty years ago. I'd only been on Blanket Bay a week before a child got swept away. I had to swim against the tide to bring him back. They paid for me to go all the way to London to collect that medal.'

Traces of the old Denzel are visible now, his face

proud. I can't tell whether it's losing his hero status to age that has caused his bitterness, or the loss of his wife, but his scowl soon returns. He traces the raised words on the medal with his fingertip. *"Quemcunque miserum videris, hominem scias."* Do you know what that says?'

'I never learned Latin.'

'It means every human in misery is known to you. It's telling us to care for our fellow men.'

I try to keep the motto in mind as I deal with Jory. His caustic personality stems from loneliness, I'm sure. He's travelled a long way from the young hero who saved lives. When I look inside the bowl on his dresser again, his RNLI medal is missing.

'Where's your other medal?'

He looks confused. 'So many people come here, bothering me. How would I know?'

'Have you shown it to anyone recently?'

'Only that lad, Damian. He's always polite so I let him see.'

'Thanks for helping us.'

The old man looks back at me, suddenly clear-eyed. 'Remember no one will rescue you if you slip into the water, Benesek. Drowning's the easiest thing in the world.'

'Is that your prophecy?'

'The sea took your father, didn't it? Likely it'll come for you too.'

'Drowning doesn't run in families, thank God.' The idea makes the skin prickle on the back of my neck.

'No one can fight their destiny, young man.'

Jory ends the conversation abruptly, by turning his radio to full volume.

It feels like I've missed something, but the old man refuses any more questions. The tide is rising when Eddie and I cross the sandbar, discussing the missing medal. I make the journey with Shadow in my arms. He's howling in protest at losing his independence, but the water sometimes rises fast enough to sweep him away. I tread carefully, as waves splash over the pathway, glad that the water's only ankle-deep. People have died trying to swim back to St Agnes, swept away by vicious currents. It's a relief to reach dry ground again, as darkness falls.

I'm about to give Eddie a lift home to Tresco, when a voice calls to us. Len Bligh cuts an odd figure, dressed in yellow shorts and Cornish flag T-shirt, his red hair dishevelled. He's babbling out words at a hundred miles an hour. My dog has picked up on his tension already, giving a howl of concern.

'My sister,' Bligh stammers. 'She's not answering her phone.'

'Take a breath, then talk us through it, step by step.'

'Molly took our boat, at two o'clock, to check on the ponies we look after here. She was due back on St Mary's hours ago, for a riding lesson, so I took the ferry over to find her.' His anxious gaze scans our faces. 'Something bad's happened, I know it.'

'She's probably just visiting a friend,' Eddie says, his tone gentle.

Len shifts his focus to me. 'Listen to me, please. Molly never lets people down.'

Night-time will make our search difficult. When I glance out at the sea, its appearance has changed during our time with Jory. It's become a limitless black expanse, onyx-smooth, with no light to guide our way.

35

Sam reaches the harbour early. Callum's powerboat is filthy, with food wrappers and drink cans strewn across the hold. He throws the rubbish into a bin on the quay, then swills water across the deck until the grime and mud rinses away. He'd love to own a boat, yet Moyle treats his with neglect.

His confidence falters when he checks his watch; it's 8 p.m., but the quay is empty. Maybe Danielle's got cold feet. When he spots her at last, she's rushing towards him at full pelt. Her voice is breathless when she reaches the end of the quay.

'Sorry, Sam, I got held up. I should have texted you.'

She drops onto the deck in one graceful leap, proving that she's been on boats all her life. He's about to cast off when a gruff voice calls his name. Callum Moyle steps out from the shadows.

'I'm just checking you've got enough brains to start the motor,' he sneers, then turns to Danielle. 'Hanging out with this rough diamond, are you? You could do better.'

Sam feels like pushing him into the water, to silence him, but Danielle's smile remains constant.

'Thanks for lending us your boat, Callum, but we're running late. Have a good evening, won't you?'

Moyle looks irritated by his failure to embarrass his housemate. Sam feels triumphant as they sail away, but the sensation soon fades as he remembers the reason why they're heading to St Agnes. There's little breeze as they make the crossing, the air gentle on their skin. When he notices the police boat moored below the Turk's Head, he feels like turning round. His jail sentence is a part of his life that he'd rather forget, but Danielle looks expectant.

'Let's get a drink, then chat to people. Someone must know something about Jez.'

'I don't touch booze these days, I should warn you.'

She shrugs. 'I don't like it much either.'

The pub is only half full. Sam recognises most of the faces, the rest must be guests staying in the rooms above, or the island's few holiday cottages, but the atmosphere falls flat when people spot him. A few greet Danielle warmly, but the rest fall silent. Even Debbie Brookes takes ages to rise from her stool behind the bar, her expression weary.

'What can I get you both?'

'Orange juice, please,' Sam replies.

Danielle is already chatting to an old fisherman, asking about the last time he saw Jez, but the conversation runs dry as Sam approaches, as if the old-timer has taken a vow of silence.

36

I lead the way inland, looking for Molly Bligh. Len still looks panicked, but he's holding himself together as we retrace his sister's steps. She called him at 3 p.m. saying she was about to sail home from St Agnes. He keeps on stressing that she never misses a lesson. Eddie looks anxious as we use my torch to follow a bridleway past Lowertown Farm, but I'm keeping an open mind. Shadow has calmed down, but he's keeping a close watch over Bligh, like it's his duty to protect the vulnerable.

'Here are the ponies,' Len says. 'They've been fed, but where is she?'

Bligh's stammer is becoming more pronounced with each word. We follow the edge of the field, looking for signs of his sister's presence. The animals seem glad of our company, trotting over to greet us like they're expecting another feed. Bligh appears calmer as he leans down to rub their muzzles.

'Can you think of anyone Molly would visit on St Agnes, Len?'

He raises his hands, showing empty palms. 'She knows everyone, but she'd have rung me to cancel the lesson.'

'Let's find your boat. Where does she usually moor?'

'By the Turk's Head, or in Blanket Bay if the tide's low.'

'Let's check the bay first, shall we?'

The three of us move at a steady jog, downhill to the island's west coast, which only takes five minutes. It's beautiful, even at night. Stars illuminate the bay, with no houses in sight, the sand littered with fist-sized pebbles. Burnt Hill guards the inlet like a sentinel, but there's no sign of the Blighs' boat among the fishing smacks adrift on long mooring ropes. I'd recognise the old trawler they converted, with its hold turned into a pair of horseboxes. I was hoping Molly had simply moored up, to escape her obligations for once, but my concerns are growing.

'Ring her again, Len. If she doesn't answer this time, we'll call the lifeboat.'

Bligh keeps his phone pressed to his ear. The air is so still, I can hear the ringtone echoing; Molly is either unwilling or unable to answer. He's still clutching his phone when I call Liam Quick. The coxswain's voice is hushed when he says the Blighs' vessel is missing from Hugh Town harbour. I hear him sound the alarm at the boathouse, a shrill whistle from the tannoy, ringing out across the town. My own RNLI pager buzzes in my pocket, but other volunteers on St Mary's will have to take our places tonight.

It's after 9 p.m. when we return to the police launch. Len seems to have retreated into silence; I'm keen to get him back to St Mary's, where friends and family can offer him support. Eddie sits with him in the wheel-house as I steer, while Shadow stands on the prow, scenting the air. The outboard motor strains as we cross the strait. It lifts my spirits to see the lifeboat race past in the opposite direction. Liam will circle St Agnes then expand the search, following his knowledge of local tides. The unspoken truth hits me at last: today's events match the previous search too closely, before Jez's body was found.

A small crowd is waiting on the slipway when we get back, to support Len Bligh, while the search for Molly gathers speed. Members of the lifeboat support team hurry down to greet us as I moor the policeboat, with Janet Fearnley taking Len under her wing. The atmosphere in the lifeboat house is jittery. It's always the same during a shout; those left stranded on dry land are powerless, while the radio blares out white noise, mimicking the sea. Half a dozen volunteers, including me, will keep Len Bligh company for as long as it takes. We've got no chance of sleep until the boat returns.

I'm trying to get comfortable in an armchair, with Shadow sprawled across my feet when a familiar figure appears in the doorway. My boss is instantly recognisable. He's dressed in a blazer and chinos, rather than the shorts any normal human would wear on a hot summer evening. The only sign of informality is his deck shoes, instead of his usual Oxford brogues, polished to a mirror shine. I always know when he's about to deliver a lecture. His face is stony as he summons me outside with a stern nod, like I've failed to do my homework.

'I'm surprised you're here, sir. We only just got back.'

'The search could last all night, Kitto. Go home, immediately, and take Shadow with you. Why do you never follow orders? He's not meant to accompany you on police duties.'

'That's irrelevant now, sir. Molly Bligh hasn't been seen for hours. Another young lifeboat officer going missing at sea must be connected to the murder case. We have to find her, before it's too late.'

He makes a loud tutting sound. 'Your duty is on land, not at sea, as I said before. No one can investigate what's happened until her boat's found. Get some sleep, then hit the ground running in the morning.'

'I can't just—'

'Rest now, so you can perform your duties properly tomorrow, do you hear? Eddie will do the same.'

'If you insist, sir. Give me a minute to gather my things.'

His grey eyes narrow to slits. 'I'm not moving until you leave this place.'

My teeth grind, but I manage not to snap. The man's got a point; there's little we can do until Molly's boat is recovered, but the lifeboat team is like an extended family. It feels wrong to desert them but there's no point in fighting Madron's decision. I give Eddie the news that the DCI is sending us home. He gives me a look of disbelief, but he can fight his own battle. Madron's immovable once his mind's made up. I bundle my things together then step back outside.

'Goodnight, sir,' I mutter.

The man offers a curt nod. 'Until tomorrow, Kitto.'

I'm still on edge when I sail back to Bryher. There's no sign of the rescue mission now, just the lights of Tresco hovering in the distance like a swarm of glow worms. The only sound is my boat's engine's low drone. My stomach feels as if it's been tied in knots, like the ligature that severed Jez Cardew's hand.

I'd feel better if I could understand the connection between two young RNLI officers suddenly going missing within days of each other. Both disappearances happening while the festival is running may be significant. So many events taking place across the five inhabited islands are a reminder of the lifeboat's central role in all our lives.

Shadow bounds down the quay when we reach Bryher, clearly overjoyed to be on home soil, but I'm slower to relax. Frustration is still churning inside my gut. It crosses my mind to strip down to my boxers and swim it out, but I head for home instead. I'm greeted by a peel of laughter when I approach our cottage. It's set back from Hell Bay by a narrow strip of garden, the lawn unravelling into sand. I stand at the point where land meets shore, unwilling to enter, even though my three favourite people are inside. I can see Nina and

Zoe through the window, stretched out on our sofa, with wine glasses in hand. Zoe looks brighter than before, as if my fiancée's calm has rubbed off on her, and Noah has probably been asleep for hours.

I'm about to push the door open for Shadow when a sudden noise breaks the silence; it's the mechanical hum of the coastguard's helicopter. Its fierce down-draught chills the back of my neck as it swings low over Bryher, scouring the coastline. Frustration tightens the muscles in my jaw, mixed with a dose of shame, and I understand Liam Quick's mindset at last. There's nothing worse than being unable to help. I should be on that lifeboat, not hiding on dry land, while another crew member fights for her life.

37

Sam and Danielle arrive back at Hugh Town harbour at 11 p.m. Their pagers both sounded while they were on St Agnes, but they couldn't have got back in time for the shout.

'I hope it's nothing serious,' Danielle says. 'Poor dad's running on empty. He hasn't been himself for months.'

'How do you mean?'

'He worries about coxing the lifeboat. It's such a huge responsibility, and it weighs on him even more since Mum left. I'm afraid it'll break him one day.'

'That won't happen. Liam's as tough as they come.'

'I love him to bits; let's hope you're right.'

'Thanks for coming tonight, Danielle. Sorry it was a waste of time.'

'I don't expect quick answers, and neither should you. It's the island way to guard secrets.'

'The whole bar went silent when we arrived. It's like I'm carrying a deadly disease.'

'It'll get easier.' When her phone buzzes in her bag, she checks the message. 'Jesus, Sam, it's Molly Bligh that's missing.'

Sam stares back at her. 'It can't be happening again.'

'I hope not. Molly's been a mate since our school days.'

'I still can't believe Jez is gone.'

'Me neither.' Danielle looks up at him, her face beautiful in the semi-darkness. 'Do you suspect anyone, Sam? You two were so close, you must know if he's upset someone.'

'Only Liam Moyle, but he'd have to be nuts to kill his own tenant. The answer must be on St Agnes. It drew him there, like a magnet.'

'Maybe he went there to avoid Anna.'

'There was no need. She stays in most nights, with her daughter.'

Danielle's hand rests on his arm. 'Do you think Callum could be involved? It wasn't just Jez, he's not keen on the whole lifeboat crew.'

'How do you know?'

'Dad would hate me telling you, but he applied to join us last year. The RNLI selection panel judged him unstable, so they turned him down. Callum questioned their decision, apparently. They still said no.'

Sam stares down at her. 'That explains why he's bitter, but it's no reason to kill someone, is it?' When he scans the quay again, there's still no sign of Moyle. 'Come on, I'll walk you home.'

'I can find my way, don't worry.'

'Crew members are being targeted, Danielle. The police told us not to spend time alone, especially if we've had one of those packs full of badges.'

'Like me and dad.' Her smile slowly revives. 'Go on then, Sir Galahad.'

They climb the hill together, while Sam remembers the past. He used to dream of walking Danielle Quick home from school, but never plucked up the courage. She keeps the conversation light, chatting about her new job. It's only when they reach the house she shares with her dad near Carn Gwaval that her face turns serious.

'If I ask a personal question, will you give me an honest answer, Sam?'

'That depends.'

'Did you send me a Valentine card, in year nine?'

'Why do you ask?' He's too embarrassed to admit it.

'You watched me sometimes, but never said a word. I hoped it was from you all the same.'

'That's hard to believe, but you guessed right. I went to Mumford's really early to buy it, so no one saw me.'

'I went to all your football games.' She grins at him. 'I had such a crush on you back then. You were in that band too, the Treasure Seekers, the moody bass guitarist. Girls in my class had your name written all over their exercise books.'

'Now you're kidding me.' He comes to a sudden halt. 'Why are you bothering with an ex-con? You could have anyone.'

'There's goodness in you, Sam. The way you're hunting for Jez's killer proves it. Plus you still look the same, all quiet and intense.'

'Everyone else sees me as a bad penny.'

'That's Callum, not you. I still think he's involved.'

'We can't prove it, but I'll keep watch, don't worry.'

'Shut up and kiss me, will you?'

Sam hesitates, because he's waited for this moment so

long. He keeps the kiss gentle, his hands cradling her face. Her response is warm, his past mistakes seeming to fall away. 'I promise we'll find the truth, Danielle. I won't stop looking.'

When she says goodnight, his heart's pounding. It seems disloyal to be so happy when his best friend's gone, and Molly's missing, but his priorities are changing. If Danielle believes in him, maybe it's time to forgive himself.

38

Wednesday 30 August

I wake early from a bad dream. The sea is crashing around me, and thunderclaps echo across the sky, but when my eyes open, it's just Shadow outside our bedroom, barking at top volume. It's a fierce, keening howl, like a wolf crying for its mate. Nina's stirring awake, but there's no sound from Noah next door; our son could sleep through an earthquake. I pull on boxer shorts, to find out why Shadow's agitated.

'Shut up, monster,' I hiss. 'It's the crack of dawn.'

He releases another blood-curdling howl. When I open the front door, he flies out then runs back to me, barking wildly. I'll get no peace unless I follow wherever he's heading, and my curiosity's rising. My dog has an uncanny sense for danger. He's helped me out too many times in the past to let me ignore his antics now. I pull on jeans and a T-shirt, ram my feet into trainers, and set off. Shadow chases inland, stopping occasionally to check I'm keeping up. I catch sight of the daymark on Watch Hill against the dawn sky as I sprint over Shipman Head Down. It's obsolete now, like so much of island life, but it once served as a beacon for mariners stranded in fog on New Grimsby Sound. I'm panting for breath when Shadow finally comes to a halt on the shore outside Maggie's pub, the Rock. If he's led me on a half-mile sprint just for fun, I won't be amused. He's sitting on his haunches staring out at Hangman Island. 'What the hell is it?'

He growls at me again, for no clear reason. I'm about to abandon him and return home when he leaps in front of me, teeth bared.

'For God's sake, Shadow. Show me what's wrong, or go home.'

He darts towards the island, and something catches my attention. There's a pale shape stretched across the rocks, too far off to see clearly, and my stomach balls into a fist. It's exactly the same place where we found Jez. The tide is still out, so I can clamber over to the island on rocks exposed by the receding waves.

'Stay there,' I yell to Shadow. 'You'll get swept away.'

I'm ten metres out from shore when he races past, his paws slipping on seaweed that reeks of ammonia. The creature never follows orders, but it's hard to stay angry, even though he takes stupid risks.

I stumble while clambering over the jagged rocks. They're coated with bladderwrack which sticks to the soles of my shoes. This journey would be impossible in winter, but summer's low tide is a blessing. My skin prickles, even though the air's warm. Maybe it's just my memory of finding Jez Cardew's broken body here, or the haunted atmosphere left by hundreds of executions. It looks like I've wasted my time. The pale outline isn't a body after all, it's just some fabric abandoned by the waves. My heart beats faster when footsteps pound towards me, until I realise it's just the wooden yardarm overhead, rocking in the breeze.

When I gather up the fabric, I see it's the dress Molly Bligh wore last time we met. It's torn to shreds, yet the pale green shade appears identical. My concern increases when I see a medallion pinned to the hem. It's another lifeguard's award, like the one I saw at Denzel Jory's house, with the name scratched from the back.

Instinct makes me scan the rocks as I scramble round the edge of the island looking for her body, with the yardarm creaking louder than before.

'Who the fuck's doing this?' I hiss under my breath.

Molly Bligh may have met the same fate as Jez Cardew, but my only proof is a torn dress. Her body could already have been carried deep into the Atlantic. But why would anyone target such a popular young woman? Frustration leaves a sour taste in my mouth as I return to dry land, clutching the dress. Shadow is behaving normally again, playing games on the shore, rolling himself in foul-smelling seaweed, meaning that I'll have to hose him down when we get home. I have no idea how he knew to bring me here. He must have the keenest sense of smell imaginable to catch the scent of one of his favourite islanders. Either that, or the sound of a boat's engine woke him from sleep.

I call in my find to the station, leaving a message on the answer machine. There's no point in waking Eddie because the dress isn't definitive proof that Molly has drowned. I phone the coastguard next, and the news is sobering. The remnants of a converted trawler just like the Blighs' have been sighted by a fisherman in the shipping lane. They'll need to be brought to shore before we can confirm the truth, but I'm willing to bet Molly was dragged onto another boat, then hers was left adrift until a transatlantic freighter broke it apart.

I've got time to kill before my breakfast meeting with Liz Gannick, so I carry my bad mood to my uncle's boatyard. It's only a short walk south, past the next headland, where Norrard Rocks jut from the water like rusting spears. Ray is sitting on a bench by the quay, drinking coffee from an old tin cup. He always rises obscenely early. He doesn't speak when I arrive, but when he gives a low whistle, Shadow settles at his feet. My uncle is the one person my dog always obeys, without even a hint of resentment.

'There's coffee on the burner,' he says.

I half fill a cup with his vile brew. It's as black as tar and tastes like rocket fuel, but it's better than nothing. Then I sit beside him on the bench, hoping to absorb some of his calm. Ray is capable of sitting motionless for hours, with his gaze trained on the sea. He glances at the fabric I'm clutching, but still doesn't speak.

'Molly Bligh was wearing this yesterday,' I say. 'I found it on Hangman Island just now. That medal is like the one Denzel Jory got from the Royal Life Saving Society, but the name's been scraped off the back.'

'It could be hers.'

'Really?'

'She won a lifeguard's medal six or seven years ago, when you were living in London. A lad had an asthma attack in the water. She swam against the riptide to fetch him, without help from anyone.'

'So she's a hero too?'

'No doubt about it,' Ray says.

'It sounds like the coastguard have found the remains of her boat.'

His face gives little away. 'Remember I told you the currents circle back here this time of year because of the eddies at Kettle Point? All manner of things end up in New Grimsby Sound.'

'It was always the best time for beachcombing, but I'm looking for a body, not oyster shells.'

'The poor girl might have washed up on Tean or North Wethel.'

'I'll take a look later this morning. Have you got some clean plastic I can use to wrap the dress?'

He rises to his feet. 'I'll find some. Do you want me to sail over to Tean this morning to have a look?'

'That would help a lot.'

'It's no trouble, for a girl like her.'

Sadness resonates in Ray's voice, but there's no visible sign of distress. It used to bother me, until I realised he was just protecting himself from the worst kind of hurt. I believed he was unfeeling, but I've seen the way he holds Noah to his chest, keeping him from harm. Emotions must lie inside his hard shell after all.

I'm preparing to leave, when Ray screens his eyes from the sun's glare with his hand.

'Leave Shadow with me today. I know he gets under your feet.'

'He helped me out this morning, but thanks. I appreciate it.'

I know from experience that anyone who messes with Liz Gannick is in trouble, so I climb onto my boat and cast off, before Shadow can follow. His furious bark echoes across the water, protesting that I've abandoned him, straight after he's proved himself smarter than the entire canine search and rescue unit.

The water is still so tranquil, I only need one hand on the wheel as I head for St Mary's, leaving me free to ring Eddie. It's a surprise to hear that he refused Madron's order to go home last night, which is another rite of passage. Until now, he's followed every instruction from the DCI without question.

There's been no outcome from the search for Molly. He curses out loud when he hears I've found her dress, and the likelihood that her boat was destroyed. He's been mild-mannered for years, yet now he's like a grenade, primed to detonate.

'Ray's going to search the northern waters this morning. Catch the ferry to St Agnes, can you? We need an outcome from the CPS today, and chase the graphologist again. We need her report on the notes urgently. I'm meeting Liz for a catch-up, then going to the hospital.'

I'll be attending Jez's post-mortem later this morning, but mentioning it would only raise Eddie's stress levels.

I slip my phone back into my pocket as I pass Garrison Point and sail into harbour. The lobstermen and crab boats unloaded their creels hours ago, but half a dozen fishermen remain on the quay, with ice boxes at their feet, selling their catch to anyone willing to queue. The islanders are happy to rise early for the freshest fish, but I'm certain the news about Molly going missing would wipe the smiles off their faces.

Liz Gannick is alone in the dining hall at the Tregarthen Hotel because it's too early for any sane holidaymaker to eat breakfast. The hotel has stood at the end of the quay for almost two hundred years, since a ship's captain tired of sailing the world and opened his house to paying guests. It's absorbed several neighbouring cottages, the whole edifice painted a glittering white. The dining hall can hold a hundred guests comfortably. There's a direct view across the harbour, with Tresco straight ahead, and the pale outline of St

Martin's visible in the distance. Gannick is tapping out a message on her phone, too busy to care about the landscape. From a distance, she looks like a teenage rebel, with locks of bright pink hair framing her face. When I drop onto the seat opposite, she keeps her gaze locked on the screen.

'You're late, as bloody usual,' she mutters.

'I brought you something, worn by the second victim. It washed up on Hangman Island.'

'Where you found the first body? Hand it over.'

Gannick's eyes glint with interest as she peers at the dress through the transparent plastic. 'Saltwater dissolves most substances fast, but there's an outside chance of blood traces.'

'This time's different. The killer left Jez's cruiser for us to find, but this time I bet he steered it into the shipping lane. It was smashed apart by a freighter last night, from the sounds of it.'

She winces. 'The pieces won't be much use to us; salt water's perfect for washing away clues. Have you got permission for my search at Jez Cardew's house-share yet?'

'The CPS still aren't playing ball.'

'For fuck's sake,' she snaps. 'You have to tell them who's boss. It feels like I'm running a sodding marathon, without any back-up.'

A waitress stops laying tables and turns round, curious to watch our tiff unfold.

'Keep it down, Liz. Both victims are friends of mine,

from the lifeboat crew. We're all working our arses off. Blame the CPS, not me. They love wielding their power.'

'Let me sort it, for God's sake.'

I wait in silence while she makes a phone call, her voice so full of malice, the poor guy at the end of the line must be terrified. She gives a victory smile when she stuffs her phone back in her pocket.

'He's emailing the warrant now; I'll head there next.'

'Does anyone ever refuse you, Liz?'

'Only the brave.'

'Not even your husband?'

She looks amused. 'Do you seriously think I'd marry someone who enjoyed the upper hand?'

'Unlikely.'

'Damn right.' She leans towards me, her face calmer. 'Find out what connects your two victims. It's bigger than that lifeboat; someone on the island has been hurt so badly, they can't see past it.'

'I figured that out already, Liz.'

'So act on it,' she says, her tone imperious. 'Killers only carry out ritualised killings when passion's involved, don't they? It took effort to clean that boat with paraffin, and scrape the names off those medals.'

'If I was a pillar of the community I'd throw everything at staying out of jail too. The killer's showing how clever they are, by sending quotes about the sea from a play few people have read. They could unlock the case, but let's stick to evidence for now. What have you found so far, Liz?'

'The note from Cardew's boat had no fingerprints, sadly. It's coated with clay dust which must be imported. These islands are pure limestone and granite.'

I remember Lewis Marling, the only potter working full-time on St Agnes, and fire off a quick text to Eddie. 'That could be a breakthrough, Liz.'

'I fucking hope so, after all my work. What do you want for breakfast?'

'Coffee, no milk.'

'You normally devour the whole menu.'

'Not today. It's best to enter the jaws of hell on an empty stomach.'

'Is it Cardew's autopsy next? You poor bastard.' Gannick produces a narrow smile for the waitress. 'One fried egg sandwich, and two double espressos, please.'

The smell of food turns my stomach when her order arrives, the coffee leaving a sour tang in my mouth, but at least I've got another lead to chase.

39

Gareth Keillor is laying out tools in the hospital mortuary. He's dressed in scrubs and surgical gloves, his sparse grey hair covered by a surgeon's cap. He gives me a jaunty salute when I reach for my overalls. I peer down at his array of picks, saws and drills while my stomach performs somersaults. I've only attended a few autopsies when the victim is familiar, but this one's the worst. I've spent plenty of evenings in the Atlantic pub with Jez and the rest of the lifeboat crew, including Molly Bligh. It hasn't fully registered yet that she may have gone the same way. The harsh overhead light leaves me with nowhere to hide; my desire to solve the case before another crew member gets hurt tightens.

Keillor approaches the operating table to start work, but something makes him hesitate.

'Jez was a friend of yours, wasn't he, Ben?'

'I didn't know him that well, but I liked him. He encouraged me a lot on my first few shouts.'

'You shouldn't be here, but the DCI refused to send

a substitute. Frankly I'm amazed he didn't volunteer to take your place.'

'He never leaves his desk, Gareth, but it's a kind thought.'

'I can't rush this, I'm afraid. There's no shame in sitting down, if it helps.'

'I'm better off standing, thanks.'

Keillor puts on a surgical mask, then draws back the sheet. I drag in a deep breath before studying Jez's body. It looks different from when I saw it in the half-dark, covered in seaweed and tar. The damage looks worse now his wounds are clean, his battered flesh fully exposed. The pathologist is circling the table, my presence already forgotten, his eyes alight with interest. He's as committed to his profession as Gannick, but not the obsessive type. He plays golf to a high standard all year round, and spends weeks visiting his grown-up kids on the mainland, but this morning I can tell he's in the zone. He is already dictating notes into the micro-phone that hangs from the ceiling: hypoxia, thoracic abrasions, pulmonary oedema. I can only hope he'll explain everything in plain English at the end.

'Still on your feet?' he asks.

'More or less.'

'It gets easier after the Y section.'

'That's what I keep telling myself.'

I lean against the wall when Keillor uses a saw to open the chest wall after making a long incision. It sick-ens me at first, but he's right about the process getting easier. The corpse on the table no longer resembles the young lifeboatman I admired. When I open my eyes again, Keillor has removed his heart, lungs and liver. The organs lie in metal dishes on a trolley a few metres away. I transfer my gaze to the polished lino at my feet. Anger rises in my throat, too hot to suppress. Jez Cardew has been reduced to base matter. His vital organs will soon be placed in the hospital's refrigeration unit, and samples sent to the lab, while the killer relaxes on the islands' beaches, building up a tan.

'Not long now,' Keillor says. 'Almost there.'

He takes fifteen more minutes to sew up the wounds on Cardew's chest and abdomen, then place a fresh sheet over his body. His expression is sober when he stands at the sink, scrubbing his hands clean with carbolic soap.

'The death industry tires me these days,' he says.

'You always say that, but you'll never retire.'

'Don't be so sure. The wife wants to move to Portsmouth, to be near the kids, and maybe she's right. This job used to be easy, Ben. Cause of death was my only concern. I'd do two autopsies every afternoon and still sleep like a baby. Now, all that wasted potential keeps me awake.'

'Let's quit work and go on a Florida golf tour.'

'Tempting.' His smile slowly revives. 'What do you want to know?

'Cause of death, ideally.'

'Hypoxic oedema, which is a fancy name for

drowning. Jez was alive when he entered the water, and Gannick's theory that he was dragged behind a boat is correct, in my view. His left shoulder was dislocated by the force.' He stares down at his clipboard, full of scribbled notes. 'You can drown in several ways. Dry drowning happens when your larynx goes into spasm, from cold water shock. Secondary drowning happens to victims who are pulled from the water alive, only to die later because of damage from inhaling brine. Jez's death was rapid; his lungs were saturated.'

'That's a grim way to go.'

'I can think of worse. People who survive near-drowning sometimes describe a sense of euphoria before losing consciousness. The amygdala is so overstimulated by panic, it floods the system with serotonin, the feel-good hormone that produces happiness.'

'Replacing fear with joy?'

'The phenomenon's well documented.'

'I hope he didn't suffer. We still don't know if he was lured onto another boat. Whoever killed him may have gone on board his to attack him, then dragged him along behind it at full speed. Did you notice any defensive wounds?'

'He may have been coshed around the head. There's a deep wound at the back of his skull, but that could have come from bumping over rocks. I can't tell you which came first. It's possible he ingested a sedative, or was injected, although the toxicology report may not be conclusive. His body was found too long after the event.'

'Thanks for trying, Gareth.'

When I stumble outside, sunlight burns my retinas. It's the killer's total lack of empathy that bothers me most. They may have enjoyed the first murder so much, Molly's life could already be lost.

40

It's 9.30 a.m. when Sam prepares to leave the house with Moyle. His landlord has spent the last half hour haranguing suppliers about missing shipments of paint, plaster and timber. Sam knows the man's mood is toxic, before he opens his mouth.

'I'm dropping your hourly rate this week. I was mad to take on a novice, you're way too slow.'

'You can't do that, I'm already on minimum wage.'

'Watch me. I get fuck all in return, and remember who's put a roof over your head.'

Something inside Sam's chest snaps at last. 'Stick your job then, I'm moving out.'

His landlord's face darkens. 'What are you on about?'

'I don't have to take shit from you.'

'Is that right?' Moyle's hands are bunched into fists, ready to throw a punch. 'Who else would have you around?'

'No one, probably, but I'll take my chances.' Sam draws himself upright. 'I don't need your bullshit. You pretended the lifeboat didn't matter to you, but you tried to join up. Did you fancy being a hero, like Jez?'

'Shut up,' Callum hisses. 'Just pack your things and go.'

'You're a sad, lonely bastard. I bet Jez getting that medal hurt worse than him dating Anna. How about Molly Bligh? Did you fancy her too?'

'You're talking bollocks. Clear your junk out today, or it's going to the dump.'

The two men stare at each other, the air humming with anger, until someone pounds on the front door. Moyle takes his time answering. Sergeant Lawrie Deane is waiting in the porch with a woman who's balancing on crutches. She's got the petite frame of a child, but up close her face is world-weary and etched with lines.

'Callum Moyle?' she asks. 'I've got a warrant to conduct a forensic search on your property, in relation to Jez Cardew's death.'

His voice is suddenly polite. 'Will it take long?'

'I can't say. Vacate the place now, please, and stay away until we text you.'

'I need my jacket from upstairs, then it's all yours. My tenant's moving out anyway.'

Sam collects his wallet from the hall table, and his phone. His landlord shoulders him off the path, like he's blocking his road to success.

'Don't bother coming to work,' Moyle says. 'I only kept you on out of pity.'

He marches away, leaving Sam shaken. He glances across the road at Father Michael's church, Our Lady Star of the Sea. The building looks more like a fisherman's white-walled cottage than a place of worship, but the scent of incense is overpowering when he steps inside. He needs to understand how Jez died, even more urgently, but he'll have to enlist help from someone he trusts.

41

Eddie has made adjustments at the Turk's Head by the time I reach St Agnes. The air still smells of stale beer even with the windows open, there are piles of old bar stools, and dust motes glitter in the sunlight, but my deputy seems oblivious. He's shunted the snooker table into a corner and set up a trestle table for his printer and laptop, with papers stacked around him in orderly piles.

'I've had a few glitches, boss.' His voice is still brittle with stress. 'The graphologist sent us her new report.'

'What does it say?'

'The notes to the crew are all by the same person. It's likely they were written left-handed, by someone who normally uses their right, as a disguise. The love note we found on Jez's boat was definitely from someone else.'

'How about Jez's phone record?'

'I've got that too.'

He passes me a ream of numbers, listing each call's duration and the texts sent and received. He has already scribbled names against most of the numbers. I can see that Jez was in frequent contact with some of his pals from the lifeboat crew. He made plenty of calls to Molly Bligh, but they had reduced recently. The records show that Anna Dawlish continued texting him right up until his death, even though he never replied.

'How many times did Anna ring him in the past fortnight, Eddie?'

'Almost every day, but that's nothing. She sent over a hundred texts, the day Jez ended it. That makes her a stalker, doesn't it?'

'Anna could have used Janet Fearnley's boat. I think we should talk to her again, and find out what all those messages said.'

'Come on, Eddie. Anna's moved on and found a new bloke.'

'That could just be a cover.'

I can tell he won't rest until we talk to her again. 'Okay, set up another interview, just to be certain. I want to see Jez's pal, the potter on St Agnes too. He may have known about his relationship.'

'I've left half a dozen messages for Lewis Marling, but he's not answering. His number shows up on Jez's phone record. Some weeks they spoke two or three times.'

'The clay dust Gannick found on that note has to mean something, Eddie.'

His gaze meets mine properly for the first time today.

'Do you think Molly's been attacked the same way as Jez?'

'All we know is that her dress ended up where his body landed. It's not absolute proof she's dead.'

'The killer's got a thing about Hangman's Island, hasn't he? That's why the symbol's on all our notes.'

'I can see why he'd plant Molly's dress there, if he's angry. Traitors were executed there by the dozen in Cromwell's day. Their bodies were left hanging, as a warning. Maybe the killer feels betrayed.'

Eddie's about to speak again when his phone rings. 'That'll be Madron, he's been calling for hours.'

'Better find out what he wants.'

Eddie grimaces as he accepts the call. I watch him grip his phone tightly; he listens in silence, absorbing every detail.

'A fisherman's seen something on Annet that looks like a body. The lifeboat's on its way.'

'We'll get there first if we take my boat.'

We race downstairs, passing Debbie Brookes at the bottom. It's possible the landlady was eavesdropping about the case, but right now that doesn't matter. Eddie's already jumping onto my bowrider, then starting the outboard motor with the key I left in the ignition. I drop onto the bench and let him steer.

We'll reach Annet fifteen minutes before the lifeboat because the island lies due east of St Agnes. It's one of Scilly's largest uninhabited islands, almost a kilometre long. The place fascinated me as a boy because going

265

ashore was forbidden; it's a site of special scientific interest. I wanted to check out the grey seal colony, and underground nests of shearwaters and storm petrels, but the shore is too rocky for easy landing. The sea's dazzle is blinding as we cut through shallow waves. We're travelling at top speed, with the engine straining. I'd hate to find Molly Bligh's body torn apart like Jez's – I'd hate to find her body in any condition – but I keep my eyes trained on the island's coast.

I catch sight of the seals first. They're sunbathing on outcrops that jut high above the water, and Eddie is forced to slow to a standstill. There are so many sub-merged crags and boulders, he could easily damage the outboard motor, but the seals don't seem concerned. They're having the time of their lives. I count a dozen, at least, their grey velvet hides glossy with health. A few swim closer to inspect us, curious to witness an alien species.

'What can you see?' Eddie calls out, too busy study-ing the water for hazards to look up.

'Nothing yet. Can you get any closer?'

'We'll run aground.'

'I'll wade there.' I dump my wallet and phone on deck, then swing my legs over the gunwale.

'It's too rocky to anchor, boss. I'll have to stay in deeper water.'

I miss my footing, landing waist deep in brine, making me curse out loud. The shoreline is made up of boulders, with little bare sand between, so walking's a challenge, my feet sliding on wet seaweed. The island's native population seems angered by my arrival. Black-backed gulls dive-bomb me, then a shearwater flies at my face, protecting her nesting site. I'm aware of the damage I'm causing to their habitat, my feet crunching over buried nests until I reach dry ground, but there's no avoiding them today. There's no sign of a body, so I clamber on top of the largest boulder in sight, to scan Annet's eastern coast.

I'm still looking when several gulls descend on me at once, wings flapping in my face. Their screams sound like Noah yelling in the night. I bat the creatures away and gaze further ahead, until I spot an orange pinprick in the distance. I'm almost certain it's Molly Bligh's bright red hair. I scramble across the beach, squinting into the sunlight, with the birds' high-pitched warnings ringing in my ears.

42

Sam waits for Father Michael in his small church. He's never been a believer, but the pure light spilling through the round stained-glass window overhead forces him to search his conscience. Was he a good enough friend? Maybe Jez was in trouble and he never realised. If he'd known, he could have defended him. It's a relief when the priest finally arrives.

Father Michael listens intently while he explains his situation.

'What will you do for work now, Sam?'

'Anything, Father. I'm not choosy, I just need to stay in Scilly.'

'I'll ask around for vacancies. Will you live with Rose?'

'Mum's cabin's too small. I want to spend more time on Bryher, but there's not enough space for both of us.'

'What made you leave Callum's today?'

'He treated me like dirt.'

The priest gives a slow nod. 'Then you did the right thing. We all deserve respect.'

'He argued with Jez all the time. I think he was jealous, because he failed the lifeboat selection test.'

'What are you saying, Sam?'

'Maybe Callum killed him, but Stuart Cardew's convinced it was me. The police would never believe me. Talk to them, Father, please. I have to clear my name.'

'Come next door, we can talk easier there. You're welcome to use my spare room till you're back on your feet.'

The burden Sam's been carrying lightens immediately. The priest's home is small and simply furnished, yet he feels relaxed for the first time in days. Father Mike's spare room reminds him of his old prison cell, with a narrow bed, a chair, and a cupboard for his possessions.

'It's pretty basic,' Father Michael says. 'The diocese doesn't believe in luxuries, I'm afraid.'

'I'm just grateful for a place to sleep.'

The priest looks at him again. 'Have you ever considered starting afresh on the mainland? I'd miss you, and so would your mother, but life might be easier for you there.'

'I couldn't leave Mum, and there's a girl I like too. She's special, I want to see where it goes.'

'Those are good reasons to stay. Just promise me you'll keep attending your AA meetings.'

'You know I will, Father.'

'Good, now tell me why you think Callum hurt Jez.'

Sam blurts out every detail, from the rows he witnessed, to the lies Callum's told about Jez being a womaniser, and stealing his possessions. He's certain Callum has a drug habit that's eating all his money. That's why he takes his boat out, late at night.

'Those are serious allegations. Do you really think he's that violent?'

'I've seen him blow up plenty of times, for no reason. His attitude to Jez changed from friendly to bitter. The bloke's a toxic force when he's angry.'

'I'll speak to Ben Kitto. Is there anything else you need?'

Sam hesitates. 'A boat tonight, if I can get one.'

'Use mine if it's important. The key's in the kitchen drawer, but make sure you're back here by ten. And stay out of the investigation, Sam. Let the police find the killer.'

Father Mike hurries downstairs, leaving Sam in the small bedroom. When he looks out of the window, Sergeant Lawrie Deane is standing guard outside Callum Moyle's house while the forensics expert searches the building. It's just as well he's got nothing to hide.

43

I call out to Eddie, telling him to sail further up the shoreline. My progress is slowed by the boulders underfoot, glistening with seaweed. There are no visible paths because few people visit Annet, apart from the RSPB, checking the local birdlife. I wade through sedge grass and brambles, then drop back onto the shore. I'm starting to wonder if that flash of red was just a trick of the eye. But once I've cleared the next line of boulders, I see it again. Molly is lying face down on a narrow strip of sand. Her body's motionless, but instinct makes me sprint across the narrow bay.

I'm breathing hard when I drop onto my knees to check if there's a pulse, but I know we're too late. The young woman's yellow RNLI slicker has been ripped to shreds, her exposed skin sunburnt to a dark pink. Her corpse is in better shape than Jez Cardew's, even though some of her wounds look vicious; a piece of twine has been tied round her wrist, leaving a deep cut. The line must have broken as she was dragged behind the killer's boat.

'What's this about, you bastard?' The words spill out, even though no one can hear.

When I roll Molly onto her back, I see another Royal Life Saving medallion has been tied around her neck, then water gushes from her mouth. Suddenly her eyelids flicker. When I place two fingers on her throat, there's the faintest pulse. There's a chance she can hear me, even though she's not responding.

'It's okay, I've got you now. Who did this to you, Molly?'

Her eyes open wider. I can see she's terrified, but too weak to make a sound. It's a huge risk, but her only chance of survival is getting her to hospital, before she fades away. I lift her into my arms, taking care to cradle her head, then wade out to the boat. I yell to Eddie at the top of my voice.

'She's alive! Look after her while I steer.'

Molly's chances of survival are better with him in charge. He completed his St John's Ambulance training last month and is already laying her in the recovery position as I spin the boat round. He's covered her with the towels I keep stowed in a box on the prow. I push the engine to top speed, as we head for St Mary's. The local hospital is her best chance, not the air ambulance, which would take too long.

The lifeboat is racing towards us, and we're lucky the sea is still flat calm. When it comes to a halt, Eddie and I lift her on board. I see relief on Liam Quick's face as he thanks us for our work, then Molly is on her way to safety. The lifeboat's wash almost topples my bowrider with a succession of high waves, but I couldn't care less if I get even more drenched. Eddie looks elated too, his smile wider than it's been since his cousin died.

'We got there in time,' he says. 'Thank God, Len would be lost without her.'

I could point out that Molly's not yet out of danger, but our biggest task is to learn who attacked her and why. The killer's MO has escalated since the first attack, with Molly's dress being replaced by the RNLI waterproof suit, like the ones crew wear on a shout, another medal attached to her hand before she was dragged through the waves. I need to understand why someone hates the lifeboat crew with such a passion, but that won't come from drifting on open water. I twist the wheel full circle and head back to St Agnes.

My first job once we're ashore is to phone DCI Madron. His congratulations are muted, but I know he's relieved. The whole community is relying on us to end this violence against the island's bravest members. He tells me that Father Mike has called the station, claiming that Callum Moyle could be involved in the killings. Lawrie Deane will bring Moyle to the station for an interview, to hear his alibi for yesterday after-noon, when Molly was taken. I dislike Callum Moyle on instinct, but would someone really launch a murder campaign simply because they felt excluded by a team they wanted to join?

When Eddie hears the news, he appears to feel the

same. We both know that a double attack in a three-day period means that the killer's vicious. There's every chance they'll strike again if we don't get answers soon.

'Let's get moving, Eddie. Lewis Marling might know something.'

We set off at speed, still energised by finding our crewmate alive. I know where Marling lives, even though I've spent little time in his company. The man's house lies at the edge of Garabeara on the west coast of St Agnes. The area is covered in small fields, edged by crumbling dry stone walls, home to a flock of goats. The islands' native agapanthus is in full bloom at this time of year, growing wild at the edge of the lane we follow through the island's heart. The flowers stand waist high, their heads studded with bell-like blue flowers, but I'm too distracted to admire them. I only know that Marling works as a potter, selling his wares in the gift shops of St Mary's, and further afield.

'Do you know Marling at all, Eddie?'

'No one does,' he replies. 'People are curious, but he prefers his own company. Only Jez got past his front door.'

It's taken us ten minutes to cross the island, my curiosity rising as we follow a shingle path to Marling's property. It's a two-storey version of my own, built from rough-hewn granite, with windows overlooking St Warna's cove. It seems a fitting home for a man with reclusive habits. Legends say that Saint Warna lived as a hermit beside a well nearby, and it's still a place of pilgrimage. Believers say that she purified the waters with her holy spirit, but there's little sign of piety outside Marling's home. All I can see is a tidy garden, with a rose-bed, a greenhouse, and a vegetable patch. No one appears when I press the bell, so I peer through the window into a lounge which contains few creature comforts. There's no TV or computer, just a large sofa, shelves full of books, and a cat sleeping in a patch of sunlight.

'Let's check his workshop, Eddie.'

Someone is singing as we follow the path down the side of the property, and the man I see doesn't fit my image of a hermit. He's singing an Ed Sheeran tune, as he works a lump of clay on his wheel, moulding it with the palms of his hands. It's clear he's enjoying himself. The guy's in his late thirties, like me, dark hair tied back from his face, and he's dressed for the heat. Lewis Marling's bare feet control the treadle, his T-shirt and denim cut-offs caked in clay.

He's so immersed in finishing his pitcher, he doesn't spot us by his door. I wait till the piece is complete before saying his name, but the potter almost jumps out of his skin.

'Jesus, how did you get in here? I didn't hear a sound.'

'Your work would have been spoiled if you had. I'm DI Ben Kitto, and this is Sergeant Eddie Nickell. We'd like a chat, please.'

'Can I move this first, before it sets on the wheel?'

His shock has been replaced by practical concerns; it doesn't take him long to free the pitcher with a length of wire, then place it on a shelf.

When Marling rises to his feet, he's taller than I realised, with a dancer's slim build and fluid movements. He leads us across a garden that's clearly his pride and joy, the grass mown short, his rosebeds full of blossoms in every shade of red. The man's kitchen is just as orderly. It's clear he uses it for business, with cardboard boxes stacked neatly against the wall.

'Go ahead and sit down, if there's room.'

He produces a water jug from his fridge, fills glasses with ice, then joins us at the table. Marling's discomfort only shows when I look closer. His chair is positioned at a distance, like he's surrounded by an invisible forcefield, keeping intruders at bay.

'We're here about Jez Cardew,' I tell him.

'Not misbehaving, is he? I haven't seen him in days.'

'Didn't you hear the news?'

He looks confused. 'About what? Jez normally drops by each week, but I know he's busy, doing up an old house.'

'He told you that, did he?'

'Of course, we've been friends all year.' He takes several long gulps of water, as if his work has left him parched.

'Do you mind me asking how you met?'

'He came here without invitation, curious to learn about pottery.'

'I'm sorry, this is bad news, Lewis. I assumed every-one on the island had heard by now.'

'I don't check my email or go out much when there's a big order to finish.' He's still watching me, eyebrows raised.

'We found Jez's body on Hangman Island.'

Marling's reactions slow to a standstill, his eyes glaz-ing over. 'That can't be right.'

I can't tell if he's listening when I speak again. 'Let's sit in your living room, you'll be more comfortable there. I can see you're shocked.'

Marling moves like a sleepwalker down the hallway. The man's recovering, but his expression's still dazed.

'Are you okay, Lewis?'

He frowns back at me. 'It doesn't make sense.'

'I'm afraid it's true. We think someone attacked him at sea.'

'He was murdered?' Marling's eyes screw shut. 'Christ, that makes it even worse.'

'Tell me about your friendship, please, if you're able to talk.'

He rubs his hands across his face like he's scrub-bing away cobwebs. 'Jez came to my workshop last January. He watched me at the wheel, mesmerised. I sent him away, but he kept on coming back. We swapped life stories over a few weeks. People saw him as this big hero, but that wasn't his choice. It made him uncomfortable.'

'He confided in you?'

'We trusted each other instinctively. There's no point in concealing anything now, is there?'

'None at all.'

'Jez had relationships with women, until he met me. His world view was stuck in the last century. He thought it was unmanly to fall for a guy, but it happened anyway, almost overnight. I was reluctant to get involved because my last relationship was a disaster, but he was hard to resist. He said it was love at first sight.'

My gaze catches on a slip of paper on Marling's coffee table, covered in a hectic scrawl. I don't need a graphologist to see that it's a direct match for the note left on Jez's boat. 'I'm sorry, Lewis. This must be terrible for you.'

A tear spills from the corner of his eye. 'It doesn't seem real.'

'Why did you keep your relationship secret?'

'His choice, not mine. I had to respect his decision. It started with me teaching him pottery, and progressed from there. He was a natural. It's like he was born knowing how to handle clay.'

'I never knew he was creative.'

'Jez had a gift. I taught him free after the first few lessons, because of his talent. I even helped him complete his application form.' Words spill from his mouth. 'He'd won a place at Falmouth School of Art, to study ceramics, starting next month. I even lent him half the fees for his first year. He was skint because his student loan hadn't arrived. He needed to pay for the first term's accommodation in advance.'

'So that's why he owed people money. Even Jez's parents didn't know.'

'He told his grandfather about art school, but not about us. The old bastard banished him from his house.'

'Most people here would have been proud. The islanders are more accepting than you'd think.'

'Denzel accused him of deserting the lifeboat crew. I don't think Jez cared what anyone thought about us falling in love; it was our lives, not theirs. He planned to come out to his parents then go straight to the mainland, and give them time to process it.' Marling finally meets my eye. 'We were drawn to each other, so powerfully. Nothing else mattered.'

'I still don't see why you kept it quiet.'

'Jez felt ashamed about Anna, he couldn't face telling her the truth. He ended their relationship days after we met, even though they'd been in love. He couldn't bring himself to explain, and hurt her all over again. It caused arguments between us. She deserved the truth, but I could never stay angry with him for long. I'd already scheduled my first visit to Falmouth.'

Marling falters as he approaches the mantelpiece, then passes me a figurine of a porpoise, glazed in silver. The creature's body is arched, like it's leaping through waves. It's beautifully made; the clay is so fine its weight barely registers on my palm.

KATE RHODES

'Jez made that for me. I liberated him, he said, from a life that never felt true.'

There's a depth of sorrow in Marling's voice that I've rarely heard. His story about mentoring Jez and falling in love sounds convincing, yet he's still reluctant to meet my eye. That could be down to shyness, or because he's lying through his teeth.

'How did you conceal it in a place this small?'

'He came here at first, but we'd begun meeting at sea. I took my boat out to meet his, then we moored in a quiet bay, away from prying eyes. I left a note for him on Friday night, but he never showed up. He was paranoid about being seen, and sometimes got cold feet.'

'Did you ring him at all?

He nods. 'Just once. I was trying not to pressure him; our relationship was so intense, I thought he needed space.'

'Where do you keep your boat, Lewis?'

'On the beach, behind my house. It's called the *Demelza*. I use a quad bike to drag it down to the water.'

'Can we take a look? We'll need to do a forensic search tomorrow.'

'Go ahead, but can I be alone now, please?' His manner is cooling, now he realises he's a suspect, his skin turning pale.

'You don't look well, Lewis. Do you want me to call someone?'

'I'm better off alone.'

280

'I need your last address on the mainland, please, before we go.'

He hesitates before speaking. 'I hate people digging around in my past. It leaves a trail, for people to follow.'

'How do you mean?'

'I was hounded out of my last place. No one knows I'm here.'

'We'll keep it private, if we can.'

The man's shaking when he rises to his feet. His story will be easy to check. If Jez really did win a place at art school, the admissions department will give us the truth. I can't prove the man's innocence, but he seems an unlikely killer, unless Jez ended the relationship fast, like with Anna. But he's got no clear motive to attack Molly Bligh, and the graphologist's report insisted that the love note and threats to the crew were written by different people.

Marling looks relieved to say goodbye. We leave him with his cat mewing bitterly at his feet, like it hates intruders too. Eddie and I go straight to the beach, where the *Demelza* stands on its trailer. I can tell he's been rocked by the news of Jez's plans for art school, and his relationship with Marling. He looks dumbfounded, but his expression soon clears.

'I knew Jez was changing, he even hinted that I'd be surprised when it all came out. He always wanted to do something creative, but I don't blame him for keeping it quiet. Some of the crew would have joked about him falling for a bloke, wouldn't they?'

'Plenty wouldn't have cared one way or the other.'

'Come on, they'd have laughed at him for weeks. His mum and dad are pretty traditional too. They'd have taken a while to accept it fully.'

I'm still thinking about Jez's secrets when I put on plastic gloves and overshoes to check Marling's cabin cruiser. The keys are in the ignition, like most boats in Scilly. Anyone could have hotwired his quadbike and hauled it down to the sea at night, after he returned from meeting Jez. It's a hundred yards from the potter's home; he wouldn't have heard them set out to hunt for Jez's boat on open water. I bet there are other vessels on St Agnes's beaches that could have been borrowed in exactly the same way.

Eddie seems preoccupied. 'The thing is, boss, Marling could be a psycho. If Jez ended it between them, like with Anna, he'd have one hell of a motive, wouldn't he?'

'Marling's handwriting's different from whoever sent the crew those badges.'

'Maybe the graphologist's got it wrong.'

I'm still considering the idea of Marling as Jez's killer, when my phone vibrates in my pocket. The text sends my spirits plummeting. Molly Bligh is in hospital, but it's touch and go. She's been trying to talk, without success, her condition fragile.

44

I leave Eddie on St Agnes then return to St Mary's with the afternoon sun hot on the back of my neck. Hugh Town is in full holiday mode as I jump off my boat. A queue of day-trippers extends down the quay, ready to climb back on board the *Scillonian* for the return crossing to Penzance, clutching mementoes and take-away coffees.

My size comes in handy when I need to get some-where fast. Most people step back when they see a man of six foot five, built like a rugby full back, barrelling towards them. It works like a charm as I hurry to the police station. I'm due to interview Callum Moyle, but my mind is still processing Lewis Marling's claims. Jez's status as the islands' hero might have been tar-nished in some people's eyes simply because he was gay, in a place that can appear decades behind the times.

Denzel Jory's caustic comments make more sense now. The old man has a sour word to say about most people, but Jez's news about going to art school would have met a brick wall of opposition. Denzel's views hark back to the days when island men all performed hard labour, fishing or farming, and leaving Scilly was viewed as desertion.

Lawrie Deane gives me a baleful look when I arrive, as if Callum Moyle has already tested his patience. One of the island's two practising solicitors has arrived already. Louise Walbert is an experienced middle-aged professional, and her appearance is always eye-catching. She has a penchant for bright colours; today she's wearing a scarlet dress, coupled with a yellow hairband and electric-blue beads, but her expression is sober.

'Callum's not under arrest, Louise, I just need answers to some questions.'

'He's calling it victimisation, claiming you never explained why his house was searched.' She gives me a sympathetic glance. 'Your forensics expert ransacked the place, according to him.'

'Jez was murdered. His home might contain valuable information about why he died, I'm sure he appreciates that. Can we interview him now?'

She gives a brisk nod. 'He may not play ball, but let's hope I'm wrong.'

Callum Moyle's bad mood shows when Deane leads him into the station's interview room, his face a dull red. He glowers at me when I sit opposite him and Joanna, with a metre-wide table separating us. Moyle interrupts before I finish explaining the purpose of our interview.

'It's Sam you should go after, not me.'

'I'm just gathering information, Callum. It's possible someone entered your home to steal Jez's medal, but you could have taken it yourself. Sam's claiming you went through his things, the night Jez went missing. We know it was done systematically, the place stank of bleach. You've also been seen on the water late at night. You could have intercepted Jez's boat, the night he died.'

'Sam loves making up stories. He's a liar, but you know that already. You put him away for three years, didn't you? If anyone's done wrong it's him, not me.'

'We'll find out, don't worry. Evidence always gets left behind.' I glance down at my notes from the case file. 'You pursued Anna Dawlish, but Jez had more luck with women, didn't he? It must have hurt you when they got together.'

'Plenty of things annoy me, but I'm no killer.'

'It's interesting that you're so quick to deny it.' He refuses to meet my eye. 'Did Jez irritate you even more, after your application to join the lifeboat crew was rejected?'

'That was a blessing in disguise. Work's been hectic, and it's not unusual. They turn down plenty of people each year.'

'Why do you think your housemates got selected, but not you?'

'Who cares? It didn't affect me.'

I lean closer, across the table. 'Failure hurts us all, Callum. Did you think joining the crew would help you get a girlfriend?'

'That's a stupid question.'

'Has it been hard making friends here?'

'My social life's irrelevant.'

I lean across the table, deliberately invading his space. 'How long have you been a cocaine user? It starts out fun, doesn't it? Then it spirals out of control.'

'I've never taken it in my life. I could sue you for false accusations.' His hands jitter in his lap.

'You've been picking up drugs late at night, haven't you? I imagine our forensics expert will find evidence in the fibres of your carpet, or on your boat. If tests come back positive I'll have to arrest you. Plenty of users do a bit of dealing on the side, to make ends meet.'

Callum turns to his solicitor. 'He can't say that, can he? I've done nothing wrong.'

'The police can arrest anyone on suspicion of drug dealing, I'm afraid,' she replies.

'Are you familiar with a play called *The Tempest*, Callum?'

He stares at me. 'I've never heard of it in my life.'

'Are you certain? We'll be sending your laptop and phone to the mainland for analysis.'

'That's fucking ridiculous. I need them for work.'

'You'll survive without them for a week. Tell me something, how well do you know Molly Bligh?'

'We chat now and then at the pub, that's all. I knew her at school.'

'Did you ask her out and get knocked back?'

His eyes blink rapidly, giving him away. 'You're barking up the wrong tree. I haven't seen her for weeks.'

Moyle answers my next questions with a curt 'no comment', but he'll remain a person of interest, thanks to his defensiveness. It's possible that he grew to hate Jez for his popularity and developed an obsession with all lifeboat officers. I'm about to release him, even though he's got no alibi for the afternoon Molly Bligh was abducted, claiming that he was working alone after sacking his tenant. Words only spew from his mouth after I call the interview to an end.

'I was crazy to let an ex-con into my house, but I fell for his sob story. Sam's up to his old tricks, so I gave him the push.'

'He's been attending addiction therapy sessions every week, so that's hard to believe. What are you using, Callum? Coke or MDMA?'

'That's ridiculous. How could I run my business with a habit?'

'Plenty manage it fine. We'll need a blood sample before you leave; don't worry it's just a pinprick, but the toxicology tests are pinpoint accurate. It'll take three days at the lab. We'll find out then, even if your last fix was forty-eight hours ago.'

Moyle shoots me another filthy look before leaving the room. I still hope that Sam Austell is innocent, but I may have to eat my words if Liz Gannick's search fails to find conclusive evidence against his old landlord. I'll call at the hospital before speaking to her, to check on Molly Bligh's condition.

Dr Ginny Tremayne is the first person I see in reception. Isla's mother is the hospital's chief medic, with the same unflappable manner as her daughter. She's a plump figure, in a white coat that's a size too small, grey hair pulled back in an untidy ponytail. Ginny seems in a hurry to usher me down the corridor to her consulting room.

'There's no point in sitting by Molly's bedside today, Ben.'

'How's she doing?'

'She's very weak, which isn't surprising. Molly was tied to a boat and hauled through the water. The pressure fractured her left wrist, but you could say she was lucky. The twine snapped, and she swam for her life.'

'Did she tell you all this?'

The medic nods rapidly. 'She was delirious, until her blood oxygen levels plummeted. That's typical with secondary drowning.'

'Remind me what that means, please, Ginny.'

'It's when a casualty inhales too much seawater. Without oxygen, their lungs can collapse. It's a miracle you found her alive.' She glances down at her clipboard.

'What did Molly say exactly, before she passed out?'

'She swam for hours. I'm giving her high-pressure oxygen now, and a glucose drip to give her strength, but she's struggling.'

'What are her chances?'

'Molly's a fighter, which increases the odds.' The medic hesitates before she replies. 'If she can survive tonight, things will improve.'

'Where's Len?'

'At her bedside. Paul Keast's supporting them both. I know you want answers, but promise me not to bother her, until she recovers.' She peers at me over her clipboard.

'None of us will.'

The medic suddenly looks exhausted. 'Who would do that to a girl like Molly? I've seen how she and Len care for their horses; they live for those animals.'

'We'll find out what happened, I promise.'

'You look tired, Ben, I can tell you're worried. Do you want to see Molly just for a minute, when I check on her again?'

'That might help, thanks.'

'Give me a minute to check on my other patients.'

Ginny bustles away, leaving me in her consulting room, which hasn't changed much since my mother brought me here as a kid for a tetanus jab. Her pin board is still covered in thank you cards, the air smelling of Savlon and kindness. I steal one of the boiled sweets she uses as rewards for her youngest patients, still trying to piece together why Jez and Molly were targeted. I can see plenty of reasons why Callum Moyle would attack his housemate, and I'm willing to bet Molly turned him down, just like Anna.

I'm still churning through possibilities when I follow

Ginny down the hospital corridor, to Molly's room. Len is sitting at his sister's bedside, with arms folded tight across his chest. His sister's face is hidden by her oxygen mask. She's hooked to monitors, which make the scene look like an episode of *Casualty*. Numbers flash as oxygen wheezes from the machine in slow gasps, and my feet have frozen to the spot. I want to stay here, in case the monster who dragged my crewmate through the water returns, even though she's in safe hands.

I bump into Paul Keast on my way out. I'm amazed he's taken time away from his farm to support the Blighs, but my old school friend is full of surprises. He doesn't seem the kind to join a committee, yet he's been instrumental in planning the lifeboat festival. He's clutching a bag from the Island Deli. I bet it's food for Len, so he can stay at his sister's bedside.

'I brought Molly here, from the lifeboat,' he says. 'None of this makes sense. What the fuck's going on?'

'Someone's targeting the crew; half of us have been sent RNLI badges and threatening notes. I just need to know why.'

'Did you hear about Jez and Molly going out together in their teens?'

'Len mentioned it.'

'It was pretty intense, I think, even though they were kids.'

'They're the same personality type, aren't they? Strong-minded, brave, and keen to help others.'

Suddenly I remember Anna Dawlish, unable to forgive Jez for walking away, while her good friend Molly still met him regularly. When I study Paul again, his anxiety shows. 'What else is bothering you?'

'It's not about Molly. She's tough, I know she'll pull through.'

'What then?'

'She told me someone followed her home from the pub, about a week ago. I didn't take it seriously enough. She left the Atlantic after Len, and heard footsteps as she was heading for Old Town Bay, but when she looked back, no one was there.' His frown deepens. 'Some bastard could have been watching her for days.'

'Don't torture yourself, Paul. It's not your fault.' I study his face again. 'Is it serious between you and Anna?'

'I've liked her for ages. I'm lucky she noticed me.'

'How do you mean?'

'Shyness often trips me up, but she saw past it.'

'Didn't her attitude to Jez bother you?'

'I knew she'd get over it, if I treat her right.'

I give a brisk nod. 'Thanks for looking after Molly and Len. Text me updates, okay?'

He straightens his back, like a weight's been lifted from his shoulders, then hurries inside the hospital. The expression on Paul's face concerns me. I can tell he's fallen for Anna, hook, line and sinker. I'm certain he'd do anything she asked, including giving her a fake alibi.

I'd like to stick around until Molly Bligh can face questions, but the sun is already dropping, and Ginny Tremayne is waving me goodbye with a shooing motion, like she's banishing a stray cat. The islands are awash with gold when I head back to the harbour, yet the landscape's beauty feels like a pointless distraction. I need to dig under its surface, to expose the human ugliness it hides.

45

Dusk is settling over St Agnes when Sam moors Father Michael's boat by the quay. He's grateful for the loan, but the old speedboat is on its last legs. The engine coughed and spluttered all the way, and his ride home could be perilous. He leaves the key in the ignition, then climbs the slope to the Turk's Head. The place looks empty, but when he peers through the window, the landlady is sitting alone, head bowed. She looks heartbroken. He's got questions to ask, because he knows Jez liked her and senses she might help, even though few people trust him. But she might clam up completely if she feels vulnerable alone with him. It's best to find Sharon Cosgrove first, then return after more punters have arrived.

He hurries uphill towards Middle Town, past the old light-house he loved as a boy. Its tall form still dominates the landscape, as it did three hundred years ago, but it's failed to safeguard the community this time. Someone murdered Jez without anyone noticing, and now Molly Bligh's fighting for her life.

Sam knows the killer might be watching him as well. He pulls in a long breath to calm himself. It's his duty to find out why Jez died. His friend trusted Sharon Cosgrove, and his own life is on hold until his name is cleared.

The post office is empty of customers. Sharon is sweeping the floor, her expression startled when she catches sight of him. She puts the broom down immediately, then retreats behind the counter.

'We're shut,' she says. 'I was just closing.'

'I need a quick word, please, about Jez.'

She shakes her head. 'You shouldn't be sniffing around. People here don't like busybodies.'

'Jez mentioned your name a few times. He really enjoyed talking to you.'

'Why are you hassling me?'

'I won't tell anyone, I promise. Please just help me understand.'

'We were acquaintances, that's all. I studied art in Edinburgh. He was interested in that, not me.' Her hands rise to cover her face, her voice suddenly high and child-like. 'Leave, now, please. I hate talking about it.'

'I only want the facts, Sharon. Don't you care about Jez dying?'

'Of course, but talking won't bring him back. It just puts me in danger. Leave now, please,' she says, pointing at the door.

Sam's frustration curdles in his stomach. It's grown dark while he was inside, cooler air greeting him as the door shuts. He pulls his torch from his pocket, but footsteps are approaching, so he leaves it unlit and ducks behind some bushes. Damian Cosgrove marches past, scowling. Sam can't understand why Sharon's husband appears on edge. He'll have to stay on the island until all Jez's secrets are exposed.

46

I'm back on St Agnes with Eddie as the late-summer dark thickens. We're reviewing evidence in the pub's old snooker room. The killer seems obsessed with his victims' status as members of the lifeboat crew, but that could disguise a more personal obsession. I still don't fully understand why bravery medals are being left on their bodies, unless the murderer is taunting us. The quotes from *The Tempest* still nag at me. Maybe the killer feels like Prospero, ruling a magical island, but exiled from the life he desires.

Eddie appears frustrated, his hand tapping out a rapid tattoo as he skims through witness reports. The case has grown more complex now that Jez Cardew's secret has been exposed. He appeared so easy-going, yet there was more to him than anyone realised. He hid his feelings for Lewis Marling from everyone, and it takes commitment to master a challenging new skill. He had enough guts to contemplate leaving his old life behind.

'Could Jez and Molly's friendship have caused all this?' Eddie asks.

'I think it's their status that bothers the killer, not their relationship. Why do all that elaborate staging with the medals unless they mean something? We know the killer has access to a boat, powerful enough to drag someone through the water, and they posted RNLI badges to crew members, including both victims. You and I are on his list, like Isla, Sam Austell, and the Quicks. We all have to watch our backs.'

'You're certain the killer's planning more attacks?'

'Maybe he chose the lifeboat festival to make a statement, starting with our biggest heroes. No one else on the crew has received a medal. It could make us less vulnerable.'

'Thank God Molly survived.' My deputy looks so worn down, I keep the severity of her condition to myself.

'Should I be worried about you, Eddie?'

'No, boss. I may look like crap, but I'm okay.'

'Let's run through our suspects then. You go first.'

'Sam Austell's my first choice, then Callum and Anna,' he says, flicking through his papers again. 'Jez was steady till Sam came back. Then he turned secretive, and started messing people around.'

'Or maybe Jez was twitchy about revealing his first relationship with a man. I keep telling you, Sam's not the killer. He got a lift back to St Mary's hours before Jez was seen sailing west from here.'

'You've got a blind spot about him,' Eddie says, his voice a flat monotone. 'He could have borrowed another boat and sailed straight back here. Sam's screwed up, isn't he? His dad abandoned him, his mum's a witch, and drugs have fried his brain. If he was pissed off with Jez, he'd want to get even.'

'Come on, Eddie. Rose looked after him well as a kid. They were poor, but she did her best. Sam went off the rails like plenty of teenagers, and he's paid the price. Anna Dawlish was treated badly. She had a right to pursue Jez for answers. I suppose she could have borrowed Janet Fearnley's boat that night. I just can't see her boarding Jez's boat straight after he left Lewis Marling, then whacking him with a crowbar before drowning him.'

'No one wants to think their high school sweetheart's capable of murder. She's agreed to come to the station for an interview tomorrow, by the way.'

'She'd never attack Molly. They've been mates for years.'

'Maybe Anna couldn't forgive her for staying close to Jez. Paul could have helped her too. It sounds like he's putty in her hands.'

Instinct tells me that a man I've known all my life would never play a part in a gruesome murder. I'm so frustrated by blind corners, I feel like diving into the sea to cool off, but time's against us.

'Did you find out why Lewis Marling didn't want us checking out his past, Eddie?'

'He ended up in Plymouth hospital after his last relationship finished, with broken ribs,' Eddie says, grimacing. 'There's a twist unfortunately. His boyfriend was a married copper, trying to keep things quiet.'

'Jesus, Marling must be wary of all police by now, but he did a good job of covering it. We can't rule him out either. Anyone would resent having to conceal a perfectly legitimate relationship. Maybe Jez crossed some invisible line and he went ballistic.'

'The guy's solitary. I bet he's never even met Molly Bligh.' Eddie throws up his hands. 'We're going round in circles.'

'Liz should have news on the forensics front today, that'll help. Did you have any luck with who could have stolen Denzel Jory's medal?'

'The field's too wide. No one likes the old bastard, but half the island visits him, out of duty.' My deputy's head is hanging so low, it's almost resting on the table.

'Go home, Eddie, that's an order. Tomorrow we'll interview Sam Austell again, I promise.'

He manages a smile before leaving, but it only lasts a micro-second. Grief for his cousin, mixed with frustration, seems to be wearing him down, and only finding the killer will cure it.

My legs ache from sitting down too long, and I can't stay here doing nothing while the killer lines up their next target. More boats have sailed here while we've been inside. I can see a few converted fishing smacks and an old cabin cruiser from the window. The owners will be in the bar downstairs, having a quiet drink, while I trawl through a quagmire of information. I'm surprised to see Father Mike's cruiser, the *Disciple*, moored by the quay. The priest normally only uses it for daytime visits to the sick and elderly.

It's 9 p.m. when I sail home to Bryher. I'm only half-way across the island when I hear Shadow barking at top volume, like when he chases seagulls. I can tell he's overexcited when he appears on the path ahead. His frantic barking continues, leaving me mystified. He's normally overjoyed to see me, but not tonight. He keeps trying to make me retrace my steps. When I push past, he bares his teeth and snarls.

'What's wrong, Shadow? Have you found something?'

He releases another fierce growl, but finally lets me pass. He falls silent as I drop down the path to Hell Bay, where the tide is rushing inland. Maybe he's just complaining that I've been away too long.

I pause to listen to the shirring sound of pebbles being dragged ashore. The noise always calmed me as a boy; it meant that nothing had to change. The waves carry stones inland, but they're always replaced by the next tide. I take a few deep breaths, and my spirits lift when I check my phone. Paul Keast has texted me about Molly Bligh: she's recovering, and fully conscious again. The killer will be furious. There's a chance he'll act even quicker, now that his second victim has escaped his grasp.

I don't call out when I get indoors, aware that Noah

must be asleep. It bothers me that Nina's left the front door unlocked, despite my warning to keep the house secure. There's a smile on her face when she emerges from the spare bedroom.

'Don't look in there, Ben. You can't see the dress before the wedding, it's bad luck.'

'I didn't know you were superstitious.'

'My Italian grandparents filled my head with notions about fate and destiny, but humour me, okay?'

'I promise not to go in there.'

'Give me a minute, I'll just check on Noah.'

The pressure of her footsteps on the floorboards makes the door swing open as she hurries away. I try to keep my gaze averted, but catch sight of a column of ivory lace hanging from the wardrobe door before I can shut my eyes.

Shadow growls in disgust, then retreats to his basket. I close the door fast, but it's too late. If bad luck exists, I've just welcomed it into our lives with open arms.

47

Sam spends his evening exploring every corner of St Agnes. Only the centre is inhabited, the north and south undisturbed. The place looks ghostly when he skirts round Porth Killier. Vertical slabs of rock on the beach look like sculptures in the darkness. When he scans the bay with his torch, a trick of the light seems to bring a horde of men marching closer, a platoon made from stone, intent on crushing him. He's glad that Danielle's not with him this time. If he finds the killer, she'd be in danger too.

Panic speeds up his pace as he returns to the pub. Holidaymakers sit outdoors, enjoying the evening's warmth and planning tomorrow's excursions, oblivious to Sam's presence. He'd like to know why the landlady looked so broken-hearted earlier. She's close-lipped when he buys a drink, reluctant to talk. Surely someone in Jez's favourite pub must have the answer to his drowning?

He waits ten minutes before slipping down the corridor to the fire exit, then stands in the shadows, observing the landlord. He climbs the stairs, then Sam hears him rattling

the door of the room the police are using for their investigation. When he reappears, Sam glimpses frustration on his
face. Debbie is still sitting behind the bar, only rising to serve
guests. The couple barely speak before swapping places, and
she retreats to the kitchen.

It's late when Sam goes outside to call Danielle. He's relieved
to hear that Molly is recovering. They agree to meet early
tomorrow morning, because her shift starts at 10 a.m. He tells
her about Sharon Cosgrove's odd reaction to his questions,
and she congratulates him on leaving Callum's house, to find
somewhere better. When they say goodnight, she sounds eager
to see him again, and his confidence soars. If she sticks by him,
he can achieve any goal.

He retraces his footsteps, following the path down to the
Cosgroves' house. It's in such an isolated spot the couple have
left their curtains open. They're in their living room, and raised
voices greet him. Damian is red-faced with veins standing out
on his neck.

'Blokes have been visiting while I'm on the mainland,
Sharon. The neighbours told me. How come you kept it secret?'

'Only Jez Cardew, asking me about art school.'

'Why did he care? It was a joke, wasting your time doodling.
You could have been earning a living.'

'I loved every minute.'

'People saw him here, half a dozen times.'

'Three at most. He was friendly, that's all.'

'How come he waited till I was away?'

'Because you hate sharing me. Nothing happened between
us, Damian, I promise.'

'Tell the truth for fuck's sake, you lying bitch.'

Cosgrove lands a slap on her face that sends her reeling. Sam drags in a breath. Instinct tells him to bang on the door to put an end to it, but Cosgrove slams out of the property before he can act, leaving his wife alone.

She appears rooted to the spot, her hand nursing her cheek, pale but calm, like the routine is familiar. Sam is considering ways to help when there's an odd scraping sound. Suddenly he's shoved forward, too fast to defend himself. His head hits a rock, leaving his vision blurred. He yells out, but the darkness muffles his voice. It's so thick and impenetrable, he can no longer see the stars.

PART 3

48

Liz Gannick calls me at 11 p.m. Callum Moyle's house has given her little new information. I listen in silence, trying not to wake Noah, then step outside with Shadow at my heels.

'Slow down, Liz, I missed your last sentence.'

'The place is squeaky clean. You were right about the bleach, I found washing up liquid too.'

'How about connections with the RNLI?'

'An envelope full of badges in Jez's room, but no note or medals anywhere. Those guys loves junk food. I've never seen so many Pot Noodles in one kitchen. The only useful thing is a ball of steel twine sheathed in plastic. If it matches the one round Cardew's wrist, and Molly's, we're in business. I've taken clothing samples to check them against the clay dust on the boat too.'

'No need. I found out Cardew had been visiting a pottery studio regularly.'

'One more thing, Ben. There were a few grains of cocaine in Callum's room, on a pillow.'

'How did you find something that small?'

'They call me *numero uno* for a reason, and I've got an excellent magnifier.'

'Thanks for your work, Liz. Let's meet tomorrow morning.'

I shove my phone back into my pocket, but there's no point going back indoors when I'm too wired to sleep.

At least Liz's search has given me a reason to question Callum Moyle again. His brittle confidence will crack apart if I can find conclusive proof he was involved in the attacks. I walk towards the sea, hoping the waves will work their magic, their slow murmur a natural lullaby. Shadow is on the beach, standing in a shaft of moonlight that makes his eyes gleam. He's straight-backed, his stare challenging, like he's the rightful leader of a pack of wolves.

'Come indoors,' I tell him, but he doesn't move an inch.

I'm about to grab his collar and haul him inside when my phone suddenly vibrates in my pocket. Texts often arrive late, due to the island's patchy signal. The first is another message from Paul Keast, saying that Molly's still holding her own, her blood oxygen level is slowly rising.

It's only when I read the second text that the truth emerges. Ginny Tremayne reports that Molly took a sudden downturn after Paul left. She died half an hour ago, with her brother Len at her side. The misery and shock of it makes me feel sick.

I want to chuck my phone into the ocean, but end up shouting curses at the sky instead. There's no way I can go home and climb into bed with the worst possible news swilling around in my gut. I remember Molly's quiet bravery on the lifeboat, and her gentleness towards the horses she rescued. Auto-pilot kicks in as I tiptoe indoors to collect the items I always carry: a small but powerful LED torch, and the Swiss army knife my father gave me when I turned twelve. I keep it more as a talisman than a tool, its weight reassuring in my pocket.

Shadow is waiting for me outside, as if he's known all along that going home wasn't an option. He's eager to tag along, as usual, and I know from experience that attempting to lock him away only fuels his determination to follow. There's no obvious place to go, but instinct leads me to the quay. Jez Cardew and Molly Bligh were both seen for the last time on St Agnes, and I can't stop looking. The killer may still be out there, feeling triumphant, with the next crew member in his sights.

I'm running on adrenaline as my boat's engine starts, the sound sluggish. Shadow is poised at my side, scenting adventure as we pull away. It's midnight, but the light is still on in Ray's living room above the yard. I bet he's fallen asleep watching Clint Eastwood stride across a parched landscape. I wish the islands' moral universe was as clear-cut as the old westerns Ray loves. The hero always defends the innocent, then kills the villain with no reprisals, before the inevitable happy ending. Today's picture is much too complicated for my liking.

The sea is a hard metallic white, lit up by the moon, the ultimate hostile environment. It should be a calming sight, but the news about Molly has put me beyond comfort. I'm close to St Agnes when I cut the engine to listen to the night's sounds. If someone else has been taken, they'll be in trouble already. The killer works fast, dragging his victims behind his boat until they drown, or manage to get free. My ears strain for the roar of another vessel's engine, but there's only Shadow's low whine. It sounds like he's complaining about my slow progress.

St Agnes lies in darkness as I sail closer, its shadowy outline filling the horizon. The island has a history of hiding secrets in its minute bays, where smugglers once stowed their contraband. I'm still on edge when I moor up on the quay.

I've never seen the place so quiet; the lights are out in the pub, and there are few boats, except a handful of dinghies. When I catch sight of Father Michael's boat still moored here, I feel almost certain it's happened again. Shadow chases ahead of me up the quay, like he knows exactly where the killer's hiding. He releases a shrill howl then vanishes into the night.

49

Sam is a child again now the lights are out. The past bubbles to the surface, diluting the terrors of the present. He's back in the cabin where he was born. The atmosphere is peaceful, until he hears his mother crying, the wailing sound setting his teeth on edge. When the door slams, he knows his father will never come back. He's threatened to leave many times, for reasons Sam can't understand. He complains about the lack of food on the table and money in the bank, but how could anyone bear to live in another place? Sam misses the islands whenever his mother takes him to the mainland. He counts the days before he can return to the wide-open skies and go beachcombing for shells lined with mother-of-pearl, or treasures washed ashore from old shipwrecks.

Suddenly he jolts awake. He's being dragged over rough ground by his ankles, too weak to open his eyes or yell for help. There's pain in his shoulders as his body bumps over stones, but he can't make a sound. He's just an object now, to haul from one place to the next.

311

'Where are you taking me?' His words are no more than a whisper.

There's no reply. Whoever is controlling his destiny seems to be having fun; he hears someone humming an old sea shanty. The sound soon fades. He's back in the cabin on Bryher, where the scent of his mother's herbs fills the air. Peace has returned, now his father's gone. Maybe it's the smell of dried lavender and camomile that keeps sending him to sleep? He's unconscious as the sea's waves hiss in his ears. Pictures appear then dissolve again, his thoughts too blurred to make sense.

50

Thursday 31 August

It's after midnight when I call Father Michael to check he's safe. The priest sounds startled at first, then angry that his boat is still in St Agnes harbour.

'Sam promised to bring it back hours ago.'

'Why did you lend him your boat, Father?'

'He asked me for help. Sam needs people to trust him again.'

'I'm sure he's desperate to find out why Jez died, but searching for the killer alone just puts him in danger.'

'Sam wouldn't take stupid risks. He's found a girl he likes, and seems over the moon about it. If he's missing, it's because he's in danger.'

'Call me, the minute he contacts you, please.'

My thoughts are spinning when I put down the phone. I can't prove whether Eddie is right, after all. Sam Austell could be a victim, or the killer, but instinct tells me he's innocent. The more time passes without contact, the greater chance he's been taken. I consider ringing Eddie, but I've never seen him more exhausted. If I summon him over from Tresco, he could do more harm than good. I need someone who knows the local waters and keeps a cool head. The choice is obvious. Liam Quick sounds groggy when he answers his phone, like he's been roused from his first decent sleep since Jez Cardew died. There's misery in his voice when he hears of Molly's death.

'Paul Keast said she was doing okay. I was sure she'd pull through.'

'I'm sorry, Liam. It was secondary drowning, and now Sam Austell's missing too. He should have been back on St Mary's hours ago.'

'Christ, is there no end to it?'

'I need your help, Liam. No one knows the waters like you.'

'I'm on my way. Want me to bring some crew members with me?'

'No need, just get here fast.'

When the call ends my spirits revive. Liam Quick has wanted vengeance for Jez Cardew's death since finding his body, and losing Molly Bligh will have fuelled his anger. Quick brings a hundred per cent focus to everything he does. He's my best chance of finding the killer, but it will take him thirty minutes to arrive, and I can't stand idle. The killer may already have carried Sam Austell out to sea, but I have to check inland to see who's on the move.

I stare up at the Turk's Head as I pass. All the lights are out; the pub's guests and staff must be asleep, but Tommy's open-decked boat is missing from the harbour. When I hurry inland the old lighthouse rises above me like a ghost. Then I spot a light, coming from the Cosgrove's cottage, in Perigilis. Shadow has reached the property before me. The creature has a knack of sensing where I'm going before I've made up my mind. I should be grateful for his canine sixth sense, which has kept us both out of danger in the past. My dog stares at me like I'm the slowest pupil in class. He stands at my feet, pretending to be docile as I tap on the front door, expecting to be confronted by Gareth Cosgrove. A minute passes before the door opens by a fraction.

'Let me in, please, Sharon. We need to talk.'

'Go away. You'll only get me in trouble.'

'I can't just leave without answers, I'm afraid.'

Sharon looks different from the fierce young woman I met before. Her face is blotchy with tears, her pale blue pyjamas making her look small and child-like. Suddenly the door flings open, and she launches herself at me, her face burrowing into my shoulder. This is Eddie's territory, not mine, but I put my arm round her and wait for her sobbing to end. When she finally pulls back, there's embarrassment on her face.

'I want to help, but you have to tell me what's wrong.'

When I lead her through to the kitchen, the flood-gates open. She explains that Gareth didn't seem like the jealous type at first. He'd fly out to work on the rig, then they'd spend weekends together on Orkney. The separations seemed romantic at first. His paranoia only began after they moved down to St Agnes to the house where he grew up. Now he criticises everything, from the company she keeps to the clothes she wears.

'Has Gareth ever hit you?'

'He's not like that,' she replies, her voice a fraction too loud.

'Until tonight?'

She hesitates. 'He accused me of sleeping with Jez, but that's not true. I was unhappy, that's all. I missed my friends from art school. Gareth persuaded me to abandon my studies; he made it sound like a big adventure, getting married and moving eight hundred miles away from home.'

'But his temper's worse?'

'He's convinced the baby's not his.' A flash of guilt crosses her face, then vanishes.

'It must be lonely for you here, when Gareth's away.'

Her face crumples. 'I never meant to hurt anyone. I was weak, and he was kind.'

'Who do you mean? I know it wasn't Jez.'

'I can't expose him.'

'That's up to you. Just tell me if Gareth's been behaving strangely.'

'He's out of reach. We used to take late night walks in Orkney. Gareth said it cleared his head, taking a final stroll round the island before bed, but it's different now. He goes out alone, and his anger's fiercer than ever.'

'About the rumours?'

'He says I've brought shame on him.'

I take a stab in the dark, thinking of the island's other troubled souls. 'Has he worked out you slept with Tommy Brookes?'

Her eyes widen. 'Who told you?'

'You confided in Jez about it being Tommy's child, didn't you? You saw him as a friend, and he liked you too. He was angry that Tommy took advantage of you, before you'd put down roots here. Jez confronted him, the night he died. He called Tommy a liar and a fake.'

'It was all my fault.' She's crying again, but this time her tears are silent. 'Our generator broke down, back in February, while Gareth was away. I went to the pub for help. Tommy came round after closing time. He was so kind, helping me late at night...' Her voice falls silent for a moment. 'I told him about Gareth being so possessive. We had a glass of wine, and he's such a good listener. It only happened that one time.'

'How's Gareth acted since?'

'He's sensed something's wrong. Sometimes I don't feel safe here.'

'I can't leave you and your baby at risk, so let's get you to a neighbour's house. Stay there tonight, and you can make proper plans in the morning.'

She looks afraid. 'Don't tell Gareth about Tommy, please. He'll hurt him, I know he will.'

'It sounds like your husband's behaviour's the biggest problem. We call it coercive control. You could prosecute him for it, and the attack. Where do you think he's gone?'

'He just roams around the island by himself.'

'You don't own a boat, do you?'

'Just a small launch we keep by the slipway, on Blanket Bay.'

'We'll sort all this, don't worry, Sharon. Go upstairs now and pack an overnight bag, please.'

I want to find out more about Gareth Cosgrove's late night trips, but his wife is so fragile, we'll have to move at her pace. She seems as delicate as one of Jez Cardew's figurines, easy to shatter with a harsh word. I watch Shadow guiding her upstairs to pack, aware that I've secured one islander's safety, but the killer is still out of reach. Sam Austell may already have drowned.

51

Sam feels less pain when he comes round again, with the sea murmuring in his ear. The ache in his shoulders has faded. Panic only sets in when he tries to move. It feels like he's hunched inside a box, which smells of brine and fish guts. There's a gag tied around his jaw; the material tastes of bleach and his lips are smeared with petrol. He tries to call out, but no sound emerges except a hiss of air.

When he moves his hands, the pain comes back. His wrists are bound together so tightly, even small movements burn his skin. His mind spins back to the past, protecting itself from present danger. He sees himself on his first day at school, a thin, dark-haired boy, five years old. He's dressed in hand-me-downs his mother found at a jumble sale. Some of the lads laugh at his shabby clothes, but Jez stood up for him. He told them to shut up, or he'd knock them flat. Jez was always braver than the rest. Sam was grateful for a powerful ally that day, and on all the days that followed.

He shifts and turns, unable to move more than a few inches. The space is as hot and airless as his prison cell. Next, he sees Danielle. She wore her hair long at school, in a ponytail or braid. She was a year younger than him, their paths only crossing in the playground, where she was always surrounded by friends. Their worlds were so far apart, but now she trusts him. He must get home safe for her sake.

His eyes jerk open again, hunting for light in the darkness. He's determined to stay alive. The boat's powerful motor makes his body shake, and instinct tells him the vessel is heading west. But why him? Jez and Molly were heroes, while he's an ex-con, with nothing to brag about. He clenches his teeth against the gag, fully alert at last, as the boat powers through the calm water.

52

Sharon Cosgrove's neighbours are a retired couple who used to run the Co-op on St Mary's. They appear at the door wearing their dressing gowns and slippers, bleary-eyed with sleep. They look mystified to hear that Sharon needs a bed for the night and protection from her husband. Luckily they usher her indoors immediately, with expressions of sympathy. That's how life works in Scilly. No one lasts long on a small island unless they're prepared to help a neighbour in trouble.

I almost manage to persuade Shadow to stay behind with Sharon, but he changes his mind at the last minute, bolting after me. He's still in an excitable mood, racing down the path at breakneck speed. I'd like to go straight to Blanket Bay to search for Damian Cosgrove, but Liam will arrive in the main harbour soon, so I retrace my steps to the Turk's Head. There's a faint light from inside the bar, and even though it's late, the door is unlocked. The place is so poorly lit, the bar appears empty, until I see Tommy Brookes hunched over a tumbler of whisky. The bottle at his elbow is half empty. His sorrows should have drowned long ago.

'Welcome, my friend. The bar's shut, but who cares?' His voice is slurred. 'Want to try this excellent single malt?'

'I'll pass, thanks. How come you're drinking alone?'

'Long story. I'm the villain, not the hero.'

'Why is your yacht missing in the middle of the night?'

He ignores my question, his eyes unfocused. 'Me and Debbie loved this place at first. Now it's a bloody millstone round our necks.'

I glance out of the window, but there's still no sign of Liam. I settle on a bar stool opposite Tommy, while he pours himself another shot. 'Sharon Cosgrove just told me about your one-night stand.'

His eyes screw shut. 'I knew it would come out, sooner or later.'

'Is that why you and Jez argued?'

He stares at the bar's scuffed surface. 'Sharon told him about it. He was close to my wife too, so he may have hinted at it over a beer. I don't even know if Sharon's baby is Damian's or mine.'

'Where's Debbie?'

'Upstairs, in our flat.'

'Are you sure?'

Tommy gives a slow nod. 'I've screwed up our marriage, and she's too sick to care. I caught her checking my phone the day Jez went missing. She must have her suspicions.'

'Damian Cosgrove thinks Sharon slept with Jez, not you.'

Brookes raises his head at last, his eyes bloodshot with booze. 'This mess is all my doing. You should lock me away.'

'Self-pity won't help us, Tommy. Sam Austell sailed here, but now he's missing, and so's your yacht. Did you see it leave the slipway?'

'He can't have taken it. We only have one key.'

'Check if Debbie's upstairs for me, please.'

He stumbles away. When he returns, his bleak expression tells me his wife's missing.

'Call her, straight away. If she went out the back way and took your boat, she's in real danger.'

Tommy blinks at me, still in a stupor, but at least he follows my instruction. When his wife's phone rings at top volume we both spot it, lying on the counter behind the bar.

'Why's it here? She always takes it with her,' he mutters.

'What's Debbie been doing today?'

'A mate came over. She took the night off, they had dinner in the flat.'

'Who's the friend?'

'Anna Dawlish. They've been close for years.'

The picture suddenly makes sense. If Debbie knows about Tommy's infidelity, she could be nursing the same fury Anna felt towards Jez, both women bitter about painful betrayals. They may have united around

323

a common cause, but their logic's skewed. I can see why Anna would target Jez, but not Molly Bligh, unless she's mad enough to see her friendship with him as a betrayal.

Boat lights glint in the distance. Liam Quick is arriving at last, but it does nothing to temper my fear for Sam.

'Wait here, Tommy. Call me if she comes back, and stop drinking, for God's sake. I need you sober.'

Shadow releases a loud bark of agreement. He always senses when I'm angry with someone, so it's lucky Tommy Brookes is safe behind his bar, or my dog would be snapping at his heels.

53

Sam feels the boat slowing down. The sea's rocking motion increases as the vessel heaves against its anchor, and it's lucky he doesn't suffer from seasickness. He keeps panic at bay by trying to escape. His ankles are bound together, but he can still rock his body weight against the door at his side. He's so full of pent-up energy, surely the catch will give if he keeps on pushing?

He stops to catch his breath. A thread of light needles through a gap in the door, but when he presses his face to the crack he sees nothing at first. Suddenly he spots a flash of colour. A shoe lies on the floor of the hold; it's one of Jez's favourite sky-blue trainers. He wore them on the last day they spent together. Sam teased him about paying a fortune for them online. It proves that Jez was held here too. Sam catches a glimpse through the porthole of the dark ocean beyond, with no land in sight.

'Why the fuck are you doing this?' Sam's words are smothered by his gag.

His energy returns in a burst, fuelled by anger and fear.

It doesn't matter who shoved him into this airless cupboard. He's not prepared to drown, like Jez. Sam's hip thuds against the door, using all his strength, but the lock still won't budge.

54

I leave Tommy Brookes nursing his misery. I can't guess whether he picked a vulnerable newcomer as his conquest because she was an easy mark, or he fancied her too much to resist. Reasons are irrelevant now. I'm a hundred per cent focused on finding his wife and Sam Austell.

I stand on the pub's terrace, scanning the water for lights, with no definite proof of the killer's identity. Anna and Debbie could be together on the Brookes' boat, yet the idea of them as killers seems far-fetched. Hating your partner for cheating is far more likely to provoke violence in a man.

My heart's beating too fast as I march down the slipway, but Shadow's enjoying the adventure. He bounds onto Liam Quick's boat and gives him a boisterous greeting, almost knocking him over, his barking high and loud. Liam's boat is typical of the islands. There are dozens of twin-engine cruisers like it in Scilly, well designed for island hopping.

'Get back here, Shadow. Stay on dry land,' I call out.

'Let him come,' Quick says. 'He might even help us.'

The reason for the cox's nickname, Hawkeye, is obvious when his gaze locks onto mine; he scarcely blinks when I share details of Sam's disappearance and Debbie Brookes going missing on her boat. The only sign of anxiety is that tell-tale muscle ticking in his jaw when we leave harbour.

I scan the water again, as wind furrows its surface. The air feels warm, but the Atlantic is unpredictable, even in summer. Choppy waves splash over the bow as we set off. Shadow howls even louder as we leave the island's protection, clearly thrilled by our new voyage. I'd feel better if we had a clear destination, but the Atlantic never looked bigger. It unrolls in every direction, an infinite skein of black silk, rippled by the breeze.

'Which way first?' Quick asks.

'They've probably gone west, to avoid being seen.'

He swings the wheel hard to starboard. 'What are we chasing?'

'The *Seal Watcher*, it's the Brookes' motor yacht.'

'It's slow in the water, we'll soon catch up.' He reaches inside his oilskin to hand me some binoculars. 'Scan for lights as we sail, can you?'

I'd rather steer because Quick's vision is more acute, but he's focused on piloting his boat at top speed. I keep my eyes on the water when I call Sam again. There's still no reply, but his fate is in safe hands if he's with Liam. The cox's knowledge of local waters is even better than Ray's. He glances at his GPS monitor occasionally, following coordinates internalised over the years. Shadow seems peaceful for the first time in days, curled up under a bench, despite the engine's scream.

We've been sailing for ten minutes before Quick asks for more information about the missing crewman.

'Sam's not answering his phone,' I reply. 'Anna Dawlish, Damian Cosgrove and Debbie Brookes could all be on that boat.'

'You think one of them's the killer?'

'It might be a duo.'

'That's hard to believe.'

'Killers often go unnoticed for years. Have any of them got reason to attack the lifeboat crew?'

'Anna hated Jez for dumping her.' Quick looks thoughtful. 'But that's no reason, unless it was one rejection too many. She wouldn't lay a finger on Molly.'

'Have you spoken to Anna recently?'

'We had a brief chat last week. She asked me about joining the lifeboat crew, but I give all single parents the same advice. Two thousand people drown in British waters every year. You remember the Penlee disaster, don't you?'

'When lifeboatmen died?'

'They lost the whole crew.' He keeps his gaze on the water ahead. 'What would happen to Kylie if Anna drowned?'

'You were a single dad, after your divorce. How come you ignored your own advice?'

'Danielle was twenty-three when my wife left, but I see your point. My daughter knows the lifeboat's my vocation. She'd hate me to leave, and our whole family would rally round if anything happened to me. Anna's got no one except Janet Fearnley.'

I study the horizon again through the binoculars. Quick's words stay in my head. Why Anna would ask to join the crew, then launch vicious attacks on its members? I'm still trying to work out a motive when a faint light appears in the north.

'There, Liam,' I call out.

The boat is already swinging in a new direction, but something's wrong as we approach. The Brookes' motor yacht is on a long anchor chain, rising and falling with each swell, only a dim light burning in the hold. It seems to have been abandoned, in a seaworthy state, like a modern-day *Mary Celeste*.

55

Sam is growing tired. The oxygen inside the confined space is almost gone, affecting his ability to concentrate. He imagines voices drifting from the deck above, but it might only be the wind's murmur. Conditions are changing out there; the boat lists from starboard to port more quickly, the engine whining in his ears. When he heaves his weight against the plywood door again, the lock strains but refuses to give.

He lies on his back, panting for air, and suddenly Jez appears out of nowhere. He's flesh and blood this time, not a flimsy ghost. His friend looked the same whenever he visited him in prison: tall, with a surfer's mess of blond hair, and an easy smile.

'I let you down,' Sam whispers, his tongue dry against the gag. 'Forgive me, please.'

'Shut up, you idiot, it wasn't your fault. Listen to me, there's a way you can survive.'

'How?'

'You'll only get one chance, Sam. Keep pushing, hard, then fight for your life.'

Jez vanishes, but Sam can still hear his voice promising to stay close. He's struggling to breathe, but his energy has returned. He throws his weight against the door again. It springs open at last on his fifth attempt. He lands on the floor, face first. The pain is brutal. He knows something's broken: his eye socket or cheekbone. But at least he can breathe. He lies still until the pain subsides to a throb, but how can he fight back? His hands are bound so tightly, his fingers are numb.

56

'It's like the first time, isn't it?' Quick says.

I share his sense of déjà vu as we approach the Brookes' boat. The deck is empty as it rides each swell, currents dragging its prow east to face the islands. St Mary's is so far away, its lights are white pinpricks in the distance, and the knot in my stomach tightens. Sam Austell's body may already have been dragged under the water. Quick sounds his horn, but the piercing sound makes no difference.

'Get me closer, can you, Liam? I'll check on board.'

I'm about to step over the rail onto the yacht when Debbie Brookes emerges from the hold.

'Stay back,' she snaps. 'I don't need rescuing.'

'We just want to check you're okay, Debbie.'

'Leave me alone. Can't you see I want peace and quiet?'

She looks different to the last time we met. Her professional smile is missing; she's sober and dry-eyed, unlike her husband. But there's something broken behind that stare. She stands her ground, making a stop sign with the palms of her hands.

'You can't board my yacht without permission,' she says. 'You don't have a search warrant.'

'It's for your own welfare. I won't hurt you, I promise.'

'No one can. I'm beyond that now.'

She stands in front of the door, blocking the hold. A sound comes from below, the dull thud of metal on metal. Debbie grabs a broom from a clip on the wall and brandishes it at my face. I could easily push past, but instinct tells me to proceed with caution. Her partner in crime must be watching from below, prepared to kill Sam Austell if I make a mistake.

'Let's talk, please, Debbie. Then I'll go, I promise.'

I drop onto the bench in the bow, giving her the advantage. I learned the trick on a police training course about body language: submission can be the best form of defence in a volatile situation. Make yourself appear weaker than your opponent, so they drop their guard. Debbie is still clutching her broom like a hunter with a shotgun.

'Why did you come out here?' I ask.

'To clear my head. No matter how bad life gets, the ocean washes it clean.'

'But it's dangerous, especially at night. Is Anna with you?'

'She sailed back to St Mary's hours ago. This isn't her fault.' She lays down the broom at last. 'I couldn't face going home.'

'Jez spoke to you about going to the mainland, and his relationship with Lewis Marling, didn't he?'

'He told me about Tommy being unfaithful too. I was grateful, even though it broke me.'

'Jez knew you wouldn't judge him, and he thought you deserved the truth.'

Her smile revives for an instant. 'People always tell me their secrets.'

'That must be a burden sometimes.'

'Go home, please.' Her face crumples. 'You're not safe out here. You're more vulnerable than anyone.'

'Why, exactly?'

'Because you're a hero, like Jez and Molly.'

'That's not true.'

'We all read about you getting the Queen's medal at Scotland Yard in the local papers. It's the highest honour for a serving officer, isn't it?'

'That was years ago, and my partner did most of the work.'

'No one gets a medal unless they've faced serious danger.' Her eyes glitter with feelings I don't understand.

'Let me search your boat, Debbie. Then you should go home.'

'To what, exactly? My health's gone, and so's my marriage.' She seizes the broom again. 'Keep away from me.'

I rise to my feet slowly, trying not to fuel her panic, then I push past, down the steps to the hold. It's pitch dark compared to the starlit deck, so I use my torch to scan the interior. Adrenalin makes my heart kick against my ribs. I'm expecting to see Sam Austell's body as my eyes slowly adjust, but the space is empty, apart from a few bits of furniture. I must have imagined the noise from below deck – it could have just been the anchor chain hitting the prow. Papers lie strewn across a small table, and Debbie Brookes's solitary voyage makes sense to me at last. She sailed out to open water with the end in mind. She's written a suicide note, blaming the husband she no longer trusts.

I rush back on deck, in time to see her jump overboard. I kick off my boots, ready to swim, but Liam Quick dives first. I scrabble for my phone to call the coastguard. Debbie seemed so desperate, I can tell she'll keep on jumping if Liam manages to drag her back on deck.

Debbie seems determined to drown. There's no sign of panic when she disappears under the waves. I yell directions to Liam, pointing at the spot where she vanished. His face is grim with determination as he keeps on diving. Finally he rises with the woman in his arms, coughing up water. He catches my lifeline and I haul them both on board. When I lay her on the deck, Debbie is barely conscious, shivering with shock.

'You're safe now,' I say, kneeling at her side. 'But you need a doctor. The helicopter's on its way.'

The coxswain looks relieved, as if rescuing a victim from the sea's clutches has eased the guilt he carries, for lives no one could save. He wraps a silver emergency blanket round Debbie's shoulders, sheltering her from the breeze. The wait feels endless until the emergency helicopter hovers over us. It feels like we're trapped in the eye of a storm, with a cyclone drenching my skin. I give the winchman the thumbs-up, while Liam comforts Debbie. It only takes five minutes for the paramedic to drop onto the deck, then place her in a safety harness and winch her to safety. I hope she gets the support she needs, to realise she's got a future.

Quick watches the helicopter spin east, back towards the mainland, his demeanour calm. My respect for him rises by another notch. You'd never guess he's just risked his life to save another, until you look at him head on. His eyes blaze with excitement, like tonight's adventure has only just begun.

57

Sam looks around the hold. It's almost bare, apart from half a dozen portholes with a view of the coal black sea. Engine noise reverberates from the stern, while the pain in his cheek throbs like his skin's been branded. Jez's voice keeps whispering in his mind, but self-defence won't be easy. He looks around for something to free his hands, but there's nothing sharp enough. He must rely on his fingers alone. Sam can reach just far enough to loosen the knotted wire around his ankles. Several minutes pass before his feet slip free.

'Fight for your life.' Sam whispers Jez's advice like a mantra.

He manages to lever himself onto his feet, to search again for a weapon. All he finds is a cardboard box full of RNLI badges, a life jacket and Jez's abandoned trainer.

Footsteps thud across the deck, directly above his head. He may have to defend himself soon, but how, exactly? An idea arrives out of the blue. The hold is lit by a single light bulb screwed into the ceiling. He raises his bound hands and knocks it hard with his fist, until it shatters. There's a last fizz of light, then he's cast into darkness so complete he can't even see his

338

hands. At least he'll have one advantage over the killer; his eyes will have got used to the dark. He'll be ready to attack whoever stumbles through the door, and his best chance is to keep trying to get free. He raises his hands to his face, using his teeth to loosen the knotted wire. The pain in his cheek burns like hellfire, but it's his only hope.

58

'What now?' Quick asks.

The coxswain is still dripping wet from rescuing Debbie Brookes, but finding Sam could be even harder. Shadow has picked up on my worries. He jumps onto the prow and howls at the moon, until I warn him to come down. He slinks at my feet with his head down like a sulky teenager.

'We keep looking for Damian Cosgrove. He thinks Sharon was sleeping with Jez Cardew. Maybe he's trying to wipe out his whole circle of friends. He could have ambushed Sam then brought him out to sea.'

'Where do you think he's gone?'

'The Atlantic Strait, like the other times. Let me steer, your sight's way better than mine.'

I push the boat's engine into overdrive as we head west. My hands grip the wheel so tightly the knuckles whiten. I keep my eyes trained on the water, but there's nothing except reflected starlight, and matchbox-sized freighters lit brightly on the horizon, like a string of pearls.

Liam is kneeling on the prow, gazing through the binoculars like nothing could ever distract him. The muscles in my chest relax at last. I can only pray we're sailing in the right direction, with the tide increasing our speed.

59

Sam is drowning in dark air. He can no longer tell if the boat is idling, or cutting through deep water. The pain in his cheek is sharper than before, and his hands are still tightly bound. A flash of moonlight illuminates the cabin, and he catches sight of something on the floor. It's his phone; it must have fallen from his pocket when the killer dragged him into the hold. He manages to call Danielle's number, breathing a sigh of relief when she answers.

'What's happened, Sam? Are you okay?'

'I'm trapped on a boat. Jez was held here too, you have to call the RNLI.'

She sounds terrified. 'Dad's at sea. He must be looking for you already, with Ben Kitto. I'll use the radio to contact them.'

'Tell them to look for a two-berth cruiser with a powerful engine. I think we're heading west. We've travelled miles, I can't see the islands anymore.'

'I'll do it now. Keep safe, Sam. Don't take any risks.'

The signal dies before he can reply, casting him back into darkness, but he feels stronger. If the islands' best lifeboatmen are searching for him, he's got a fighting chance. But they need to work fast. This pitch-black hold is no place to die, with a madman stamping across the deck overhead. Sam keeps searching for a weapon. His fingers grope in the dark, but touch only the floor, grimy with sand and dirt.

60

We've covered miles. Our chances of immediate support from search and rescue have vanished too: they need to drop Debbie at St Ives hospital, twenty minutes away, before refuelling and flying back to help us again. Shadow is skulking at my feet, growling to himself.

'Shut it,' I tell him. 'You should have stayed on land.'

Shadow gazes up at me, his eyes bleached white by the moon. Liam is still crouched on the prow, binoculars glued to his face, even when his phone rings. He uses his free hand to take it from his pocket and answer, then he calls back to me.

'Sam's been taken. He was able to call Danielle – he's trapped in a boat travelling west.'

The news makes me shift the boat's engine to full power. The ocean looks empty, like an endless sheet of pewter, slick with starlight. It's a relief when Quick finally spots something. He yells out, then points due east.

'Follow those lights. Can you see? It's half a mile away.'

My night vision fails me. I can't see anything except the black ocean, as I swing the wheel until we're circling back to the islands, grateful that the cox's experience has worked its magic. We've been chasing in the wrong direction. I've covered a nautical mile before I realise he could be mistaken. When I check the fuel gauge again, it's running empty, forcing me to slow down.

'Did we overshoot? I can't see the light.'

The coxswain's face blanks. 'That's because there's nothing here.'

'Why send us this way then?'

'Can't you guess? I've faced danger all my life, Ben. It cost me my marriage, but no one rewarded my sacrifice. True bravery comes from facing your demons every day, without ever turning your back.'

My skin prickles with tension. 'Is this a confession, Liam?'

'Not at all. My actions weren't crimes.'

'If you killed Jez and Molly, what else do you call them?'

Quick's eyes are full of hatred, and it's starting to make sense. The man's obsession with saving lives has converted to madness. Now he's claiming them for his own, like trophies. There's a metal wrench in his hands, and I can only rely on the ocean's cruelty. I step back, trying to think more clearly, but the coastguard helicopter is nowhere in sight.

'How could you attack your own crew?'

'Jez and Molly both planned to leave, yet people

called them heroes. No one should grieve for turncoats like them.'

'Is that why I'm here? You guessed I'd resign after having Noah?'

'Your kind disgust me,' he sneers. 'You get all the respect, for no reason.'

'I had no plan to leave. Where's Sam Austell?'

'Who cares?' Quick says, his eyes narrowing. 'I won't have some drug dealer chasing my daughter.'

'Jez was your best crew member, for God's sake. He respected you more than anyone.'

'He begged to join the crew full-time, then changed his mind, at the last minute. Jez was fickle. Can't you see?'

'He and Molly resigned from the lifeboat crew, so you killed them?' I ask in disbelief, but he's slipped out of reach.

'Real heroism comes from a lifetime at sea, like mine. Those two deserved to drown.'

His madness shows when I catch the joy on his face as he hurtles towards me. I land the first punch, but his wrench strikes my shoulder, then hits my temple. I lose consciousness for a moment, the world turning black. When my eyes open again, I'm hunched across the gunwale, too stunned to fight.

My body is still braced for the next punch when I'm pitched overboard. Quick's manic laughter follows me, then Shadow's howl echoing, like a long goodbye. The water feels bitter, even though it's late summer. Its voice roars in my ears. Suddenly the waves churn around me and there's pain in my left wrist as I'm dragged along, behind the boat. I fight to keep my head above water. It takes all my strength to grab the wire and haul myself to the surface, as the engine quickens. Denzel Jory's prediction that drowning runs in families echoes round my head as spray blinds me.

I flip onto my back, hoping to stay on top of the water, but I'm soon pulled under again. My eyes fix on the moon's round face as I struggle to breathe. I keep thinking of Nina and our boy, waiting for me at home. The helicopter needs to arrive fast, but saving myself may be my only chance.

61

Sam hears a high-pitched squeal, like a child bawling for its mother. But when he listens again, it's a wolf's howl. The haunting sound adds to his fear. He's standing in the hold, his body shaking with pent-up adrenaline, then everything changes. The door is wrenched open and the space floods with torchlight, almost blinding him. He sticks out his leg tripping a man as he races down the steps, sending him sprawling. The killer is soon on his feet again, grabbing Sam by the throat as the torch rolls at their feet. Sam can't see the man's features as he lashes out with all his strength. His attacker lands a blow on his torso, almost toppling him, but Jez's voice cheers him on. He releases his hardest punch. The man's head snaps back, then he drops to the floor, out cold.

Sam stares down at his captor, certain he's made a mistake. It's Liam Quick. Danielle will be horrified. The cox must have come to his rescue with Kitto, his attacker already disarmed.

When he runs on deck, Shadow is still howling, but Kitto isn't on board. The boat is travelling at top speed, with no one at the wheel. Sam uses his bound hands to twist the key in the ignition until the engine dies, yet the dog's frenzy grows. It grabs his sleeve in its jaws and drags him to the bow. Sam catches sight of Kitto lying in the water twenty metres away.

'Keep your head up, I'll pull you in,' he yells, but he's terrified it's too late.

Kitto is stretched out, motionless, like a giant gazing at the stars. Sam is frantic now, trying to pull the taut wire to reel him in, but his hands are too tightly bound. His gaze lands on a Swiss army knife glinting at his feet. He grasps it between his fingers to try and free himself, hands fumbling in the cold.

62

Gareth Keillor was right about drowning. The pathologist told me that acceptance arrives as life slips away. The sea feels warmer now; the fear's gone too, like I've drunk a pint of Zoe's best vodka. My mouth is full of brine, and my strength's deserted me. My gaze fixes on the night sky. There's not even a shred of cloud, just the Milky Way stretched gossamer thin, a fishing net awash with stars. It's time to let go. I'm halfway there already, my thoughts spinning back through childhood to infancy. The last time I swam like this was with Noah on my chest, carrying him home. His image brings my thoughts back into focus.

My family's waiting for me on Bryher. We make our own luck in this world, and Denzel Jory is no fortune teller. He's just a bitter old man who's lost his power.

I thrash through the water again. My only hope is to get back to the boat, but at least someone's rooting for me. Shadow is barking non-stop, and Sam Austell is hauling the wire that trails from the bow, dragging me closer. I raise my head to call out a warning, but he doesn't hear. There's a figure behind him on the deck, and suddenly the line falls slack.

63

Sam spins round when someone grasps his shoulder, just as his hands work free. Liam Quick is back on his feet; there's madness in his eyes, and fury. The coxswain is gripping a boat hook, the tool sharp enough to claw out his eyes. Sam ducks out of reach as Quick strikes him. All he can do is take evasive action, but the man's enjoying his revenge for being knocked out. Quick has spent his whole life on boats, giving him a big advantage. He laughs when Sam loses his footing. He stands over him now, the hook inches from his face.

'Pathetic, aren't you?' Quick hisses. 'I'd never let you steal Danielle from me.'

'This'll break her heart, you monster!' Sam yells in his face.

'It won't; Danielle understands duty and honour.' Quick lashes out with the hook again, the blow hitting Sam's shoulder.

Everything changes in an instant. Shadow sinks his teeth into Quick's ankle, making him scream with fury and pain, giving Sam time to regroup. But Quick is still fighting. He kicks the dog away and hits out again, but Sam grabs the boat hook and throws it overboard.

'Now it's just you and me. I bet you're not even brave enough to fight.'

'Shut up, you idiot.'

'Prison's hell for men like you. The weak don't survive.'

Quick hurtles towards him, but he's moving too fast. When Sam steps aside, he plummets head-first over the gunwale. He tries to swim to the boat, but Sam kicks him back into the water.

'Take some of your own medicine, Hawkeye.'

Sam returns to pulling Kitto through the water. It's easier now his hands are free, but it may be too late. He's suddenly aware of the silence. There's only the hiss of waves slapping the ship's bow. Shadow has stopped howling, and when he scans the deck again, the creature has vanished.

64

I can't keep my head above water as Sam heaves on the line, pulling me closer. The boat is still ten metres away. I can see Liam Quick in the water too. He tries to haul himself up the ladder that hangs from the bow, but Sam kicks him back into the waves. I want to cheer, but it would waste the last of my energy. My chest aches, and each breath is harder than before.

I'm slipping under when something nudges me back to the surface until my skin meets cold air. It's Shadow, of course. I'm amazed he waited so long to dive overboard. He doesn't normally show any restraint.

'You took your time,' I whisper.

He swims hard when my hands close round his collar, keeping me afloat as the distance narrows. When I look up again, the coastguard helicopter is in sight, and relief provides the last kick of adrenaline I need, then Sam drags me on board. I land on deck like a line-caught fish, too weak to move as the helicopter raises a tornado of spray.

I catch the disgust on Sam Austell's face when he finally allows Quick back onto the boat, and Shadow appears to feel the same, yet the killer can't accept the game's up. When he lashes out again, the dog bites his raised hand, his jaws locking shut. I could call him off, but defending a murderer from pain isn't my first priority. When Quick releases a howl of pain, it's music to my ears. Sam appears to feel the same. There's blood dripping from a wound on his cheek, but it's not slowing him down.

He grabs my arm. 'Your breathing sounds bad, let's get that seawater out of you.'

Sam forces me to lean on the gunwale, facing the waves. Nausea hits me suddenly. I retch a pint of brine into the ocean, with Austell thumping my back until my chest empties, and my head clears.

When I finally swing round, he looks different from the lad I arrested years ago. He's come of age at last, aware that others' lives matter, as well as our own. Maybe he deserves a medal for that realisation alone.

'Everyone's going to hear what you did, Sam,' I say.

'It doesn't matter, just keep breathing. What's that on your wrist?'

I see metal glinting in the starlight. Quick attached a medal to my arm, like he did to his two other victims, bitter about other people's heroism, despite being called one all his working life. Now the tables have turned. There's nothing valiant about the coxswain tonight. He's hunched in a corner of the deck, his hands protecting his face, as Shadow barks out a fierce rebuke.

'Come away,' I call out, at last. 'He can't hurt us now.'

Shadow looks disappointed, but settles at my side. Quick doesn't move. He's curled in a foetal position, hiding from judgement. Maybe he's got just enough sanity left to realise the scale of his crimes; he'll spend decades in jail or a psychiatric hospital. He looks even more broken than Debbie Brookes, as though shame has caught up with him at last.

Quick's body language doesn't change as we fly back to St Mary's. He sits hunched in a ball, with his face pressed against his knees.

65

Friday 1 September

Ginny Tremayne refuses to give me the all-clear, even though I'm desperate to leave the hospital.

'Your blood oxygen level's too low, Ben. You're staying here till morning, with that mask on all night.'

'Nina must be going nuts. We're getting married the day after tomorrow.'

'Your fiancée has a cool head. I called her an hour ago to say you'll be fine, if you rest. She can fetch you in the morning.'

When my boss appears in the doorway, I know there's no point in fighting. It's still pitch dark outside the window and DCI Madron must believe the situation's serious, or he'd have stayed in bed. His appearance is smart as always, with hair combed, and shirt neatly ironed. My voice is a rusty wheeze when I try to speak.

'Rest, Kitto, no need to talk. I hear you and Sam Austell are the heroes of the hour.'

'Don't use that word, sir, please.'

'Are you well enough to hear Quick explain himself? He's keen to talk, but only if you're in the room. He claims to regret hurting you.'

Ginny Tremayne advances closer, with clipboard raised. 'Ten minutes, maximum.'

Madron gives her an unctuous smile, then indicates for me to stay where I am, while chairs are brought in from the corridor. It's a relief that no one expects me to stand. My body still feels hollow, but Liam Quick looks worse.

The coxswain is a shadow of himself as Lawrie Deane leads him inside. His forearm is bandaged, and he's hand-cuffed to Deane's wrist. I wasn't expecting to confront him again so soon. I notice that his hands are heavily bandaged. I still feel grateful to Shadow, who's curled up in the corner, asleep, after excelling himself tonight.

The DCI reads Quick his rights at a sedate pace. He barely responds when Madron explains that his confession isn't being recorded. He will be questioned again in the morning, with a solicitor present, when his statement will be legally binding. He's under no obligation to speak, but Quick appears determined.

'Get it off your chest then, Liam,' Madron says, his tone sombre. 'Tell us how it began.'

'I caused Trevor Fearnley's death. I didn't want to, but it served my purposes.'

'What do you mean? He had a heart attack, on his boat.'

'He might have survived.' Quick no longer looks angry, just gaunt with misery. 'Trevor was like a mentor to me when I started on the lifeboat. Him and Janet set up the lifeboat festival, but he lost trust in me. He said I was cracking up. Trevor told me to see a counsellor for stress, or he'd contact the RNLI and make them relieve me of my duties.'

'What did you do?'

'I couldn't lose my job. I'm the only one with enough commitment and sea knowledge to run that boat, so I delayed our launch when he called for help. I guessed he was having a heart attack or a stroke, so I sabotaged the engine, knowing his chance of survival was falling every minute. I started it up again, but the threat was over. He'd stopped breathing by the time we got there.'

'So Janet was right to complain about you,' I mutter.

'Trevor brought it on himself, for doubting me, but Jez and Molly were worse. I spent days convincing the RNLI to support another paid position on the boat. They finally agreed ten days ago, then Jez told me he was off to the mainland. He didn't even apologise. All he cared about was his stupid dream of going to art school.'

'So you planned his death?' Madron asks.

'He betrayed me. I sent those badges out to the others, to remind them it's our moral responsibility for every lifeboat officer, and lifeguard, to protect the island population from the sea. I can always tell the ones that aren't fully committed.'

'Why did you pick those quotes from *The Tempest*?'

He lips stretch into an ugly grin. 'Danielle studied that play at school. I only read it last year, but it all made sense. Prospero's the only man on his island with integrity. I'd never read Shakespeare before, but it's like he wrote it just for me. That storm at the start is just like the ones I face each winter. Prospero wants the best for his daughter, like I do for Danielle.'

'She'll be visiting you in jail from now on, and crew members are entitled to resign,' I tell him. 'We're volunteers, remember? You're the only one drawing a wage from the RNLI.'

Quick ignores my words. 'I intercepted Jez's boat easily. He was so gullible. I told him to drop anchor and help me find a man who'd fallen overboard. I beat him with a boat hook, then dragged him behind my boat, out to the Atlantic Strait. I kept going till the only thing attached to my boat was his severed hand. I chucked that back in the water for you lot to find. It seemed like poetic justice that his body washed up on Hangman Island, after his betrayal.'

'That's a terrible punishment for an innocent man.'

'He committed worse crimes than mine. Jez could have stayed here, saving lives, but he walked away. He deserved to have his left hand torn from his body.' Quick leans forward, his eyes stretched wide open. 'Judas betrayed Christ with his left hand, pointing out which man to kill. That's why I dumped Molly Bligh's dress on Hangman Island too. Traitors have always met their fate there.'

'If you really believe God was on your side, you're out of your mind. Why did you use those medals, Liam?' My voice is still a raw croak.

Quick swings in my direction, his gaze full of hate. 'You all got honoured for saving lives. People revered you, even though you showed no loyalty. But I was wrong in your case, Ben, I should have seen that. You've got no intention of leaving, whatever your wife says, because the sea took your dad.'

I don't reply, my decision not yet made.

Quick's crumbling at last, rambling to himself when he speaks again. 'The ocean steals everything we value. Our sanity, our lives. I never got any recognition from the islanders, or my wife, for facing it every day. Only Danielle understands my sacrifice. It's a travesty. Can't you see that?'

'That's rubbish; the whole community respected you,' I tell him. 'Was it your wife leaving? Did that send you over the edge?'

He looks away. 'She asked me to get a new job, go and live inland, far from the sea. My wife was jealous of the ocean's hold over me. It's my vocation, but the stupid bitch never listened. She even tried to steal Danielle.'

'Molly Bligh never hurt you.'

'I gave her a chance to change her mind about leaving the crew, when I sailed out to St Agnes, but she refused. The girl put up quite a fight, before I threw her into the water. It upset me when that wire snapped, setting her free, but I knew she'd drown eventually. The sea punishes disloyalty. It knows who's right and wrong.'

'How come you attacked Sam? He had no intention of leaving the crew.'

'He was stealing Danielle from me. Prospero would never let that happen.'

'You've lost her anyway.'

'She'll see I had no choice.'

The interview lasts another ten minutes, but Quick's argument never changes. If any member of the lifeboat crew showed any sign of leaving, they had to pay for it with their lives. I'm certain part of his motive was resentment about never getting a gallantry medal, but his wife's desertion may have been the trigger. He hated anyone else being viewed as a hero after that. He stopped feeling valued, and rejection compounded his problem. Only Danielle was safe. She never questioned her dad's obsession with the lifeboat, and neither did I. He struck me as a bona fide hero, facing the sea in its worst moods, without flinching.

It's a relief when Ginny Tremayne finally orders me back to bed. I've given up protesting about the oxygen mask she straps to my face. It feels like I'm being dragged through a force nine gale, yet I sleep anyway, my dreams full of waves crashing on the islands' shores.

I wake early with the new morning, and my breathing's eased. Last night's events feel like a weird fantasy. What made Liam Quick lose his mind? Was it the constant threat of the sea, his obsessive nature, or his wife's disloyalty? It may have been a combination of all three. He'll be flown to the mainland today, to face a double murder trial, and two more counts of attempted murder. The bedcovers shift at my feet, and when I look down, Shadow emerges, his jaws opening in a wide yawn.

'You deserve a medal,' I whisper.

He whines a quiet reply, then shuts his eyes again, determined to catch up on sleep. I'm about to do the same, when another sound rouses me. I spot Sam Austell hunched in an armchair. There's a bandage on his cheek, his right eye puffed shut.

'Is that cheekbone broken, Sam?'

'Just a hairline fracture – it looks worse than it feels. They kept me in overnight too.'

'I wouldn't be here, if you hadn't pulled me on board. When did you realise Quick was the killer?'

'Only at the end. I never saw his face when he ambushed me on St Agnes.'

'The guy's out of his mind.'

'It's Danielle I pity. By the way, I've got something of yours.' He passes me my father's Swiss army knife. 'It saved my bacon last night.'

'Thanks, it must have fallen from my pocket.' I sit up to study him more closely. 'I thought your landlord was the killer for a while. Why's Callum so bitter?'

Sam shrugs. 'Nothing's gone his way since his family left St Mary's. He wanted Anna Dawlish, but she preferred Jez, and the drugs don't help. I tried to get him to come to addiction meetings with me, but he has to admit there's a problem first.'

'What can I do in return for last night?'

He looks down at his hands. 'I just want to stay in Scilly.'

'You'll be accepted now, when everyone hears about your bravery.'

Austell's smile soon fades. 'I may have to go back to the mainland anyway. Stuart Cardew's convinced I killed Jez.'

'This changes all of it, Sam, can't you see? You were the hero last night, and you never hurt anyone. You can start over.'

'I hope you're right, but I need a new job too,' he says, rising to his feet.

'Rest for a few days at Father Mike's first.'

'I need to sort out my future.'

'Because of Danielle?'

'She's part of it, yeah, if she's still talking to me.'

A new thought enters my mind. 'Have you thought about boat-building as a career? My uncle needs an apprentice, and you've got the right skills.'

His face lights up. 'Are you serious?'

'Let's see what he says.'

I put a call through to Ray. There's a pause at the end of the line, before he replies. I listen in silence then hang up.

'You can start Monday, for a month's trial. My

godmother will give you a room at the pub on Bryher, till you find your feet.'

Sam's grin of amazement makes him wince in pain, but relief echoes in his voice when he says goodbye. He gives me a mock salute, then dashes away. Shadow continues snoring at my feet. The creature seems completely at ease, while last night's drama rattles around my head. My father's knife lies on the bedside table, with a new scratch on its casing from last night's adventure. It seems fitting that his favourite tool helped to save my life.

I pull off the oxygen mask and take my first deep breath, unaided. Sunshine pours through the thin hospital curtains, and I can't wait to sail home. I need a day on the beach with Nina and our boy, doing nothing except building sandcastles as the sun burns down.

66

Sam is still dressed in last night's clothes, the fabric gritty with sea salt. He pauses outside the smart-looking bungalow Danielle shared with her father. Curtains are pulled shut in every window, like closed eyes, and Liam Quick's Volvo is still parked on the drive, with RNLI stickers displayed in the back window.

He feels like running away, but that never helped him in the past. Danielle might hate him for hurting her father and exposing the truth, but he needs to find out.

There's so much tension in his body when he rings the doorbell, his hands bunch into fists at his sides. Danielle's expression is unreadable when she finally appears. Her face is puffy from crying, but she still looks beautiful. He wants to apologise, but there are no words to match the sadness in her voice as she greets him. It's a surprise when she flings her arms round his neck, then leads him inside. One of her aunts scuttles out of the living room to see who's arrived, then retreats to give them privacy.

It feels awkward standing in the kitchen while Danielle

cries, but he's frozen to the spot. He's almost certain she's preparing to say goodbye.

'Inspector Madron told us how you saved Ben Kitto's life. I should have done something long before, I knew Dad was close to the edge. But how could anyone hurt Jez and Molly? It doesn't make sense.' There's no blame in her expression for him bringing her father to justice, only confusion. 'I've lived with him all these years, Sam. Why didn't I realise he was falling apart?'

'Everyone trusted him, not just you. I respected him so much.'

She looks up at him, eyes glistening. 'Tell me something good, can you? I have to believe things will get better.'

'You'll survive this and come out stronger. I'm staying put, Danielle, if that helps. I've got a month's trial as an apprentice on Bryher, in Ray Kitto's boatyard. I'll make damn sure he gives me a full-time job at the end.'

'That's perfect for you.' Her hand settles on his arm. 'You won't stop seeing me because of this, will you?'

'Didn't that Valentine's card convince you I'm serious?'

She manages a smile at last. They sit together at the kitchen table, with hands linked. Sam can tell she's shocked to her core. Danielle will need to talk it out, for years to come, until it finally makes sense. He's nobody's hero, but he's a stayer at least. Sam won't give up now that he's found the right girl. She's the lifeline he's dreamed about, the one to help him keep his head above water.

67

Saturday 2 September

I'm standing by the altar in Bryher church, with Eddie
beside me, the pair of us in our matching suits. Zoe is
playing a slow version of 'Summertime' on the piano
in the nave, and my chest feels tight. I've had a full day
to recover, yet it still feels like I'm drowning. This time
it's nerves making me short of breath, not cold seawater. Every aisle is packed with islanders wearing casual
summer gear, while the sun blazes outside. I can't
explain why I'm afraid. Maybe it's because nothing else
matters as much as this. Marriage used to seem like a
long road, full of hazards, yet my spirits soar when the
music changes. Zoe launches into 'Here Comes the
Bride', and the church falls silent.

I glance back, just once. The long column of ivory
lace looks a hundred times better now that Nina's
wearing it. She's tall and elegant, with dusty sunlight
falling from the windows turning her image sepia. She's

leaning on her dad's arm, and the only unconventional thing I can see is Shadow walking at her side, sporting a white collar. We both knew he had to be part of the ceremony. If we left him at home, he'd howl for hours, then destroy the furniture.

My anxiety drops away when she draws level with me, and last week's terrible losses fade away. I lift the veil back from her face, and it feels like a homecoming, her amber-coloured eyes perfectly calm. There's no sound now. It's just us, standing here in an old church on a small island engulfed by the sea. I glance back one more time to see Noah, asleep on Maggie's lap, oblivious to the biggest day of our lives. Shadow seems glad to rest at our feet; he's in his element, his fur brushed to a dull gleam.

Our wedding goes by in a blur of hymns and promises. I only exhale properly when we cross the island with the crowd following us to the beach. By the time everyone assembles, we're barefoot, in white shorts and T-shirts, so people can spot us easily in the crowd. The air smells of barbecued chicken and newly opened wine. My brother's in the crowd somewhere with his wife and daughter, my fragmented family pieced together for once.

It's Ray who gives me the biggest surprise. He steps onto the podium, looking like a veteran movie star in his blue suit, slim and relaxed, his thatch of pure white hair tamed for once. He delivers a perfectly timed ten-minute speech, full of casual insults, begging Nina to divorce me and marry him instead. He doesn't even need to consult his notes. I can't help staring in amazement, while the crowd laughs at his jokes then breaks into a tumult of applause.

The sun is still high above us, and for once in my life I'm not asking questions or hunting for answers. Music blares out from the stereo rigged above our heads. Soon we're drunk and dancing, arms round our friends' and neighbours' shoulders, until darkness claims these islands again, and the bonfire flares into life.

I know it's stupid to wish time away when it's so precious, and yet I do. I've been surrounded by good will throughout my wedding day, as summer blazes to an end. Yet I'll be happiest when we can peel away and put Noah in his cot. We'll sit up talking through details, drink another glass of wine, then go to bed. I'll drift into sleep while the sea retreats on the ebb tide, with my wife beside me, and Shadow curled up by our door.

Acknowledgements

Thanks are due, as always, to my long-suffering husband Dave. I owe him a million cups of tea, plus many encouraging words. My whole family keeps me going whenever my confidence flags. Thanks so much to my sister Honor, and stepsons Jack, Matt and Frankie, plus Jess, Harriet, Freddie, Ruby, Florence and Minnie. You bring so much happiness into my life, it fuels my energy to keep writing! My friends Judy Logan, Penny Hancock, Michelle Spring, and Louise Millar, all kept me going as this story progressed. My dear friend Amanda Grunfeld lost her battle with cancer soon after we chatted about my new plot. Her memory, and her belief in my writing, will stay with me forever.

Thank you, Teresa Chris, for being my fabulous agent for twelve years, and telling me that you love how I write. Your encouragement means the world to me. This book marks the beginning of my relationship with Clare Hey, a great editor, with such a light touch, the process feels effortless. Jess Barratt, you always come out to bat for me on the publicity front. Thanks so much! Many thanks also to the sales and marketing teams at Simon and Schuster. I know you put in many hours on the phone, emailing and touring the country on my behalf. I appreciate all of it hugely.

Twitter may be a mixed blessing, with some folk saying daft things, but it's introduced me to many brilliant book lovers over the years. You are too big a group to mention individually, which is a pity, but many thanks to all of the following for fuelling my ego up with your lovely tweets: Janet Fearnley, Scott McKenzie, Jennie Blackwell, Jane McParkes, Caroline Casson, Ian Dixon, Jennifer Ashton, Louise Marley, Helen @Dogearedtatty, Allan B, Clive, Mary Lay, Theresa McCormick, Cressida Downing, Alain Marciano, Geoff McGiven, Nadine Brokas, Peggy Breckin, Polly Dymock, Peter Fleming, Marni Graff, Nikki reads books, Mike Rodgers, Julie Caton, Hazel Wright, Helen Jones, Julie Boon, Angela Barnes, Anna Tink, Elaine Simpson-Long, Susan Johnston.

The Prison Reform Trust helped me again in writing this book. Thanks so much for providing a set of figures about prison reoffending that even someone with dyscalculia like me could understand.

Finally, this book would not have been written without the help of Mr Peter Hicks, the serving RNLI lifeboat coxswain for the Isles of Scilly. Thanks so much for showing me your boats, the lifeboat house, and giving me a real insight into the dangers faced by all members of the RNLI. I salute your bravery. The sea terrifies me, yet you all volunteer your time and face huge storms without flinching. It goes without saying that none of the lifeboat officers imagined in this book are based on any living person in Scilly, or elsewhere.

Don't miss the other atmospheric
locked-island thrillers featuring DI Ben Kitto
from highly-acclaimed author, Kate Rhodes

'An absolute master of pace, plotting and character'
ELLY GRIFFITHS

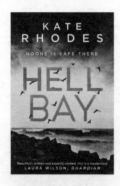
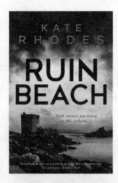
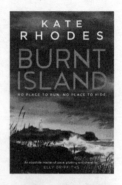

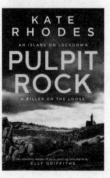
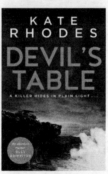
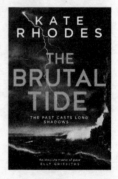

'Gripping, clever and impossible to put down' **ERIN KELLY**

'Beautifully written and expertly plotted;
this is a masterclass' *GUARDIAN*

**SIMON &
SCHUSTER**